Praise for

YOU COULD BE HAPPY HERE

"...Van Rheenen's debut novel...never goes where you think it's going, but always takes you someplace wonderful."

–Karen Joy Fowler, national bestselling author of *We Are All Completely Beside Ourselves* and *Booth*

• • •

"Populated by a cast of colorful characters, and buoyed by the customs and culture of Costa Rica, *You Could Be Happy Here* is a wonderfully insightful story of one woman's journey of discovery...an auspicious debut novel!"

–Gail Tsukiyama, national bestselling author of *The Samurai's Garden, The Color of Air,* and *The Brightest Star*

• • •

"A surprising novel about family and what it means to belong. I found myself rooting for Lucy every step of the way."

—Julia Scheeres, *NYT* bestselling author of *Jesus Land*

• • •

"A brilliant debut novel that only a traveler could have written—a beautiful blend of travelers' insights, natural history, and heartfelt truths about what it means to belong to a place—or have a place belong to you."

–Pat Murphy, Nebula-winning author of *The Adventures of Mary Darling*

• • •

"A young woman, a tropical paradise, and a past not quite become history—Erin Van Rheenen's new novel is a pleasure to read, full of satisfying complexities."

–Mary Ellen Hannibal, award-winning science writer and author of *Citizen Scientist* and *Spine of the Continent*

• • •

"...*You Could Be Happy Here* vividly captures the tension of being a privileged foreigner in another country, as well as the profound understanding that we are all in this messy life together....Beautifully written and soul-searching."

–Sharman Apt Russell, author of *An Obsession with Butterflies* and *What Walks This Way: Discovering the Wildlife Around Us Through Their Tracks and Signs*

• • •

"With familial layers and a richness of place, *You Could Be Happy Here* encompasses the universal appeal of looking for home while stepping into the unknown. I was blown away by the beauty of the prose, as well as the wonder and pathos of the story."

–Nikki Nash, author of *Collateral Stardust: Chasing Warren Beatty and Other Foolish Things*

• • •

"...this novel bridges the geographic, emotional and cultural gaps the complex characters encounter as they strive to find themselves and examine the new and historic connections that will either sustain or destroy them."

–Polly Dugan, author of *The House of Cavanaugh* and *The Sweetheart Deal*

YOU COULD BE HAPPY HERE

A Novel

ERIN VAN RHEENEN

Sibylline Press
AN IMPRINT OF ALL THINGS BOOK

Sibylline Press
Copyright © 2025 by Erin Van Rheenen
All Rights Reserved.

Published in the United States by Sibylline Press,
an imprint of All Things Book LLC, California.

Sibylline Press is dedicated to publishing the brilliant work
of women authors ages 50 and older.
www.sibyllinepress.com

Distributed to the trade by Publishers Group West.

Sibylline Press
Paperback ISBN: 9781960573476
eBook ISBN: 9781960573537
Library of Congress Control Number: 2025933660

Book and Cover Design: Alicia Feltman

This is a work of fiction. Names, characters, places, brands, media, and incidents are either the product of the author's imagination or are used fictitiously. Any resemblance to similarly named places or to persons living or deceased is unintentional.

Subjects: LCSH: General or Realistic Fiction—Women Authors; Environmental Fiction—Costa Rica; Travel—Fiction; Costa Rica—Fiction; Parent and Child—Fiction; Sisters—Fiction; Women's Adventure—Fiction

For David

para siempre

YOU COULD BE HAPPY HERE

A Novel

ERIN VAN RHEENEN

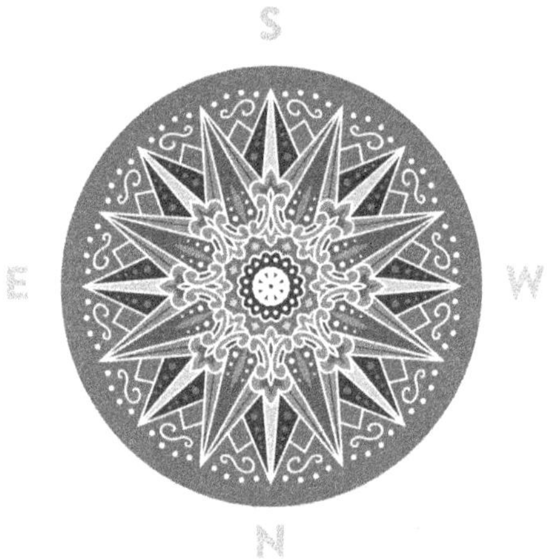
S
E
W
N

PROLOGUE

Two bodies were in the water, thousands of miles apart. One spun downstream. The other came in with the tide. Both sent out ripples in widening rings that would meet and overlap in ways none of the survivors could have imagined.

A woman in her late thirties stood on the riverbank, hood up against the wind. She watched her sister pull a bag the size of a bread loaf from a black cardboard box. They had argued about what to do with the ashes. Lucy remembered their mother wanting to be planted in the garden. Lucy's stay-at-home sister claimed to have more recent intel: Their mother wanted to be thrown—thrown, not scattered—into the Trinity River.

That rang true for Lucy. Though they harbored different versions of their mother, the sisters agreed on one thing: She had been a woman of big gestures, dying too soon and swimming too early, plunging into the river with whoops of joy when the water was still raging and ice-cold.

Spring or summer, Lucy had lagged behind. Her mother and sister would be halfway across the river as she waded in, mindful of the rocks. At first, Lucy would call to them to wait, but grew accustomed to going it alone. It had been good training for leaving home, turning the tables, becoming the one who leaves rather than the one left behind.

The wind was with the sisters as they took turns shaking ashes from the bag. They stood back from the edge. The embankment had a habit of giving way, the current undermining its base, just as Lucy's hard-won sense of self was undermined every time she came home.

Letting her hood fly back, Lucy wondered: Was she an orphan now, or had that happened a long time ago?

* * *

Three thousand miles south, Beto—whom Lucy did not know yet—walked the tideline of a Costa Rican beach. It wasn't a white-sand, turquoise-sea kind of place. There'd been a storm, and the frothy water was the same warm brown as the sand.

Down the beach was a big lump of something, wound in seagrass and half-obscured by a broken tree limb. Beto approached, tugging his earbuds out. Tinny music spilled into the morning.

With a bare foot, he nudged aside the grass and leaves. *Carajo.*

The body was naked and on its side in a larval curl, neck out of whack. The eyes, open and filmy, showed no more or less recognition of Beto than when the older man had been alive. Though they had lived for decades in the same small town, the father's gaze and paternity had slid off the son like water off coconut-oiled skin.

"If he wants to claim us," Beto's mother had said, "he knows where to find us." Her resignation had made her son's blood boil all the hotter, since he had to carry the anger for the both of them.

He switched off his music to better deliberate: What does an unclaimed son owe the father who washes up at his feet?

CHAPTER 1

> Insect larvae eat their brothers and sisters to get a bigger share of food and parental attention. Up the food chain, strawberry poison-dart frogs lay a few nonviable eggs so their recently hatched tadpoles have something to eat.
>
> —*Lucy's bug notes*

LUCY OPENED THE FRONT DOOR and out wafted her childhood: mildew and wood smoke. The house was part rickety Victorian, part cabin in the woods. High ceilings and gaps between the floorboards made it hard to heat. Stepping inside, she wondered if her sister would buy firewood this year or chainsaw it herself from downed trees on the property.

Lucy and Faith hadn't been in touch much since they'd dealt with their mother's ashes. The last time Lucy had reached out by phone, the conversation had taken a turn. When Lucy mentioned a book about the different stages of grief, Faith thought Lucy was accusing her of being in the wrong stage.

Now Faith was in a fever to "take care of business," as she put it. Lucy arranged for a sub for her science classes, wrote out lesson plans, and made the four-hour drive north from San Francisco in the rain.

On the hall table, a chipped ceramic dish held a jumble of keys and orphaned earrings. Lucy heard the shower running upstairs. Faith's utility belt hung over the back of a chair, its holster empty. Their mother, Sara, had been an outlaw of sorts, at least until weed became legal. Funny that Faith, now a sheriff, had become The Man.

The drive was catching up with Lucy. In the kitchen, there was the welcome smell of coffee brewing but also of harsh cleaners, the kind Sara hadn't allowed in the house. Coffee in hand, Lucy passed the doorway of her old room, where Faith's son now stored his junker bikes and computers, then braved Sara's old office, where the dying woman had dozed fitfully in her final weeks, unable to climb the stairs to her bedroom.

Lucy sat at the desk, not surprised that Faith had a stack of files ready for review. As she sifted through the folders—mortgage and tax stuff, receipts from the irrigation system they'd put in years ago—a musty sadness drifted up as if from the paperwork itself, the remnants of what their mother had managed to grab and hold onto in this life.

The stack was off-kilter, and now she saw why. A bulging envelope lay at the bottom of the pile. The packet's weight, color, and slick feel were just different enough that she knew it couldn't have come from the local office-supply store. Something about its foreignness put her on high alert.

Inside the envelope was a small bundle of letters she'd never seen. Her throat constricted when she saw that the top one was addressed to her, or to whom she had once been: *Luz Gale*. Lucy had been born Luz. Later she would cringe at how she had denied her true name, but in the standardizing crush of grammar school, she had opted for something less associated with the Mexicans and Central Americans who came to work in motels or to harvest and trim marijuana. The daughters and sons of those workers didn't have an easy time of it at school.

Wait. Why in the hell was there a letter to Lucy that she had never seen before?

The return address was Palmita, Costa Rica. They'd spent summers in that tiny beach town while Sara had dated a local man Lucy and Faith called Uncle Gabo. Even now, Lucy could almost feel the humid air of that place, like steam when you lift the lid of a pot.

Women there did the laundry by hand in outdoor sinks, with a stiff brush and a cake of blue-and-white marbled soap. The tide rushed in over the rocky coastline, bringing with it green coconuts and, one memorable afternoon, a brown-skinned Barbie with salt-matted hair. Lucy pictured Uncle Gabo sprinting alongside her on the beach, pumping his arms but letting her win.

Both she and Faith had been crazy about Uncle Gabo; he had been their hands-down favorite of all of Sara's boyfriends. They cried when Sara said they'd never see him again. That was before they learned not to get caught up in their mother's enthusiasms.

Lucy saw that the other letters, seven or eight of them, were addressed to Sara, and appeared to be unopened. The top letter, the one to Lucy, had a postmark from about a year ago. It had been opened hastily; there was a big rip down the front, right through her name and the address that hadn't been hers for decades.

> Querida Luz,
>
> Whatever your mother told you, know that there is a place for you and the beautiful family I am sure you have by now. I'm sorry for all I didn't do, but I can do this. Please come to see your father soon. I am not so young anymore.
>
> tu papá,
> Gabriel Mora Soto (Uncle Gabo)

Lucy sat very still, thinking of the story her mother had told them about the father who'd left, the flannel-shirted man in the Curry Village cafeteria in Yosemite Valley. Sara claimed she had approached him because they were two solitary people reading Edward Abbey's *Desert Solitaire*. The new couple took off for the Utah high desert and there conceived her, the daughter they named Luz, in honor of the light on those high, arid plains where pink sandstone reared up into strange fins and arches. Sara had dragged the man back to California. He'd been present for Lucy's birth, though Sara said he'd been useless during her labor. He stuck around a few more years, long enough to help make a second child, Faith. Then—Lucy wasn't sure of the timeline—he drove his battered pickup truck out of their lives, never to be seen again.

That was the story. Lucy had never questioned it.

Now, she wondered why she hadn't. She had vague memories of being alone with her mother in the house early on, but she'd figured childhood memories were notoriously unreliable, and that maybe her father, the flannel-shirted drifter, hadn't been around much even when he lived with them. But there were other inconsistencies Lucy had ignored, like that both Faith and Sara were tall and lanky, with hair like a palomino's tail, a round face, and placid eyes, though neither woman was anywhere near placid. Lucy had darker skin and hair and was half a foot shorter than her younger sister. Her face was sharp, her eyes watchful. A friend of Sara's had called her a "pointy little thing." Ten-year-old Lucy had cried in the gardening shed, sitting on an overturned bucket.

There was something else in the envelope. A single page so slight, she almost missed it. A will, in Spanish. Lucy's mouth went dry when she saw her own name, bolded and in capital letters. In vain she scanned for her sister's name, or her mother's, but found only Uncle Gabo's: Gabriel Mora Soto. Lucy's name was followed by "no second surname on account of her nationality" and "heir to this property."

Lucy heard movement and looked up. The hallway light showed Faith in silhouette: a lithe figure weighed down with a heavy utility belt, blocking the doorway. She seemed menacing in her crisp uniform, the bulge of the oversized flashlight in her utility belt faintly obscene.

"So you found them," Faith said.

Lucy gave her sister a hard look. She pushed the chair back from the desk but didn't stand. Faith's height gave her an unfair advantage. The girls had sparred like prize fighters when they were young. They'd also huddled together on the couch, grooming each other like chimpanzees.

Faith was at the gun safe. "I only found them last week."

Lucy gripped the arms of the chair. "Did you read the top one?"

"Yep."

"It wasn't addressed to you. But since you read it, what do you think?"

Faith was arm-deep in the safe now. "I guess our deadbeat dad is now just *my* deadbeat dad." Her offhand tone didn't fool Lucy. Faith was shaken. "And you get some sort of glamorous exotic new father."

Glamorous was a good word for Gabriel. He'd looked like a '70s rock star and moved like a pro soccer player.

"You didn't read the other letters, right? The ones to Mom? They're unopened." Lucy thumbed the stack. The envelopes were soft and limp, having absorbed the damp.

"Are you blind?" Faith jibed.

Lucy brought the letters into the light cast by the desk lamp. She saw now that they'd all been neatly slit along the top seam. The openings looked as if they'd healed themselves, knitting back together as scars formed to protect the body.

Faith shoved her gun into its holster. "What do I care about love letters to you and Mom?"

"I can't believe it," Lucy said. "How are we supposed to—"

"We?"

She was stung by her sister's tone. Even with how bad things had been lately, Lucy still felt connected to Faith, a connection of history and blood. And if that blood turned out to be more diluted than they'd thought?

"We're sisters," Lucy asserted.

"Right. You weren't much of a sister when Mom was dying. You couldn't be bothered."

"What was I supposed to do, quit my job?"

"You made your choices."

"I called," Lucy said quietly. "You hardly ever picked up. And when I came, it was like you didn't want me here."

In fact, it would take Lucy days and sometimes weeks to recover from a visit home. She felt erased, and it took time and effort to impose herself back onto the world. It wasn't a new feeling. When the sisters were in their early twenties, bonding over what a kook their mom was, Lucy had asked Faith, "When was it that Mom started favoring you and, I don't know, kind of stopped *seeing* me?" To Lucy, it was irrefutable. She'd just wanted help with the timeline.

Faith had said she didn't know what Lucy was talking about. "Mom thought you were smarter," Faith said. "But you were just a better test-taker." Lucy had no memory of being dubbed the smart one.

Sara, too, had denied she favored Faith, but Lucy saw evidence of it everywhere. Sara had said, "You don't need me like Faith does."

Lucy bought that line for a while, as she, too, was protective of her little sister. But even their daily horoscopes were an occasion for exclusion. Faith and Sara shared the sign of Sagittarius. Lucy was a Pisces.

"Water signs are inconstant," Sara used to say, as if lecturing about how depleted soil affected the marijuana crop.

"I tried to help," Lucy said now. "I kept offering. You said it would take too long to get me 'up to speed.'"

"It would have." Faith narrowed her eyes. "You know Mom wanted me to have the house."

Lucy stood, swearing as she knocked her knee on the corner of the desk. A part of her couldn't believe it. A deeper part felt her fears confirmed: Their mother had favored Faith, the girl who looked like her and never strayed far from home.

But Lucy had counted on splitting the money from the sale of the house. "The hell she did."

"You see the improvements I've made. Look at the receipts." Faith gestured at the folders on the desk. "I've used my own money."

"I'll pay you back."

"I've got to go. Some of us have to work."

Lucy followed Faith to the door to the hall. Her sister turned abruptly, blocking the way, feet planted wide like some cartoon cop.

"I was supposed to work today," Lucy snapped. "I had to get a sub."

"Too bad you didn't get a sub when Mom needed you."

"I took care of Mom a lot longer than you did," Lucy said through gritted teeth. Now thirty-eight, Lucy had been her mother's keeper from the age of eleven until she left home for college. Later, Lucy would learn the term "parentification" for when children are forced to parent their parent. It was part of why Lucy had never wanted kids herself—she'd already parented enough in this lifetime.

"Mom was always the child," Lucy continued. "How can you not know that? Then *you* were the child. Who the hell do you think took care of *you* when Mom was at her worst?"

Faith scoffed. "Yeah, you're such a mom."

"No way is this place yours. I'll hire a lawyer."

Faith headed down the hall. "With what money?" she threw back over her shoulder.

Lucy went after her. "You can't leave in the middle of this."

Faith spun around. "The middle of this? I've always been in the goddamned middle of this."

"I'm in the middle of it too." For a moment, looking into her sister's face, Lucy thought there was still a chance they could come out of this whole. She'd just lost a mother; she didn't want to lose a sister as well.

"That's just it," Faith said, somewhere between apology and gloating. "You're not."

From the front porch, Lucy watched Faith drive away, then went out into the yard to look back at the house her sister said she had no stake in. She pictured a wrecking ball careening towards the house, then her sister's face when she drove up to a pile of rubble. Or Lucy could dismantle the house piece by piece, ship it to Costa Rica, have Gabriel help her put it back together in Palmita. North Coast gothic meets the tropics.

She settled for a favorite doorknob. Lavender cut glass from the sunroom, the best place to sip coffee in the morning. She twisted the screwdriver, and the faceted globe tumbled heavily into her hand. A metal post protruded like a finger bone. The outside knob she left in place, closing the door carefully. Next time Faith tried it, the knob would come off in her hand.

Back in the city, Lucy's head buzzed like a termite nest. She second-guessed what she'd said, picked apart what her sister had claimed, glanced at the letters to Sara, then shoved them back into their envelopes. She wanted to know everything, but was afraid that *everything* might make her head explode.

During the next few weeks, Lucy called Faith, leaving message after message. She sent half a dozen emails and as many texts. Faith did not get back to her.

APRIL 2010

DAY ONE

SATURDAY

CHAPTER 2

> Some insects are born with wings, and some grow them when they need them, like aphids when the colony gets too crowded.
>
> —Lucy's bug notes

STRIKING UP A CONVERSATION with a silver-haired woman at the departure gate, Lucy tried out the line, "My mother died, but turns out, I might have a father in Costa Rica." The word *father* felt wrong in her mouth, like fruit gone bad. The woman looked at Lucy as if she'd just failed a screen test for Grieving Daughter. Wrong emphasis. Wrong tone.

"I'm on spring break," Lucy added, mostly to remind herself of how little time she had for this errand. Not counting travel time, she had just eight days to track down her alleged father and see what he had to say for himself.

An online search for Gabriel Mora Soto had turned up a Catalan poet and a guy specializing in online reputation repair. The name of the lawyer on the will hadn't yielded anything either. Apparently, some things still had to be done in person.

On the flight to Costa Rica, she finally worked up the courage to fully read the letters from Gabriel to Sara.

In his letters, Gabriel's tone was by turns angry, apologetic (for his "indiscretions"), and pleading, not for access to his supposed daughter, but for Sara to come back to him. Lucy was disappointed by how little she herself figured in these letters.

One letter, sent a year or two after their last visit to Palmita, was just one line, no greeting or sign-off. *You have ruined everything.* The pen had punched small holes in the thin paper.

In another, Gabriel wrote about Sara being pure joy. That definitely wasn't how Lucy would describe Sara, and she was pretty sure Faith wouldn't either, though they'd had their joyful moments.

Summer days, doors open, *Astral Weeks* blaring, the three of them had spent hours on their art projects. Once, they'd brushed blue poster paint all over their naked bodies and rolled designs on huge swaths of newsprint. Was that joy? The word suddenly sounded like a nonsense syllable or a bird call. *Joy joy joyjoyjoy.*

Lucy was getting used to the idea of her own absence from this correspondence when she came across a letter whose first line landed like a physical blow.

> You say she's not mine but I feel the pull of blood, even from here. I know you remember it as well as I do. The abandoned fire station in the eastern Sierra. It was baking hot, you said, and we laughed because you don't bake, so how would you know?
>
> The wooden deck smelled of creosote. Water came from a hose outside. Remember how we rinsed off between sessions? I can't remember if it was you or me who said our lovemaking felt like rock striking stone. Sparks flew and something caught fire—Luz is proof of that. The dates add up.

So Gabriel was in the US long before they all supposedly met him for the first time during their summers in Costa Rica? And he and Sara had conceived her, Lucy, during Gabriel's time in the US? Lucy could almost feel the heat of the desert, the cold water from the hose. Two flinty people colliding and sending up a spark that made her, Luz, flare into existence.

The abandoned fire station in the eastern Sierra. Was that the real-life version of Sara's story about meeting a man in Yosemite and then heading for Utah? Had Sara told a version of the truth but told it slant, the names and places changed to protect the guilty? The letter went on:

It's true we are both hard, solitary people. But that day. That day. And later, in Palmita. We both mellowed. You know we did. We were a family once. We can be a family again.

Yes, their time in Palmita had had a softness to it, Sara giving off a mellow glow Lucy hadn't seen before on her mother—and never saw again.

Lucy remembered Gabriel with what she knew now to be love. Not just fondness. She'd put the love in deep freeze when Sara dumped him and they never went back to Costa Rica. But apparently it was still there, like yucca moth larvae emerging after a decades-long dormancy.

One thing Lucy had loved about Gabriel was that he didn't condescend to her or Faith. He treated them like fully realized human beings, which they weren't, but hell, she hadn't achieved that pinnacle even now, in her late thirties.

Gabriel wasn't perfect. Sometimes he flew off the handle, letting loose a torrent of Spanish, which made Sara roll her eyes and Lucy and Faith giggle. But he was easy to cajole out of a bad mood, and he'd never seemed threatening. They'd been a foursome that felt right. Complete. Accustomed to life with just one parent, Lucy hadn't ever thought of it in terms of family.

But if Gabriel's claim of parentage were true, then the question remained: Why would Sara keep from Lucy that he was her father? Was Sara afraid Lucy would prefer him, maybe move to where he lived? Or was Gabriel so dangerous, so off-kilter, that Sara knew her daughter would be better off without him?

Lucy sat with that question for a while, not making any headway. Then she sifted through the pile for the only letter actually addressed to her, the one signed *tu papá*. Here it was, with that violent tear through her name.

The question that should have hit Lucy when she found it in her mother's office finally reared its head. Who had opened the letter? Sara could have chosen *not* to open a letter addressed to Lucy. If Faith had been the one to open it, then Sara might not have known about the will.

Lucy had to admit it: Heading for Costa Rica without first finding out everything she could back home was a little crazy. For weeks, though, Faith hadn't answered calls or texts. Should Lucy have driven north and forced Faith's hand? Probably.

But Lucy was furious with her sister, and it felt good to make big, sweeping, possibly self-destructive gestures: buying a plane ticket she couldn't afford, catapulting toward a place she remembered well that might have no memory of her. But there was someone who had not only remembered her, but had wanted Lucy to have a place there. Gabriel.

Still suspended in the air at 30,000 feet, Lucy felt a small, wavering flame of hope.

In the taxi from the international airport to the local airport where Lucy would catch a small plane, the driver blasted the AC. Tinted windows cast a pall over the six-lane highway, with billboards advertising private hospitals and gated communities. They passed sprawling industrial parks, fast-food drive-thrus, and crumbling retaining walls with balloon-letter graffiti. The view bore little resemblance to Lucy's jumble of splintered childhood memories, half-read news stories, and photos from coffee-table books that had become her idea of this place.

Before boarding the single-prop plane, the passengers had to step on a scale, as if an extra ounce might send them into a tailspin. Lucy had been living on sugary breakfast cereal, cheap wine, and big peanut butter cookies from the corner store. That diet, combined with stress and no exercise, meant that Lucy could now barely button her pants. She knew birds binged before they migrated, bulking up for long weeks or months on the wing. Was she migrating? If so, she hoped her destination would have plenty of what sent birds halfway across the world: sustenance and nesting sites.

Lucy had looked forward to the view from the small plane, but was so exhausted that she fell asleep shortly after takeoff. She awoke on the descent, feeling it in her stomach even before she opened her eyes to the deep blue of the Gulf of Nicoya. Suddenly, they were skimming low over water, the land rising up to meet them.

The bus from the landing strip barreled down the mountain toward the coast, the driver downshifting like it was an Olympic sport. Sweat poured off his broad brown face. A laminated holy card swung wildly from the rearview mirror.

Lucy's seatmate was giving her the once-over, taking in the travel-rumpled clothes and the hair plastered to her forehead. Lucy didn't return the woman's gaze or try to make herself more presentable. She was too busy peering past the woman and out the bus window, trying to see if anything looked familiar.

When the road broke from the trees, there was the indelible blue of the Pacific. Coconut palms, South Sea natives that had arrived in the ballast water of ships, vaulted out over the sand. Somewhere, Lucy had seen a dismissive description of "boilerplate tropical beauty," but this view hit her like a thump to the chest. A good term for the landscape might be *ravishing*, with all the violence the word implied. The natural world was full of ferocity, and the tropics sped up the life cycle. A plant grew faster here and died more quickly, its prime a brief moment between new growth and decay.

That was what had happened to Sara. The oncologist told them, almost cheerfully, as if knowing the truth behind dying was nearly as good as surviving, "It's about cells behaving badly. Cells are programmed to live a certain amount of time, but cancer cells don't die when they're supposed to." The cells lived too long, and Sara's life was cut short. Nature was full of such brutal trade-offs.

The woman next to Lucy fidgeted, trying to get more comfortable on the narrow bench seat. She smelled bittersweet, like orange peel. "¿Dónde están tus hijos?" she asked Lucy.

Where are your kids? Lucy translated in her head but didn't answer. She was remembering how her mother had become more maternal when Faith had a child of her own, as if grandmotherhood had made that instinct finally kick in. Having children was one more thing that bonded them and excluded Lucy. Once, Lucy had chided Faith for being besotted by the replica of herself she'd produced.

"You think big chunks of yourself will be preserved in Travis after you're gone. But sooner than you think, your precious genes will be absorbed back into the common pool."

Faith had waved the idea away. "You don't get it."

Maybe her sister was right, in this, at least. Lucy felt more kinship with trees and animals than with humankind, and had a special fondness for insects, survivors who'd been around for 400 million years. Modern humans were the newcomers, arriving just 100,000 years ago. Bugs outnumbered humans by a magnitude that was almost impossible to conceive. Lucy had recently told her students that one square mile of Costa Rican rainforest had as many insects as there were people on the planet.

Lucy wanted to linger in the realm of millions of years and billions of bugs, but what flashed though her mind was all too singular: While *she'd* lost a mother, Faith had lost both a mother and a grandmother to her son.

Lucy's seatmate jostled her companionably. The woman was probably in her early forties, older than Lucy but not by much. She wore a tight skirt that ended well above her brown dimpled knees, and a T-shirt with a big sequined heart.

"¿Mis hijos?" *My kids?* Lucy patted her suitcase. "Aquí, adentro." *They're in here.*

Her seatmate's eyes widened at the thought of transporting kids in a suitcase. She started laughing so hard that her heaving breasts made the heart on the front of her shirt look as if it were beating.

The woman gave up her window seat so Lucy could take in the view she kept craning to see. The bus crawled along, weaving around ragged islands of pavement in a sea of dirt. Plumes of dust behind the bus signaled it was still dry season. The last time she'd been here, rain had swelled the streams. They had driven fast through culverts, the splash higher than the car.

It was all coming back to her: washed-out roads, unsurfable waves, and the locals' reserve, all of which kept most tourists away from Palmita. During the summers Lucy's family had visited, she felt even more herself than she did back home, but a version of herself porous enough to let everything in: an ocean close to body temperature, waves that either slammed down like detonated buildings or sent lazy, foam-edged tongues shushing up onto the sand. When she tried to describe the feeling to her mom, Sara laughed.

"That's how it feels to be on vacation," she'd said. "Then you go back to real life."

Something odd perched on a tall post at the entrance to a steep driveway, the first paved road they'd passed since Lucy boarded the bus. It turned out to be a carousel horse, ornately carved, shell-pink and white against the blue sky. Up the drive, a uniformed worker swung a Weedwhacker whose whine added another layer to the click, whir, and rasp of the midday insect chorus.

The bus heaved to a stop, but no one got off. A rooster crowed. Suddenly, all the passengers on the right got up to crowd around the windows on the left, trying to catch a glimpse of the action: two men facing off on the side of the road. Lucy's seatmate caught her eye and chin-pointed out the window, as if to say, *This is going to be good.*

Both men wore long shorts, flip-flops, and T-shirts. Lucy wondered for a moment if the one on the left could be Gabriel, her alleged father. The lift of the chin. And his hair. Even from the bus, Lucy saw glints of copper in the dark brown, like Gabriel's hair; at least, how it had been decades ago.

But no. This man was too young. He was shorter, his skin darker than Gabriel's. Still, the way he claimed his space reminded Lucy of

Gabriel's stance, edged with belligerence, as if always asserting his right to be here.

On one of their visits, Gabriel had told her he'd grown up rich, in the capital. His was the kind of family that went on shopping sprees in Dallas or Miami. After a stint in the US (which had apparently included scattering his seed: Johnny Appleseed meets Latin Lover), he had moved to Palmita, an out-of-the-way town, never looking back. Lucy wondered if the locals ever embraced him as one of their own or kept a distance, even though they were all *paisanos*, countrymen.

The man who reminded her of Gabriel had a quivering, skin-twitching stillness, like a pit bull straining at the leash. The other man was a white man, tall and pale, a blue bandanna half-covering the bare, mottled skin of his skull. Pit Bull stood firm while Bandanna gesticulated, brandishing what looked like a chicken leg. A collective gasp went up in the bus as Bandanna brought the chicken leg within inches of Pit Bull's chest.

Pit Bull looked down at the drumstick.

"Martín tiene la ventaja," yelled a man on the bus, as if narrating a prizefight. *Martin has the advantage.*

"¡Vamos, Rafa!" another man yelled out the window and then ducked out of sight. *Let's go, Rafa!*

Rafa, aka Pit Bull, looked up, surprised, as if seeing the bus for the first time.

Like many of the passengers, Lucy had her head partway out the bus window. The air outside was hot but not as stuffy as inside the bus. When Rafa turned to look, he seemed to lock eyes with Lucy, which delivered a jolt, as if she'd grabbed a doorknob after shuffling across the carpet in her socks. When she ducked back inside, a window screw grabbed a wisp of her hair, yanking it from her head.

Lucy's hand shot to her temple. "Ow!"

Her seatmate ignored the exclamation. "¿Lo conoce?" she asked. *Do you know him?*

Lucy shook her head.

The woman smiled conspiratorially. "Es Nica," she said, "pero rica." *He's Nicaraguan, but delicious.* It sounded better in Spanish, though the "but" hinted at the Costa Rican disdain for their northern neighbors.

The driver shifted into gear, and the bus lurched forward. Lucy still had no idea why they'd stopped, unless it was to watch the drama on the side of the road. Just as they were about to round the bend, Lucy saw Rafa close one meaty hand around the chicken leg that Bandanna was pointing at his chest.

The passengers were in a good mood, now that they'd had a little entertainment. They gossiped, presumably about Rafa and the man they called Martin. Lucy couldn't think how to ask the right questions in Spanish, settling for "Lots of trouble?"

Her seatmate shrugged, then indicated a sign they were passing: Rancho Vista Dulce. *Sweet View Ranch.* Another paved drive led up the hill; the place had two entrances. "Muy caro," the woman told Lucy. *Very expensive.* As if that explained everything.

When Lucy had looked for a place to stay, she'd come across just two options near Palmita. The Rancho was the one with freestanding villas bigger than her apartment, an infinity pool, killer views, and first-world prices. Lucy had booked the other place, more of a backpacker's flophouse, or so she guessed from the rudimentary website that said each additional person upped the room rate by $5.50.

Most of the passengers, including her seatmate, had been dropped off by now, often at places that looked to be in the middle of nowhere. The bus ride was probably slower than if Lucy had chosen to walk. She checked her phone—very little juice left, no reception.

She pulled out a sketchbook, made some bug notes, thinking of her students, then tried to draw Palmita from memory. The town had stretched out along a dirt road like loose beads on a cord: church, bar, school, and soccer field. A bunker-like mini-super sold coconut popsicles and eggs so fresh they were sometimes smeared with blood and feathers.

Someone was peering over Lucy's shoulder, bringing a soap-smelling cheek close.

"Bonita," a girl's voice pronounced. *Pretty.*

"Gracias," Lucy said, turning in her seat to take in the girl's glossy bangs and freshly ironed school uniform, the countrywide combination of white blouse and dark-blue skirt. Lucy figured the girl was in second or third grade, younger than her middle-school science students back home.

"¿Vas a escuela?" Lucy asked. *Are you going to school?*

"I went," the girl continued in Spanish. "The teacher was sick."

"I'm a teacher," Lucy said, the Spanish coming easily. She felt comfortable talking to kids; they were less judgmental than adults. But she wondered how long she'd be able to claim to be a teacher.

Her job was to be eliminated, but there was another lesser position open. She was supposed to have said yes or no before spring break. She'd pleaded grief. She worried the excuse was getting old, before she'd even gotten started with the real mourning. Thinking about her mother, she usually felt numb or angry or lost. The few intimations of true grief she'd felt were like being pushed out of an airplane into something even thinner than air.

The girl looked alarmed. "They said we could go home."

Lucy pulled herself back to the present. "I'm not a teacher here. I teach in the United States."

They passed a narrow dirt road that reminded Lucy of the turnoff to Gabriel's house.

"Who lives down that road?"

The girl studied Lucy. "Nobody."

Above the rumble of the bus engine came the sound of horse hooves striking hard ground. The few remaining passengers twisted around in their seats to see a riderless buckskin galloping at full speed, as if to catch the bus, dust drifting up in its wake.

A memory washed in: Lucy cantering bareback down a road like this one, her cheek against someone's back. The feeling of safety in the midst of adventure. *Inés.* The older local girl she'd had a crush on. Sara had been suspicious of the girl, keeping an eye on her when she came to the house. But mostly the girls ran wild, on their own. The first year, they tore through the woods, banging sticks against trees and screaming like monkeys. The second, they deepened their bond by excluding Faith. The third summer, Inés took the lead in a new sort of game. They pretended to be adults, yelling at each other, then making up. Inés's scent became the smell of Palmita for Lucy. At first, it was clean sweat and rich dirt. That last summer, her friend's scent changed to something more complicated that made Lucy feel both happy and restless.

The horse clattered past the bus, a rope dragging along the ground behind. "Bobo," a few passengers said, sitting back, satisfied to have identified the runaway horse.

Several minutes later, a heavyset woman came jiggling along at a surprisingly fast clip. Soon she overtook the bus, which was moving at a snail's pace to avoid potholes and deep sand. The passengers stood to call out the windows in Spanish: "Doña Calaca! Did you lose something?"

The woman waved as she went by, dressed in rubber boots and a T-shirt knotted at the waist. Exuberant rolls spilled over the waistband of her neon-pink leggings. Lucy recalled how she'd learned on past visits to Palmita that people here appreciated a woman with curves. Gordita (fatty) was not pejorative but was a term of endearment. Meanwhile, back home, even in junior high, Lucy and most of her girlfriends obsessed over the same five or ten pounds, lost and regained in a never-ending cycle.

The woman chasing the horse wasn't even out of sight before the gossip started. Small towns. Such sniping, and, if you fell out of line, such quick and sometimes cruel reprisals. In their town, Lucy's mother had had her detractors. She wasn't nice to people who didn't interest her. More than once, there'd been anonymous complaints about her marijuana grow operation.

The upside of small towns was that it shouldn't be hard to find someone.

The bus let her off before they reached the town proper. Lucy had told the schoolgirl where she was heading and now, visibly proud of her English, the girl pronounced, "You are arrive."

CHAPTER 3

> There are ants with built-in pedometers to track how far they've traveled from their anthill. They always know exactly how many steps they are from home.
>
> —*Lucy's bug notes*

Hilda's Cabins didn't look like much from the road. A hand-painted sign nailed to a tree pointed the way down a rocky path that was hell on suitcase wheels. Another wooden sign read: Stockholm, 9903 km.

Coming to a building that looked like a shipping container, Lucy called out. "¡Upe!" *Oo-pay!* The Costa Rican version of *yoo-hoo!*

No answer except a swelling of the insect chorus, as if the heat itself were singing.

The door was open to an empty reception area—low ceiling, dust motes in the still air. Leaving her suitcase, Lucy followed another path around the side of the building to a shady complex with half a dozen cabins. Red and white hibiscus climbed the porch pillars, towels dried on railings, and a crushed-shell path gleamed in the leaf-filtered light. To one side was an open-air laundry area; to the other, a yoga platform, where a shower of white blossoms had dropped onto the tin roof. The scent wafted over: sweet cream swirled in cool water. Lucy breathed in air that seemed to have twice as much oxygen as the air back home.

A tall white woman crunched along the path in lime-green plastic clogs, snatching beach towels off porch railings. She was a walking mixed message: long silver hair in high, girlish pigtails, a deeply lined face, and a stretchy miniskirt showcasing legs that sagged at the knee. Lucy could tell the woman was neither a local nor an American. It was her world-eating stride and European irritability, as if intelligence naturally led to impatience.

She pinned the towels to a line before she noticed Lucy.

"No yoga today," she called in a voice that took a pair of pinking shears to the English language.

Lucy was grateful for the English, however accented. The pleasure she'd felt in speaking and understanding some Spanish had begun to ebb. By the end of the bus ride, the language was a muddy river, carrying unfamiliar objects that knocked against her before spinning off downstream.

"I'm checking in."

The woman looked Lucy up and down but mostly down, given her height. "Too early," she said, then took the opportunity to explain how wet towels rotted wooden railings and how some people had no respect for checkout times.

"I faxed you," Lucy said, keeping to herself her incredulity that anyone still had a fax machine. "I wired the deposit, like you—"

"No refunds on deposits."

"Why would I want a refund? I'm here."

Hilda said Lucy could leave her suitcase, but she'd have to wait several hours before the student group here checked out. Hilda let Lucy change her clothes and splash water on her face in a tiny bathroom off the shipping-container office. In a mirror above the sink, Lucy confronted a face that looked a lot like the woman who'd left San Francisco that very morning, but she didn't feel like that person. Heat and fatigue made her feel like she was oozing out of her outlines.

Waiting for Hilda to lock her suitcase safely away, Lucy read the titles of worn paperbacks on a shelf above the counter. Shiny, fat spines with big print, one so wide it sported a good-sized dragonfly. A few weeks ago, she'd told her students about how dragonflies' long-distance migrations made Monarch butterflies look like underachievers. Thousands of miles, done in relays, like her own trip to Palmita.

"You can borrow books," Hilda said, padding barefoot back into the hot room. "But if you lose, you must pay." She sang out the house rules: Keep your cabin locked, make your showers short, and no overnight nonpaying guests.

Lucy snorted at the unlikelihood of an overnight guest, out here in the middle of nowhere.

Hilda shrugged. "People are not themselves on vacation."

Lucy almost said, "I'm not on vacation," but surprised herself with, "Do you know Gabriel Mora Soto?" Saying his name conjured him. Long bangs swept back from his face like wings. Pale skin. The sun made him red, not brown.

Hilda eyed Lucy. "Why?"

Lucy hesitated. "Years ago—" she began.

Hilda looked a little more sympathetic. "You're not the only one. It is no shame. Men like that…" She trailed off.

"That's not—"

"Funny," Hilda said. "You're not really his type."

Lucy drew herself up to her full five feet, two inches. "What *is* his type?"

"Me," Hilda said. "At least until I got old."

Give the woman points for honesty.

"He was supposed to help me get my land back," Hilda added.

Lucy half-listened to a story about Hilda safeguarding the wildlife preserve her uncle had founded. Don Something-or-Other made an illegal claim on part of the preserve and a tiny island, and then sold them off as part of his family land, for a song, to none other than Gabriel, who said he'd give back the preserve part of it when—

Hilda stopped short.

Lucy hadn't meant her sigh to be that loud. But it was all crashing down on her: the shuttles and airports and layovers and buses and this squawking stork of a woman saying that she, Lucy, wasn't her father's type.

It was the first time she'd thought it outright like that. Not Uncle Gabo or Gabriel or her quasi-dad. Just her father, period. Memories of friends' fathers mingled with rosy scenes from TV and movies. *Happy-family porn*, she and her sister used to call it. But now, cynicism fell away. Lucy's eyes filled and her heart beat faster. Could it be that on the heels of losing her mother and sister, new family would rush in and fill the gap?

Damn, Lucy admonished herself as the tears started to flow. *Get a grip.*

Hilda made shushing sounds and drew Lucy to her. As Lucy laid her head against the older woman's shoulder, she recognized the body language of someone who later in life decided to be huggy. Her own family had made the switch just before Lucy entered her teens, after Sara read a book about how children deprived of regular physical contact grew up unable to fully connect.

Too late, Lucy thought, even as she clung to Hilda.

"We all miss him," Hilda soothed.

Lucy pulled back from the woman's embrace. "Did he leave? Or is he—"

"We don't know for sure."

"When was this?"

"Maybe six or seven months ago."

Around when Sara died. Had he heard about her being sick, gone north to try to see her one last time? "How can no one know—"

"Why do *you* need to know?"

Lucy didn't feel ready to reveal her connection to Gabriel. The situation seemed odd. People didn't just disappear from towns this size. "Does he have family here?"

"He didn't think so."

"What does that mean?"

Hilda waved away the question. "I have work to do. But there is someone you could talk to." She directed Lucy to a nature guide with an office past the boarded-up church. "He knew Gabriel well."

Pedaling along under a canopy of trees on a bike she'd borrowed from Hilda, Lucy rode past humpbacked cattle standing in the field as if weighing their options. The faint boom of surf came and went on the breeze. Near the beach everything was flat, but not far inland the land bunched up in steep hills, draped in a nearly vertical web of green.

Palmita wasn't exactly thriving. The church and the school were boarded up. Many houses looked abandoned. The soccer field had been converted into a parking lot for a bar. Farther on was something new, or new in the last several decades: an open-air restaurant with varnished wooden tables, old pinball machines, and, hanging from the rafters, farm tools.

The guide's office turned out to be the size of a tollbooth, surrounded by a fence of broken surfboards like huge shark teeth. A handwritten sign read BACK SOON.

Lucy ducked her head into a place down the road, another structure that was new since her last visit. The place appeared to sell everything from motor oil to DVDs to crocheted bikinis. Two tables were squeezed among the merchandise, one occupied by a man in his sixties, who looked up when Lucy called a hello. His shorts and tank top showed off a body so dark and desiccated, it looked like petrified wood. His smile was the youngest thing about him.

"Hello, darlin'," he drawled in perfect Texan. "Come on in. You're letting the air-conditioning out."

Lucy stepped inside. The relief from the heat was immediate. Goose bumps rose on her bare arms. A chalkboard menu listed ten different kinds of fruit smoothies and two kinds of coffee: with milk and without. The coffee offerings had lines drawn through them, as if they'd sold out. Too bad. She could use a jolt of caffeine.

"Do you live here?" she asked the man.

"Yes, ma'am. Which is kind of a miracle. Almost didn't make it through my first year."

"Oh?"

"Drink. The old story, with a new twist. Traded bourbon for the local brew, *guaro*. Cheaper than bottled water." He looked at her. "You in a hurry? If so, you'd be the only one between here and Houston."

Lucy laughed. "I am, sort of. I've only got about a week. I'm trying to find this guy, the nature guide with that tiny little office."

"Good choice," he said. "Best guide around. Rough around the edges, but honest. And boy, does he know his stuff. You'll find him down at Playa de los Muertos."

She didn't remember the beaches having names, beyond "where the fisherman put in" or "where they cut down all the beach almond trees."

"Go five hundred meters south, then look for the path near where the bus driver used to live."

Costa Rica didn't have number-and-street addresses and didn't think in terms of blocks, not even in the city. Directions were mostly about landmarks, often well-known buildings that had been torn down or places where people had once lived. It wasn't just space that was navigated; it was time as well.

Reluctantly, Lucy left the air-conditioned refuge and got on her bike, waving her thanks. Heading south, she wondered how the Costa Rican method would apply back home. If Faith sold the family home, would it be, "Go five hundred meters east from where you used to turn off for the old Gale house"? If Faith kept it, would she and her son soon be the only Gales anyone remembered?

She rounded a bend, the Pacific coming into view. If Lucy were in charge, what would she want? To claim the family home, move back in for a sort of childhood do-over? Sell it and split the profit, putting her share toward a new life somewhere affordable, like Palmita? Maybe start a school here or help reopen the old one?

The scenarios made her head spin. Feeling like she didn't have much say in the matter made the spin teeter, a globe off its axis. Lucy thought again about how much she could use a cup of coffee. Who was she kidding? There wasn't enough coffee in all of Costa Rica to help her figure out where in the world there was a place for her.

CHAPTER 4

> Social insects—like termites, ants, and honeybees—literally sniff out intruders. Living in close proximity means they exchange gut bacteria, creating a common microbiome, which in turn affects the pheromones they produce. When ants, which have about 400 smell receptors in their antennae alone, detect and decode the scent of intruder ants, that discovery unlocks the aggressive behavior needed to defend their nest.
>
> —*Lucy's bug notes*

Sun glinting off the water hurt her eyes. A small rocky island sat low in the water. Lucy remembered it was the town cemetery, reachable only at low tide, when the island became a peninsula. Inés used to say that if you stood on the beach at sunrise, you could hear the ghosts out there grumble about how shallow their graves were.

Lucy sat at a discreet distance to watch the soccer game in progress. A white man in lithe middle age was keeping the ball airborne, bouncing it off a bony knee, an ankle, even his wide pale forehead. The other players waited him out, deference and irritation doing battle in their faces.

Another man—brown skin, late thirties, on the shorter side of medium height—didn't want to wait. He grazed the white man's shoulder to catch the ball on his own bare chest, with a speed and grace at odds with his earthbound appearance.

The interloper let the ball he'd stolen fall to the sand with a thud. A gold eyetooth flashed as he smiled at his own skill. The others tried and failed to suppress their grins. It was clear they enjoyed seeing the white man bested.

Gold Tooth cajoled the ball down the beach, coming in Lucy's direction. As he came closer, she recognized him. It was Pit Bull, aka Rafa, of the roadside confrontation she'd seen from the bus window. He'd been menaced by a taller man, who—another stab of recognition—was the man Rafa had just stolen the ball from. People on the bus had called him Martin. Her bus seatmate had said Martin was the owner of the pricey hotel on the hill.

Rafa's long hair was pulled back into a utilitarian ponytail. His face was both exotic and familiar. Had he and Lucy really locked eyes out the bus window or had it been a trick of the light? Either way, the man was magnetic. The iron in Lucy's blood felt the pull.

"If you open your heart and let all the love you have shine," Lucy's mother used to say, "I promise that some highly dysfunctional, emotionally unavailable man will glom onto you and never let go." This was the same woman who said *Who needs men?* then had an endless string of them.

Rafa took in everyone's position; two of his teammates were open. One was a distractingly handsome man in his late twenties. When he turned, Lucy saw that he wore heavy metal plugs in his stretched-out earlobes. She'd seen similar plugs in San Francisco, where people talked about urban tribes and neo-primitivism, and called the stretching-out process "gauging." In Palmita, such plugs had actual history, dating back to the Chorotega, who arrived in the area around 800 CE. The tribe had migrated here from Mexico, Lucy had once read, lording it over other tribes until arriving Spaniards became the new overlords.

Ear Guy called out to Rafa, but the first man's words didn't carry. As fit as Ear Guy looked, there was something about him that didn't inspire confidence. Lucy noticed the other men on the field wouldn't look at him directly, but seemed to be aware of where he was, like when you keep a fly in your peripheral vision until you swat it.

Rafa turned to the one girl on the field. She looked maybe sixteen or seventeen years old. Her young face was open and appealing, her body taut with lean muscle. Rafa gave a nod and the girl took off running, each footfall spitting sand. She approached the goal. He lobbed the ball to her. Feet off the ground and hair streaming back, she punched with her forehead, spiking the ball through the span between a shirt and a piece of driftwood.

Lucy jumped to her feet and cheered, as much for Rafa not ignoring the girl on the field as for the goal. Everyone turned her way. A few men smiled. The girl flicked her eyes, suspicion shot through with curiosity. Rafa looked at Lucy longer than anyone else. She was suddenly aware of what she was wearing: cutoff jeans, too heavy in this heat, and an old T-shirt that read *My Governor Can Beat Up Your Governor*.

"¡Gobernadora!" Rafa called.

Lucy looked behind her but there was just her bike, leaning precipitously because the kickstand had sunk into the sand. Then it clicked: *gobernadora* was the feminine of *governor*. A reference to her T-shirt, with its joke from back when an Austrian bodybuilder ran California. Down here, the slogan probably just read as pride in American aggression.

The ball rolled to a stop at her feet. Rafa motioned for her to join the game.

Faith had been the star athlete, high jump and hurdles her best events. Sara went to most of Faith's meets, in part because she herself had once been something of a high-jump prodigy. Their mother professed to not understand soccer, and never went to Lucy's games, so she didn't see that her firstborn had more terrestrial talents: dribbling, passing, and body checks when the ref wasn't looking. Soccer was a good game for a short girl.

Lucy hesitated only a moment.

The sand was cool and firm from the recent high tide. She was glad they'd asked her to play, even if she suspected the plan was—as it so often is in pickup games—to show her up.

People looked different up close. Grainy, like blown-up photographs. Rafa had a scatter of acne scars under his cheekbones, and assorted other nicks on his arms and legs, as if he'd been through a woodchipper. Another man had an angry growth under one ear. The girl had a small scar on her cheek, ridged white on soft brown.

Lucy searched faces for variations on Gabriel's hooked nose and thin, curved lips. She looked so hard that people started to dissolve into individual features, a jumble of eyes, noses, and mouths, like the old Mr. Potato Head toy.

With Martin, Ear Guy, and two others, the opposing team had four players. Lucy's team had six. Rafa jutted his chin toward the girl, then the other team. Glaring, the girl headed for the other team to even up the numbers.

Lucy's plan was to stay on the margins. Maybe they'd send the ball her way; she'd trap and return it, show them she wasn't completely useless.

The girl kicked off to Martin, and the game was on.

Martin passed back to the girl, who started down the beach; Rafa indicated Lucy should cover her. The girl, half Lucy's age, easily outran her, stopping with the ball a few feet in front of her, daring Lucy to come and get it. As Lucy approached, the girl ratcheted her leg back, taking the kick.

Lucy had just enough time to turn her head so the ball hit the side of her face instead of her nose. It smacked near her ear, a hard, gritty kiss of damp leather and clinging sand. Her eyes blurred and she let out a whelp.

She caught a couple of smirks, though Martin looked outraged and Rafa pained. The girl was gone. She'd bounced the ball off Lucy and down the field, taking advantage of the lull—everyone wondering how Lucy would react—to take the shot. Now the girl was braying victory, alone at the end of the field.

"You okay?" Martin called in English.

Lucy was shocked by the girl's hostility but wasn't about to wimp out. Her mother had insisted her girls be tough, or at least pretend to be. Sara had been so proud when she found out both daughters had reputations at school. *You don't fuck with the Gale girls.* Lucy still had a small reserve of bravado to draw from when she needed it.

"Let's play!" she roared.

The game finally ended when someone kicked the ball into the surf. Lucy went after it, launching herself into the cool water, which felt wonderful. She took her time bringing the ball back in. When she regained the beach, shaking out her hair and licking salt off her lips, people were drifting away.

"Bien hecho, gobernadora," Rafa shouted. *Well done, governor.*

The girl scowled; it seemed to be her all-purpose expression. When Rafa clamped his arm around the girl and steered her down the beach, Lucy's heart wobbled like a three-legged chair. Not just because she'd imagined a connection with Rafa, but because it looked like he might be one of those men who takes up with women half his age. Not a rare thing, as she herself had experienced with a recent boyfriend who'd said he needed space and then filled it with a sweet young thing with retro leg warmers and fresher ovaries.

Martin approached. "Sorry about that rather rude welcome."

"That's okay," Lucy said, still watching Rafa and the girl. "What's with her?"

"Hell hath no fury like a lady traded to the other team. Isa's not your typical Costa Rican, avoiding conflict at all costs. And Rafa's probably got a tour to lead."

Lucy gazed at the couple heading down the beach. It suddenly came to her—the nature guide she was looking for must be this man. She went a few steps after Rafa, but someone called her over to where she'd left her bike.

Everything that had been in the bike basket was gone. Her shoes. Her blue pack. The thief had also taken the bike's pedals and the seat, leaving a rusty metal tube that reminded her of the post from the doorknob she'd stolen from her childhood home.

In the pack Lucy had had her sketchbook, a wad of local money, her room key, and—worst of all—her phone, with its contacts and backup photos of her passport and of Gabriel's will. Luckily, her credit cards, real passport, and letters from Gabriel were in Hilda's safe.

Her shoes were gone too. She didn't relish walking barefoot back to Hilda's. Visiting Palmita as a kid, she'd come out of the water one day to find her flip-flops gone. She walked home barefoot, the rocks hurting her feet. She told her mother and Gabriel that it was strange because the beach had been totally deserted.

Gabriel had snapped, "Like the New World was deserted when the Spaniards came?"

"Lástima," said a man with kind eyes and a pitted face, nodding at the empty bike basket. *A shame.*

"I'll go to the police. Where's the station?" Lucy said in Spanish.

"You could make a report in Bocas," said someone behind her, in English. It was Martin. When he spoke, everyone else's eyes went vague.

But, Martin told her, Bocas was two hours by car, three by bus, and you never knew when the police station would be open. Plus, he said, local cops couldn't investigate crimes. "You need the OIJ, Costa Rica's FBI, to do that. It would take a while for them to get here."

Lucy's exhale was somewhere between sigh and shudder.

Martin loaned Lucy a pair of battered flip-flops he pulled from the back seat and offered to take her and her wounded bike to Hilda's. When they arrived, no one was around, and Lucy no longer had her room key. Seeing her face, Martin invited her to lunch at the Rancho and said he'd drive her back to Hilda's afterward.

"That would be really nice," said Lucy, relieved.

From Lucy's high seat in the air-conditioned van, Palmita looked shabby. The flat afternoon light didn't help. They passed a house sliding off its foundation. Rusty car parts and fishing gear were half-visible in overgrown yards. A skinny horse, head down, was tied to a post.

Farther, in a tree near the road, dark shapes showed through the leaves—howler monkeys waiting out the midday heat. All the animals knew enough to get out of the sun, except an old man in a torn T-shirt on the side of the road, immobile but for his eyes following the progress of the van.

They passed the school. Part of its roof had caved in. "What happened there?" Lucy asked.

"Storm. A few years back. That's why I send some of the local kids to a private high school in the provincial capital."

She stole a sideways glance at Martin. After the game, he'd wiped himself down with a towel, trading his soccer shirt for a crisp, pale-pink button-down, tempting dust, fate, and perhaps ridicule in this hard-edged man's world.

"Very generous."

"What you have to understand," he opined, "is that people here don't value what you and I do. And sometimes it takes an outsider to see a place's potential. To drag them kicking and screaming into the modern world." His smile was self-satisfied.

"I like that Palmita hasn't changed much."

"You were here before? I think I would remember you." He gave her a sidelong glance.

Was he flirting? The man was dapper but seemed sexless.

"A long time ago. I knew a man named Gabriel Mora—"

Martin let out a sharp grunt, a sound that didn't match his spotless pink shirt.

"Hilda said he was—well, gone, which I took to mean he's maybe dead."

"Hilda." His mouth pruned.

"So he's not dead?"

Martin slowed the van and looked at her. "What's your interest in this man?"

Lucy kept quiet. She hadn't told Hilda her connection to Gabriel, and she trusted Martin even less. The lawyer listed on the will would give her the straight story. She asked if Martin knew him.

The van strained on the uphill now, tires crunching gravel. "Never heard of him."

They passed the gleaming carousel horse that marked the entrance to the Rancho. Lucy craned her head around for a better view.

"A winged horse," Lucy marveled, trying to smooth over the moment.

"So she can escape when Interpol tracks her down." Martin laughed. "But seriously, I want people to know that once they get to the Rancho, gravity no longer applies." He gunned the engine to make it up the steep paved drive. "We get a lot of seekers here."

Lucy remembered telling Faith her plan to walk Spain's Camino de Santiago. Faith had hurled that word—*seeker*—at her, making it sound ridiculous and pretentious. That was long after Lucy, home from college, had tried to convince Faith to get out of their hometown, telling her she wouldn't become fully herself until she escaped their mother's orbit.

Faith had looked puzzled. "But I already am myself."

That was when Lucy realized that some people were actually born themselves, and others—like her—had to do the hard work of chasing themselves down.

CHAPTER 5

> Millions of insects migrate, most in huge swarms. But once, an insect trap on a plane caught an outlier: a single termite flying at 19,000 feet. It was up there alone, hoping for the best.
>
> —Lucy's bug notes

IN TERMS OF LAYOUT, the Rancho resembled Hilda's: a main building flanked by half a dozen freestanding cabins. But up here, the cabins were villas, with peaked roofs, wraparound decks, and carved wood detailing somewhere between Balinese temple and gingerbread house. Pathways wound through grounds landscaped to look wild but with none of the messiness of unimproved nature.

The most remarkable thing, though, was the view. On three sides, all you could see was blue. No coastline was visible—just ocean. It was dizzying.

Martin followed her gaze. "It takes some getting used to."

Workers rushed by, carrying buckets of cleaning supplies, armloads of flowers, stacks of clean towels.

"A group arrives tonight," said Martin. "It's all hands on deck." He stopped a woman carrying a tub of fruit. She kept her eyes on the mangos and pineapples as he rattled off instructions in Spanish.

"She'll make us a late lunch," he told Lucy. "Do you want to freshen up first?"

She smiled at the old-lady phrase. "I'd just have to put back on my dirty clothes."

"You wouldn't believe our lost-and-found."

The shower had two heads and an ocean view. Lucy stood at the intersection of sprays and closed her eyes in pleasure. The long, dusty day spun down the drain.

When she'd seen the towels folded like swans, Lucy had objected, "They'll have to clean the room again." She'd been a maid for two summers during high school and now tipped well whenever she stayed in a motel.

"They're happy to have work," Martin had said, leaving her alone in the kind of luxury she would never be able to afford. Usually she was fine with that, even made a virtue of necessity, convincing herself that wealth lulled people into a kind of stupor. But every now and again, she wondered how different her life would be if she had money to burn.

The towels would be better, for one thing. These were like the clouds she'd flown through to get here. The beds were turned down and it took an act of will to resist slipping between high-thread-count sheets and closing her eyes.

Even the weather up here was better, ocean breezes making the temperature just about perfect.

Funny how beautiful surroundings could make you feel prettier. It helped that the dress from the lost-and-found was sexier than anything she'd choose for herself. Martin looked better now, too. He was lord of the manor here, at home in his authority. His body seemed to gain actual heft as he directed the activity of what had to be at least a dozen staff.

Martin and Lucy sat at a table by the infinity pool and were served course after course: a plate of papaya, greens with beefy tomato, grilled fish with mango salsa, sides of sautéed spinach and roasted sweet potatoes. He'd offered Belgian beer or Argentine wine; she went with the beer.

"Not your usual local lunch," Lucy said. She remembered the

typical meal here from her childhood visits: tough meat, warmed-over rice and beans, and a limp slaw of shredded cabbage.

"And thank God for that." Martin raised his glass.

They toasted. Her second beer was just as cold and sharply delicious as the first.

"And to how this country lets you reinvent yourself," he added, and they toasted again.

Lucy felt as expansive as the view.

Martin pushed his plate away. "So. What brings you to Palmita?"

How civilized to feed and clothe a guest before asking why they were here. Such generosity made her want to tell Martin the full story. "I grew up in Northern California," she began.

"San Francisco?"

"No." She hesitated.

Martin waited.

"Farther north. Small town—"

"Big hell," Martin interjected.

Lucy laughed. She looked out at the view, but she was picturing the field near the family house, how it sloped up to a stand of trees. Past that, mountains jagged into the sky. Even living in the city, commuting to her teaching job on the bus, Lucy had been propped up by the shape of that landscape, more real to her than the city's avenues and coffee shops and bars. Now, the thought of having no stake in her family's piece of that landscape made her feel formless, as if she were collapsing into herself. The loss felt retroactive.

It wasn't just that she no longer came from that place; it was that maybe she never had. She was as lonely as a bee whose hive had been knocked out of a tree. Turning back to Martin and to the reality of the present, Lucy told herself that coming down here had been the right move.

As if he knew what she was thinking, Martin was talking now about how where you came from didn't determine who you were. How your birth and your parents were accidents you could recover from.

"Amen to that," Lucy said. *Since when do I say* amen?

"And think about this," Martin said. "Pizarro was a bastard from Extremadura who never learned to read. He went on to conquer the Inca Empire with one hundred and fifty men and a handful of horses. Cortez? A sickly child who his own parents couldn't stand. Did that stop him from marching into the very heart of Mexico, where the Aztecs thought he was some sort of god? That's what I love about this place."

"What's that?" Lucy had lost the thread.

"You make your own reality here."

Lucy considered this.

"So," Martin said. "What reality do you hope to make here in Palmita?"

Sailing the old family house down the coast and planting it here, in a totally new place, probably wouldn't happen, but—

Before she could finish her thought, a bird the size of a man's meaty forearm swooped in, the hinge of its wing a foot from Lucy's face. It landed at the edge of the table, talons scrabbling against glass. Lucy scraped her chair back, away from the blue-and-white bird that looked like a monstrous jay. Martin jumped up to try to scare it away, then yelled at a man nearby Lucy hadn't noticed before. The man approached, and the bird flew off.

"Sorry," Martin said, as they settled back in. "You okay?"

"Of course," Lucy said, though in fact, the bird had shaken her up. "I guess it wanted the food left on the plates?"

"This place is full of scavengers."

"I wanted to ask—is there a lot of theft in Palmita?"

Martin looked at her blankly.

"My pack."

"Let's not ruin our meal," he said, waving another worker over to the table. "Two coffees," he told the woman. "And this time, see if you can steam the milk right."

The tone Martin took with his employee seemed harsh and condescending. The warmth Lucy had felt for him began to cool.

Martin said the Rancho Vista Dulce had the fastest internet in town, which was like saying Sloth A would totally cream Sloth B in a race to the next branch. The computer was in an alcove off the open-air dining room. The chatter of workers drifted in, as did a nice breeze, which dried the sweat behind Lucy's knees. She was still stuffed and half-drunk from the meal by the pool.

Lucy thought of her desk back home. If her computer had a Breathalyzer, she probably wouldn't be here right now. She'd booked the full-priced flight after a third glass of wine.

Here were her emails. Finally.

Lucy's boss, the school principal, wanted to know ASAP if she'd decided about the new position. He'd given her until after spring break but now, apparently, there was another candidate. Another candidate? Hardly a week had passed since the principal called Lucy to his office to say the school could no longer afford a dedicated science teacher. He'd offered her a tech consultant job instead.

Lucy hadn't grown up longing to teach, so was surprised by how well she took to getting up in front of a class, making science into a sort of song and dance. Two years running, she'd won Teacher of the Year, displaying the plaques proudly until they took away her classroom, a refuge filled with Coke-bottle ant farms and posters of the butterfly life cycle. She was allowed a wheeled cart overloaded with specimens in jars, rock samples, and laminated species sheets. Between visits to homerooms, the cart lived in the mop closet.

She had asked the principal, "Could I keep my cart?"

"You could keep your bug blog."

"I was planning to expand that, maybe include birds."

"Best to stay on brand."

Lucy had made a noncommittal sound. She would keep taking notes for her blog—in fact, she was always jotting down ideas—but not post anything to the school's site until she knew her job was secure. She could always start her own bug blog, separate from the school. But if she had no science students, who would read it?

"The details are still in the works," the principal had said. "If approved, the position would allow for great flexibility. You wouldn't have to work more than nineteen hours a week, and some weeks you'd have complete freedom."

That meant no guaranteed hours, no health insurance, and no vacation or sick days. The private school had no union.

Lucy had forced a smile. "Tell me more about the new job." Her mother, who'd never had to deform herself for a real job, would turn over in her grave if she heard her daughter's groveling falsity.

Now, Lucy scrolled through more emails: newsletters, ads, and fundraising appeals. Oh, God. Here was an email from her sister. So now Faith decides to get in touch.

> Mom wrote us a letter. It's not a will or anything but you might want to take a look. Also I think she wanted you to have some of the books & rugs & I wanted to tell you Travis is having some problems.

Moth-eaten rugs and mildewed paperbacks from decades back, all wife-swapping and masturbation. No, thank you. And where was the *It was all a big mistake, my claiming the house. Come home and we'll make it right.*

Lucy did worry about her nephew. She felt a special connection to Travis, in spite of—or maybe because of—him being a hornet's nest of perpetual trouble. What a funny kid he'd been, spinning around in the yard until he toppled over, hanging out the car window, panting like a dog. Raw delight transformed his sweet, chubby face. By the time he thinned out, he was a thrill-seeker of a different stripe. His mother blamed drugs, but Lucy sensed something deeper: a rush towards any brink, as if he longed to free-fall off the edge of the map. She knew that feeling, even if his mother didn't.

Martin leaned into the alcove. "You lost your notebook, you said? Here's one that a guest left behind. Totally blank."

"Thanks!" She took it, annoyed that she had to be even more grateful to him now but happy she could keep up with her bug notes. Her mind went straight to insect lore when she felt anxious or confused, and it soothed her to get it down on paper. The tidbits came unbidden, as if out of the recesses of her unconscious, though she suspected they were facts she'd learned and then forgotten. And if Lucy didn't immediately recognize their parallels to her own all-too-human drama, the fun bug facts were more than fun: they pointed her towards a pan-species understanding of just how strangely living creatures can behave.

"I'd better run you down the hill before guests start arriving," Martin said.

"That would be great. Just give me a minute to finish this email." *Now I'm begging him. Jeez.*

Tell me this, Lucy replied to her sister. *Did you open that letter from Gabriel to me or did Mom? And yes, fax me her letter. Do a web search for Hilda's Cabins, in Palmita.* There were easier ways for Faith to get her a copy of the letter, but Lucy wanted her sister to wonder what part she'd played in driving Lucy not just away from home, but out of the country.

CHAPTER 6

> Ants may raid the colonies of other ant species to steal young workers. The kidnapped ants labor the rest of their days in what is essentially a foreign country, working for the survival of a species and culture not their own.
>
> —*Lucy's bug notes*

AT THE SOCCER GAME, Martin hadn't told Beto to steal Lucy's pack. He'd whispered, *Something's not right with that chick. See what you can find out.* Martin knew Beto would take the hint, still craving as he did the older man's approval, even as their relationship stretched towards its breaking point.

Beto had sensed Lucy scanning him, her gaze snagging on his ear plugs, then dismissing him. It was the warmth of attention given, the chill of it being withdrawn. Not unlike how Martin's interest had receded as Beto morphed from boy to man. Martin had always walked the line between affection and abuse, but lately there'd been more stick than carrot. Just a word to his buddy, a local functionary, Martin said, and they'd make good on the federal government's threat to bulldoze all structures within 200 meters of the high-tide mark.

Beto's place was right on the water, a simple wooden structure up on stilts in case the tide got ambitious. It wasn't much, but it was all he had.

Lucy's gaze sliding over him, Martin's desire drying up, the town itself looking the other way—it all made Beto's job easier. Invisibility had its perks. He'd wager that no one had seen him strip Lucy's bike, much less swipe her backpack.

The breeze lifted the rice-sack curtains his mother had made. Out the window, the sea and the cemetery island. At low tide it was a peninsula, connected to the mainland by a slippery rock spine. If the sea level rose, it would become a true island, like Chira Island up north. In the 1500s, Spaniards kept Indians captive on Chira before they sent them to work as slaves in Panama's silver mines.

Okay, maybe his cemetery island was a little less tragic than Chira. But it still had its restive spirits, in large part due to Beto's grandfather, who'd dug up the graves so he could sell the place. It was illegal to sell land where bodies were buried.

Speaking of buried bodies, Beto had recently had a flash of understanding. Martin had unearthed him as a boy, only to start heaping dirt on him as he grew up.

At the beginning, there had been the pain that gave way to pleasure. The sense that here, at last, was someone who truly wanted him.

Martin groomed a preadolescent Beto by indulging the boy's obsession with all things indigenous. Together they searched remote beaches for a special kind of sea snail, *plicopurpura pansa*, used since pre-Columbian times to dye cloth. Martin said they could milk the mollusks and then put them back in their crevices so they could produce more of the viscous compound that turned cloth yellow, then green, and finally a vivid purple that didn't wash out or fade. Utterly sustainable, Martin had said, even as he crunched the mollusks underfoot.

One year, Martin drove them to Nicoya for the spring pilgrimage to the hilltop where a priest said an outdoor Mass rooted in a much older tradition: Placating the gargantuan feathered serpent that lived under the hill. Martin and Beto had worn feathered Mardi Gras masks for the climb, drawing stares.

Once he had the boy in thrall, Martin's interest in such things disappeared. Then began the belittlement and threats. Martin's goal now was to make Beto feel as if no one else could ever love him.

Beto kept going up the hill to the Rancho because it was the closest thing to getting out of town, or even the country. Martin had taught Beto his near-perfect English but also encouraged Beto to "self-identify" as an indigenous artist, and to perform his identity for the Rancho's guests. Tourists from Europe, the US, and Japan were smitten, sometimes to the tune of a hundred dollars for less than an hour's work. They told him how lucky he was, living in this unspoiled place, even as they gave him tastes of their powders and left behind their books and clothes and bright ideas, such as how Beto should move to New York or Berlin to be an artist. Like visas grew on strangler fig trees and everyone had money.

Beto turned to the task at hand. The backpack's zippered compartments prolonged the sense of discovery. In the front pocket, a wad of local bills. In another compartment was a key attached to a small fishing float. Everyone knew those were from Hilda's cabins, where in fact you didn't need a key—all you did was push hard near the knob, and the door gave way.

There was a phone, of course; no tourist went anywhere without one, even though you had to go over the hill for reception. Beto had a box of phones he'd collected over the years, charging them at a rickety machine he'd made of a stationary bike and a car battery. He kept his favorite ones juiced up so he could look at the pictures and reread the texts, windows into other people's worlds.

Here was a sketchbook with scribbled notes and pen-and-ink drawings, one of Palmita: church and school, paths leading to various beaches. Calaca's restaurant was missing, but the drawing gave off something powerful. The trees along the road felt alive. The hill to the north looked just as it did when Beto was walking alone in the early morning, wondering why he'd been born in this particular place at this particular time, and not centuries earlier, into a small, tight-knit band who always stuck together. He'd heard rumors that across the Nicaraguan border, in some of the more remote towns, the older people still spoke the native language.

If he heard the old language, would it sound familiar after centuries of lying dormant in his brain? His mother was indigenous, though only one side of her family admitted to it. She had no interest in that heritage. It was Beto, who called himself an outcast half-breed, who obsessed over a time of wholeness, when everybody had their place and their role.

What would he be in such a world? He didn't have many skills, but he had a talent for how colors and shapes worked together. Maybe he could decorate canoes or houses, or be a shaman, if that was what they called it back then. Someone who had permission to wander through the neglected layers of reality, bringing back to the group a more complicated way of seeing.

During Martin's last visit, Beto had been excited to show him his new project, even as he braced for indifference or worse. He'd led Martin through fishbone mobiles and strings of stacked iridescent beetles hung from branches. Beach rocks balanced in little pagodas. Nested in a fraying hammock lay a cluster of giant eggs—coconuts stitched into canvas covers. A guest at the Rancho had told him about Christo's wrapped bridges and islands. Beto liked the idea but thought he'd start small.

Beto had pulled a tarp from what had started life as a stand-up paddleboard. On the front end he'd bolted the head and shoulders of a woman carved from driftwood. The figurehead's eyes were green beach glass, and her ears were pale-pink shells. Where someone would stand up on the board, symbols ran in a spiral.

Squatting, Beto traced his finger along the curve of glyphs. "You know how every year in Puntarenas, they have the fishing boats all done up with decorations, and they ask the Virgin for her blessing? I was thinking I could be a part of that," he had said to Martin.

"Beto." The tone was as familiar as it was wounding. It said, *You, poor boy, are pathetic. You are nothing.*

Some days, Beto knew he wasn't nothing. His work wasn't nothing. Today wasn't turning out to be one of those days.

"These are Mayan hieroglyphs," he said stubbornly. "It's not really so far-fetched when you think about it, because the Chorotega shared certain traits with the Maya."

Martin looked bored.

"You probably can't read Mayan glyphs, so I'll translate: 'Flee, interlopers, or heads will roll.'"

Martin gazed at the sculpture again, as if to give it a second chance. "Well, look who's growing a spine. But, *mi hijo*, you can't disguise a pile of crap, no matter how many hieroglyphs you throw at it."

Beto thought he'd steeled himself against the man's casual cruelty but was stung just the same. Martin used to call him his little inventor. Said he had real talent. Growing up didn't pay. Whatever promise people thought you had, they liked nothing better than to break it.

The ceiling fan in Cabin 6 had two speeds: limp-along and whirlwind. The latter made the apparatus rattle so hard, Lucy wondered if it would shake loose and send blades flying.

On the unpainted windowsill was the glass doorknob from home. She'd thought of it as a talisman, a reminder that you can salvage stuff from an old life to help build a new one. But the metal post sticking out the back looked ugly, the mechanics of detachment laid bare.

She lay on the bed as memories circled in the churned-up air. Spring in the woods behind the family house. The scent of sun-warmed bark. The air a loose weave of cobwebs, caterpillar silk, and soft clouds of tiny, tender flies.

For a while, they'd had an old convertible with a cloth top so threadbare they never put it up, even when it rained. Lucy's job was to sit behind the driver's seat, holding her mother's hair in her fist. There was a lot of it to hold. In the wind, it was like wrestling with something alive. Faith was in the front seat, her longer legs earning her that privilege.

Lucy woke in the dark of the cabin. She stumbled to the bathroom and switched on the light. After splashing cold water on her face, she noticed a small framed landscape on the wall, its colors pulsating, especially the blue-black clouds on the horizon.

Was it a photo or a painting? When she took it off the wall to get a closer look, the picture exploded. Black bits sprayed onto her face, crawled up her arms, and flew into her mouth. She dropped the picture in the sink, swatting at herself and spitting out tiny bitter somethings. What were they? Flies?

She wailed, backing out of the room, shivering with bone-deep disgust. Bug love had limits. But it was more than that. The exploding landscape made her think of back home, of a familiar scene undermined. Something eating at you from the inside out: the cancer in Sara's breast, or a father you didn't know worming his way out of old letters. The picture appeared to be whole until you looked closer, and then it blew up in your face.

Lucy flung the cabin door open and leapt down the stairs in one bound. Hilda came running, machete in hand.

Ants, Hilda explained wearily, after making sure it wasn't something serious, like an intruder. Flying ants apparently made nests in unlikely places. She went to get a spray bottle with a green leaf on the label that smelled suspiciously like Raid.

"Maybe take off for a while," Hilda said. "Give this stuff a chance to work."

"Take off? In the middle of the night?"

Turned out it wasn't even nine o'clock yet. There was a dance tonight, Hilda said, at the local bar. It wasn't far.

Eyes stinging from insecticide fumes, Lucy squirmed into the closest thing at hand, the long clingy dress from the Rancho's lost-and-found. The effect was dampened somewhat by her beat-up running shoes.

The dress was like the one her friend Jane loaned her on her birthday a few years back. They'd dolled up to go out, not knowing it would be the last time. Lucy had met Erik that night. He was nursing a ginger ale, waiting for the first act to finish so his band could go on.

"We're Blue Division," he told her. "Bluegrass versions of old Joy

Division songs." He turned out to be the king of odd combinations. A talented guitarist who made his living babysitting developmentally disabled adults, he also surfed rough-and-tumble Ocean Beach but claimed he wasn't a surfer.

"Surfers tend to be idiots," he said. "I aspire to not be an idiot." But when Lucy spent the night at his place, they were plagued by early-morning calls about wave and wind conditions and whether it was worth a paddle out.

All that was fine, but not long into their relationship, Erik decided that in fact he did want kids. "I can't believe you don't," he said. "You'd be great at it."

"It," Lucy echoed. "You know how butterflies have kids?"

"Nope."

"They squeeze out hundreds of eggs, then take off, hoping some of them will make it."

"Okay," he said, with a flatness she'd never heard before.

"But not really caring one way or the other." Lucy wanted the last word, for all the good it did her.

Not long after, Lucy lost her best friend as well. Jane had married one of the few women CEOs in tech, had a baby, and become an even more traditional wife and mother than if she'd married a man and been wary of falling into that role. Jane was unhappy but wouldn't admit it; she thought that would be like saying she was sorry she had a child.

Instead, Jane insisted Lucy must be unhappy, alone as she was, and was angry when Lucy didn't agree. Lucy countered by saying that even roaches and beetles knew how to co-parent; why couldn't Jane's wife do the same? Lucy later apologized, but things were never the same between them.

On the walk into town, wielding a borrowed flashlight, Lucy thought she saw a pair of eyes pulsating in a shoulder-high bush.

"Mom," she whispered.

Something crashed in the underbrush. Goose bumps erupted on her bare arms.

"Hello?" breathed a voice so softly, Lucy doubted its reality.

"Yes?" Lucy whispered.

The moon came out from behind the trees. Bluish light washed across the dirt road. Into that light stepped a figure.

But it was a girl, in a dirty T-shirt and ragged shorts. Hair clumped with rats' nests and cheeks smeared with mud. She took Lucy's measure with a practiced once-over that seemed beyond her years. "Are you lost?" she asked in Spanish, as if being lost were a moral failing.

"I saw something. I thought it was, um, an animal." Lucy said.

"La Mona Bruja." *The monkey witch.*

The girl told her about a woman who shed her skin, grew fur, and transformed into a horrific monkey-woman. La Mona moved so quickly through the trees that she was just a shrieking blur. At least, that's what Lucy thought the girl said.

"She mostly attacks men. But not always."

"Oh," was all Lucy could muster.

"Look at your face!" the girl exclaimed. "Don't worry. It was probably a kinkajou."

Lucy had heard of kinkajous but forgot exactly what they looked like and whether they traveled in packs. They were related to raccoons and coatis—she knew that much—and were also called "honey bears" for their golden-brown fur. The girl was racing ahead now, as if she herself wasn't convinced the noise in the bushes had been a little honey bear.

They headed for town together. Soon there were fewer trees, and more lights. The girl tried to match Lucy's stride, even as Lucy slowed on account of the girl's shorter legs. They noticed each other's efforts and exaggerated their own. The girl's walk became a series of spastic leaps. Lucy minced along like a secretary in a pencil skirt.

"You're crazy." The girl was delighted. "Big and crazy."

Lucy mimed outrage. "You're small but your crazy is big. I bet they call you, um, Big Little Crazy."

"No!" crowed the girl. "I'm Pilar. And I know your name."

Lucy stopped. So the entire town already knew her on her first day here?

The girl stopped too. "You told me on the bus."

Could this grubby kid be the soap-smelling girl in the spotless school uniform? "Where are your parents?" She'd meant to work up to that question, but the gap between the girl's daytime and nighttime appearance sped up the timetable.

"They're—sick."

Lucy nodded. The parents were either drunk or drugged, or maybe just in a mood. You made yourself scarce and hoped when you got back, they were back to their better selves. Times like those, you wished for butterfly parents who fluttered off and left you to your own devices.

"I'm going to Tia Calaca's. She has a pinball machine." Pilar used the English word but pronounced it *peen-bahl*.

"I love pinball." Lucy echoed Pilar's pronunciation.

CHAPTER 7

> On a field trip to the rainforest dome, my fifth-grade class pushed through a heavy rubber curtain and into a steamy world of tanagers, blue macaws, and hundreds of butterflies that flickered like chemically induced flames. The guide told us the butterflies were FedExed in chrysalis form from farms in Costa Rica. If they were lucky enough to hatch, they lasted a few weeks, living out their short lives in exile.
>
> —*Lucy's bug notes*

ISA WAS CUTTING ONIONS as slowly as humanly possible.

So fast on the soccer field, Rafa thought, so slow in the kitchen. He'd been making her help with dinner lately, especially when he cooked the few Nicaraguan dishes he remembered helping his mother with when he was Isa's age. He wasn't going to be around forever.

As a teenager, he too had rolled his eyes when his mother tried to teach him the difference between Costa Rican gallo pinto and the Nicaraguan version, the latter with red instead of black beans. The name for the rice-and-bean staple translated as *painted rooster*.

"Each country paints its rooster differently," Rafa told Isa, echoing what his mother had once told him.

"Could you believe that lady's T-shirt, the gringa?"

Rafa knew his daughter. No doubt she hoped the memory of the *My governor can beat up yours* slogan would get him in a lather about imperialism and off her back about her supposed heritage. Isa had never lived in Nicaragua and probably never would. And her mother, whom she barely remembered, had been from France, a country Isa told Rafa she thought of as nothing more than a shape on a map.

Choosing a red pepper from a chipped blue bowl, Rafa steadied it on a cutting board he himself had made, and neatly sliced off the stem.

"So that's why you kicked the ball into that lady's face?"

Isa closed her eyes to sooth the onion sting. "It was an accident."

Just this year, Isa's voice had gone from squeaky to deep and melodious. It was often at odds with what she was actually saying, which should by rights have come out in an adolescent whine.

He checked the pot of beans; the earthy aroma made him picture his mother lifting the lid on just such a pot. "You know, *mi amor*, we were once strangers here, too."

"Whatever," Isa said, frowning.

"Were you mad I put you on the other team?"

Isa brought her knife down hard. "That's why your team lost. We won!" She pumped her fist, still clutching the knife. "Thanks to me. And Martin."

The Rancho's owner was a sore point between them that Isa sometimes liked to prod. Rafa knew Isa saw Martin as a harmless old man who paid good wages. She'd told Rafa that her friend Deysi worked at the Rancho part time, said it was easy money.

"You don't want to be one of his foot soldiers," he had warned. Then he'd had to explain to her what foot soldiers were.

But he also knew that the more he told her to stay away from the Rancho, the stronger the lure would become. Parenting had somehow become counterintuitive, whereas before he could trust his instincts.

Rafa needed a drink. No, he needed a meeting. His sponsor, Keith, was hard to find these days. Used to be he was always at the thatch-roofed bar with cable sports. Now he could be anywhere. Sober people were unpredictable.

"You know how I told you my uncle was like a gar, and my mom was a—"

"Machaca," Isa said without much interest. "Grandma Machaca."

Rafa had told Isa the kid's-book version of his past. That he'd grown up across the border, upriver. That he used to compare people he knew to fish. His uncle, who took tourists sportfishing, was all smiles until it came time to tally the bill; he was a sly, toothy alligator gar. His mother was a machaca, sister to the piranha, small and plump but a real fighter.

Rafa had told Isa that his mom worked at a remote fishing lodge, but not that the building had doubled as a brothel, or that his mother didn't know for sure who Rafa's father was.

Isa had asked girlish questions about Rafa's mother: What was her favorite color? How had she worn her hair? Rafa answered as if reading a bedtime story. Isa had said that him not having a dad was like her not having a mom. People who needed more than one parent were just greedy.

Rafa didn't mention that his father might have been the night manager sent from Bluefields, a big, gentle man who, like most of that town, was descended from shipwrecked slaves, English pirates, and Rama, Sumo, or Miskito Indians.

Just when Rafa wanted to update the stories, mark the fact that Isa would soon be a woman, her interest had all but evaporated. He'd never told her, for instance, that another uncle had been an interrogator for the paramilitaries.

"How many men in your unit?" the uncle had asked two prisoners. When neither answered, he shot one dead and then asked the other, "Now how many men in your unit?"

"A machaca, right?" Isa had stopped cutting onions. She looked at Rafa with concern.

"Right," said Rafa, rifling through bottles in the wood crate where he kept spices and sauces. "What I was going to say is that Martin is like—"

"A shark?" Isa asked slyly. Rafa had told her that as a boy, he'd wanted to be like the bull shark, thick-skinned, at home in both the river and the sea.

"More like a vampire bat," Rafa said.

Isa groaned. "Deysi's right. Old people can't help but be melodramatic."

He laughed in spite of himself. "Did I tell you that your old man got more sign-ups for the night hike?" He took over the onions, gently pushing her aside. "But there's still room for you."

"You know I'm not into nature anymore."

"Not into nature? You *are* nature, my love. The very best nature has to offer."

Isa couldn't help but smile. "You have to say that."

"I do. But it also happens to be true."

He let her go see Deysi while dinner was cooking. Rafa stood at the raw wood bookshelf he'd been meaning to paint, paging through the books Gabriel had brought over one by one, a slow-motion bequeathal of his library—novels and bird books and essay collections in Spanish and English, favorite parts underlined in fading ink. Some of the underlined passages made Rafa feel closer to his friend than he had while the man was still around, being his standoffish self.

A few lines in Edward Abbey's *Desert Solitaire* drew his attention. Gabriel had once read the passage aloud, acting the part of blustering gringo. "I like my job. The pay is generous; I might even say munificent: $1.95 per hour, earned or not, backed solidly by the world's most powerful Air Force, biggest national debt, and grossest national product."

The details—especially the hourly wage—made Rafa smile. Gabriel had told Rafa about his US road trip in the early 1970s. The sweep of the place made Gabriel think his own life could be more spacious, even epic. At the time, Gabriel said, Americans were breaking out of the thought prison of consumerism and national pride. This author, Abbey, had been of that ilk, a ranger in the desert drawing a government paycheck while criticizing that same government. Rafa wondered what it would be like to be born in a country so strong, it would pay you to disparage it.

He put the book back on the shelf. A vein in his temple throbbed.

Maybe it was missing Gabriel, or the fact that the book's print was so small. Or maybe it was how the writer, Rafa now realized, worked so hard to disguise his privilege as rebellion.

After dinner, he decided, he'd head over to Beto's. Someone from the soccer game had said Beto was up to his old thieving tricks. Gabriel would have wanted Rafa to be the one to confront him. Then he'd check out the party at the bar. Just the other day, Gabriel had reminded him that he, Rafa, was not just a father but also a man. And that he needed a woman, not women.

How can a dead man give advice? Easy. Rafa now heard Gabriel in the grumble of his truck engine or the screech of worn brake pads. The other day Rafa thought he heard Gabriel say, *Be there for Beto*, something Gabo himself could never do.

Beto opened his door a crack. He opened it wider when he saw Rafa, but not wide enough for his friend to see the backpack on the table.

Rafa gently pushed the door the rest of the way open. As he'd suspected, there were the telltale signs of Beto's recent thievery. Rafa sighed. "We talked about this."

"*You* talked about it." Beto went back inside and sat at the table. "Anyway, it's just a tourist."

Rafa took the other chair, across from Beto. "She's not just a tourist. You know that."

Beto picked up Lucy's sketch book and put it back down. "She might as well be. She doesn't belong here."

"She came all this way. Throw her a bone. At least tell her where Gabriel ended up."

When Beto shook his head, his ear plugs swayed. "She didn't ask."

"She doesn't know to ask you. Do you want me to tell her?"

Beto glowered. "You said it was my story to tell. When I was ready."

"I stand by that." Rafa gazed through the open window. "But when do you think you're going to be ready?"

"I've got a lot to do."

"Like what?"

"I told Calaca I'd stop by to help with the broken pinball machine," Beto said. He hadn't called Calaca "Mom" since she'd said she thought Martin, his tormentor, was a good influence on him.

Calaca wiped her hands on her apron, leaving streaks of oily grime. Once again, she'd managed to fix the *tragamoneda*—the coin guzzler, aka the pinball machine, the pride of her open-air restaurant. Fifteen years of humidity and hard use and the bells still dinged, most of the lights still flashed, and the cracked and faded flippers still flipped.

She needed help getting it back up on its legs.

"¿Me puedan ayudar?" *Can I get some help here?*

She eyed her son and then her father, each at his usual table. Beto had come to help, he said, then had sat down to draw. He and his grandfather were old and young versions of the same man: lanky, handsome, and lazy as the day was long.

"Sí, Calaca," Beto said grudgingly, setting down his pen.

"Sí, mi hija," Don Diego said, shuffling a sheaf of papers, limp with age.

Calaca loved them both so fiercely that she welcomed the day one or both of them were gone. Loving shattered men was backbreaking work.

Calaca clucked softly to her scarlet macaw, who became agitated whenever his archrivals, the other men in Calaca's life, got too close to her. Once the bird saw the old man raise a hand to his daughter, and it flew straight at Don Diego's bald head. He still had the scar.

"On the count of three," Calaca said in Spanish.

Open to the night air, Calaca's Place had a dozen tables, each with a flowered oilcloth covering and a big jar of pickled carrots, onions, and peppers.

Not much business tonight. People were probably at the bar down the street.

From the open-air kitchen came the smell of pan-fried chicken.

A subtler scent of drying herbs wafted from the room out back. Most people in Palmita had visited that room at some point. Her bestseller was Sleep Tea, though she was still tinkering with the formula. A small percentage of users reported hallucinations. Her friend Marta said that colors and textures had pulsated, and the air had felt quilted.

Most of Calaca's medicines were more straightforward: cures for everything from pink eye to unwanted pregnancies. She assisted at births too, though those who could afford it drove to the provincial capital and paid for a caesarean. Doctors pushed caesareans because they could schedule them, avoiding a long and unpredictable labor.

At the other end of the life cycle, the townspeople with money had their loved one prepped for burial by a professional. The rest of the locals went the traditional route of washing the body and getting it in the ground as soon as possible. Calaca was known for making a special herb-infused wash that kept the bodies smelling sweeter longer. Beto once told her he'd read that the Chorotega embalmed bodies with tree resin and she should try that, though he wasn't sure what tree the resin came from. She'd made her usual shooing gesture and he'd gone back to his drawing.

As if the town's garbage were an extension of the messy life cycle of the human body, Calaca had also solved Palmita's trash-pickup problem, bribing the beer deliveryman to cart the trash to an illegal dump site over the hill.

Beto and Don Diego were back at their separate tables when Lucy and Pilar arrived. The macaw half-opened his wings, squawking a warning. Calaca shushed the bird and pulled Pilar to her, stroking her hair, studying Lucy over the top of the girl's head.

Lucy thought there was something familiar about this woman, with her hair standing up like a hedgehog's and a shrewd but kind look in her eyes. Even her bright pink leggings rang a distant bell.

"Pilar scared me on my walk to town," Lucy said. She hoped she was getting her Spanish verb tenses right.

"*She* scared *you*?" Calaca said.

"I did!" Pilar unclamped from Calaca to look up into her face. "I was like La Mona."

Calaca gripped the girl's arms. "You know we don't joke about—*her*."

Pilar looked at her feet.

Lucy now recalled where she'd seen Calaca—out the bus window, chasing a runaway horse. But there was something else, maybe from further back.

"¿Donación para la entrada?" A skinny old man in an ancient suit coat fluttered some papers in Lucy's face. She hadn't seen him when she walked in, though she had noticed a young guy in the corner, his head bobbing to music from his earbuds.

"There's a fee to enter?" Lucy said in Spanish.

Calaca stepped between Lucy and her father. "He wants to build an entryway, a gate, to the island."

Lucy cocked her head.

"The cemetery island," Calaca explained. "You remember."

Lucy did, in fact, remember the cemetery island. But how—

"An entryway, to make it look like a cemetery again. Those are sketches of the different designs. My father is asking for a donation. But first"—she turned to her father—"we introduce ourselves."

The old man said nothing.

"This is my father," Calaca sighed. "Don Diego."

"Mucho gusto," said Lucy, extending her hand. *Pleased to meet you.*

The man didn't take her hand. "Donación para la entrada?"

Lucy dug a few bills out of her pocket.

"I'll get you a receipt," Calaca said.

Lucy told her there was no need, but Calaca was already heading for the back, Pilar at her heels.

Lucy looked around. The restaurant was a pleasant place, open to the cool night breeze, though of course it couldn't compare to the Rancho up the hill. And how did they even attract customers here, with that racket from the bar down the street? That must be where the dance was.

Calaca's father didn't seem to mind. He was back at his table, shuffling papers.

"Señor," Lucy called out in Spanish. "Do you know a Gabriel Mora Soto?"

The old man ignored her, but the young man across the room looked up from his sketchbook. He pulled one of his earbuds free, leaving the other in. His earlobes were stretched to accommodate plugs the size of half dollars.

It was the guy from the soccer game. The good-looking one no one would pass the ball to. She approached his table. Seeing her coming, he slammed his book shut. Lucy thought she'd been right in her first assessment: handsome on the surface but furtive underneath, like a scenic lake with dangerous undercurrents. He angled his face toward her without actually looking up.

"English?" Lucy wanted a break from being at a disadvantage.

"Who did you say you were looking for?" he said in English that was almost accent-free, not meeting her eye.

"Gabriel Mora Soto."

Beto didn't answer.

Lucy said the name a third time, in case her pronunciation was the problem. Should she be rolling the *r* in Mora? My God. She didn't even know how to pronounce the name that might, in fact, be hers.

Beto started humming along to the faint music coming from the dangling earbud.

"What are you listening to?"

Now he looked at her. "Peen Floy."

"Who?"

"Peen Floy. *Dark Side of the Moon.*"

"Pink Floyd." Lucy sat down at his table. He looked at her like she'd just pushed into an already full lifeboat. "Are you going to the dance? It's at the bar, right? Just down the street?"

"Looking for Rafa?" Beto always knew who wanted whom. Feeling unwanted himself, he'd developed that sensitivity. Of course, the way she'd looked at Rafa during the game, everyone else in town probably knew it too.

Lucy shook her head, but the wheels were turning. She'd missed talking to Rafa at the soccer game. Here was another opportunity.

"I see you've met my son." Calaca was back. "Introduce yourself!"

"Beto," said Beto, sounding as if he weren't entirely convinced.

"Lucy." She wasn't going to make the same mistake twice; she didn't extend her hand. "Nice to meet you," she lied.

CHAPTER 8

> Kissing bugs come for you at night. If you scratch the bite, the Chagas disease the bugs carry can get in. You may be tired for a while, then the symptoms disappear. But bugs are patient. Thirty years later, your heart might enlarge—lovers think that's good, but doctors know better—and then just stop.
>
> —*Lucy's bug notes*

THE BAR DOORS SWUNG like in an Old West saloon. Heads turned when Lucy pushed through. She fought the impulse to look down at her feet. *Be brave.*

A thatched roof vaulted above and the walls were of green plastic netting, which thwarted bugs and the larger dust particles. Wooden tables were crowded with empty bottles, evidence for the closing-time tally. Most of the customers slumped on stools; the few chairs with backs were hot commodities, especially as the night wore on.

On a TV suspended above the bar, men chased a ball across an electric green field, with movements that looked, to those who'd been drinking since sundown, perfectly choreographed to the salsa music thumping from speakers the size of steamer trunks.

An old couple danced with a casual authority that made them beautiful. Another couple drooped against each other like two beanbag chairs. Her cheek against the man's shoulder, the woman raised a brow plucked clean and redrawn, peaked as a teepee. That was the extent of the "dance" Hilda had told her about.

Lucy ordered a beer and scanned the room. Unless drink utterly transformed the man, Rafa wasn't here.

The music changed to electronica so loud, the empty bottles trembled, but the dancers hewed stubbornly to the previous beat. Lucy was about to leave when in flounced a group of people even more out of place than she was.

They moved like a tumble of puppies, skin and hair color in every imaginable shade. Two shirtless boys in harem pants mock-wrestled as they walked. Three girls in strappy sandals strutted arm in arm, as if down a Paris catwalk.

The dancing couples froze. Eyebrow Woman glared at Lucy, as if she'd been the advance guard for these dazzling intruders who made everyone else look like week-old fish.

More people arrived from the same crew, along with an older man with a white bandanna knotted on his head. It was Martin from the Rancho, herding the others to the bar. He leaned in close to a girl who was the Euro version of the soccer-playing girl on the beach, the one who'd kicked the ball in Lucy's face. Accidents of birth. This Euro girl could fly across the ocean and push into a local bar like the world was hers for the taking. The local girl—well, who could blame her if she felt so trapped that she took it out on blundering newcomers like Lucy?

Martin caught sight of Lucy and joined her.

"Babysitting is hell," he said, though he was clearly enjoying himself. His cologne had notes of pine that evoked a more northerly landscape and made Lucy homesick. "They arrived early for the workshop. Said they were itching for something authentic. That they wanted to see the real Palmita."

"Is this it?"

They watched as one of the girls pulled a local man from his stool to dance.

"Not anymore," said Martin.

An hour later, Lucy realized she was having a good time. She'd had shouting conversations with an Israeli about the girl's stint in the army, with a local about how the new president was a *marioneta* of the old one, and with Martin about the Google ranking of the Rancho's website.

The bartender put on a CD that one of Martin's people had brought along, vintage ska so infectious, everyone got up and tried to slot their bodies in between the beats. Lucy danced with a girl, then a boy, then a group that moved together in a syncopated scrum that at one point lifted her off her feet.

Lucy danced hard, shucking off the city's demand that all movements be small, whether on the bus or the sidewalk or in a crowded restaurant. In her own apartment, she had to keep her music down and her tread light, lest the downstairs neighbors complain.

It felt good to let loose.

Someone complimented her on her dress. She suspected she was a little drunk when she plucked at the clingy fabric and yelled at Martin across the room, "Lost-and-found!"

No one paid any attention to her; all eyes swiveled to watch the woman bursting through the swinging doors. Wait, it wasn't a woman; it was a girl. Pilar. She went straight to a local man dancing with one of the Rancho guests. Looking sadly at Pilar, the man held thumb and forefinger an inch apart, begging for a little more time. Pilar stared, and the man Lucy assumed was her father relented, shambling after his daughter as she headed out the door.

Pilar might need help. Lucy was almost to the door when another man pushed through. It was Rafa, hair down, eyes wild.

Like Pilar, he was here on a mission. He caught sight of the young woman from Martin's crew who looked like Rafa's soccer girl and was across the room before Lucy could warn him, *She's not who you think*.

But apparently, she was. The girl's face said she'd been found out. Her body language changed in a heartbeat—from defiant to repentant to defiant again.

The girl said something that made Rafa's eyes widen and his mouth thin to a trembling line.

Martin stepped between them, his face inches from Rafa's.

Rafa took a step back, not in retreat but to assess the fool who dared come between him and his girl.

The locals tuned in to the confrontation. Lucy remembered the passengers on the bus flowing to the side for front-row seats at the two men's earlier roadside conflict. There was that same collective eagerness now, amped up by alcohol and a girl to fight over.

Lucy's vision narrowed to one detail: a brown hand on a white neck.

The girl intervened, like girls in bars all over the world were doing at that very moment. She put herself between the men.

Like Pilar before her, the girl headed for the door, Rafa close behind.

On his way out, Rafa spotted Lucy and took her by the arm. "You don't belong here either." She let him pull her along, not sure whether to be outraged or thrilled.

The truck cab was thick with tension, though Lucy, wedged between Rafa and the girl, was drunk enough to treat it like weather, a massing of clouds that had nothing to do with her. What these two were to each other—what they were fighting about—Lucy didn't know. They didn't really act like lovers.

They bounced along in silence. Lucy tried to distract herself from her attraction to Rafa by puzzling over why the bar owner had gone to so much trouble enclosing the place in plastic netting when the open spaces above and below the saloon doors let in whatever bugs or rodents or snakes wanted to come to the party.

She scratched a few places on her bare leg, suddenly and acutely aware of Rafa's arm and leg just inches from hers.

The last time Lucy had felt this attracted to a stranger was a few weeks after her mother died. Standing-room only on the express bus, on the way home from work, mashed up against a man she pegged as a traveler. No luggage to give him away, just an openness of expression that said he could risk really seeing the people around him because he would soon be on his way. How long they held each other's gaze told them all they needed to know.

What a relief it had been, to be with someone who didn't know she should be a wreck, in deep mourning. When he liberated his penis from his pants, it bounced up like an apartment dog desperate for a walk. Together they rolled a thin sheath down its bowed length. It was good to have real live human weight on her. She'd been dragging around ghost baggage. Losing her mother had opened the door to all loss across time, hollowing her out so that grief finally had enough room to resonate.

Lucy made sure she came; she needed the release. The man from the bus thought her sobs were part of her orgasm. When they didn't let up, he pulled out.

"It's okay," Lucy said, guiding him back in, turning her wet face to the side. She didn't want to leave him hanging, and she sure as hell didn't want to talk about it.

The truck lurched, and Lucy was thrown into the girl, who was pressed against the passenger-side door. Lucy's foot kicked something in the footwell, a paperback with a bird on its cover, fluttering amid a jumble of tools and trash.

Lucy remembered the man on the bus back home. *This time, I'm the traveler.* The one with the clarity of the outsider. Except that any clarity was clouded by alcohol and desire.

A bark sounded in back of her. A short-legged dog was in the truck bed, trying to keep his footing as they bounced over ruts and swerved around potholes.

"Mario should be up here," the girl said.

Rafa grunted.

The dog barked again, high and shrill.

"I can walk," Lucy said.

"She can walk," the girl taunted.

"It's no trouble," Rafa said, though it was clear her presence was nothing but.

There was no one else on the road. The truck's passing rousted a bird that flew along with them for a while, swooping in and out of the headlight beams, picking off bugs.

At Hilda's, the girl had to climb down from the cab to let Lucy out. Sullen, she went to the back of the truck to check on the dog. Rafa clamped a hand on Lucy's knee.

She giggled; she was ticklish.

"Be careful," he said. "This place—"

She let out an exasperated grunt, the polar opposite of her giggle. Why did women traveling alone have to field so many vague warnings about what might befall them?

Lucy leaned over and kissed him. Why wait for danger to find her? She kissed with her eyes open, looking through the dust-pocked back window at the girl, who was having her own intimate moment, her face buried in the dog's fur.

The kiss petered out. "Good night," Lucy said stiffly. "Thank you for the ride."

"Buenas noches, señora." He matched her tone. *Good night, ma'am.*

Bastard. She was pretty sure she was younger than he was. He could have at least flattered her with a *señorita*—young lady.

She was almost to her cabin when she realized she'd forgotten to ask Rafa about Gabriel.

DAY TWO

SUNDAY

CHAPTER 9

> Despite its name, the gregarious cockroach is a homebody that doesn't venture far from the intergenerational nest. It can be hard to know who's related in that seethe of siblings and cousins, so they've developed special kin-recognition abilities to avoid inbreeding. The trick is, you have to know yourself in order to sniff out similar traits in others.
>
> —*Lucy's bug notes*

SHE SLEPT THROUGH her second day in Palmita.

A maid knocked on the door around noon, calling out that she was here to clean. Lucy asked her to come back later, and the visitor went away.

In Lucy's cabin, the curtains were drawn, the interior dim. The overhead fan slowed in response to some invisible fluctuation in power, then sped up again. A car crawled by, tires chewing gravel like a cow chews its cud.

Lucy dreamed of her mother. Sara's presence was so palpable that Lucy, knowing she was dreaming, willed herself to not wake up. Lucy was in the old house and although Faith insisted they were alone, Lucy could feel another person there. Out of the corner of her eye, she saw her mother in a chair no one ever sat in. Sara shifted from one buttock to the other. *It doesn't hurt*, she said without saying anything. *But it's kind of uncomfortable.*

Lucy woke up angry and sad. Even in dreams, Sara missed her opportunity to come clean—to reveal Lucy's true parentage and beg forgiveness for keeping it from her for so long.

Growing up, Lucy had been pinned at the intersection of two feelings: that she'd been done wrong, and that she herself had done irreparable wrong. She felt unloved, even though if asked, she would have told you that of course her mother loved her. Lucy also felt guilt for not loving her mother well enough. For not saving her. From what? Men. Loneliness. Death. Maybe even from her own daughters, who were so obviously not enough for Sara.

Lucy was just fourteen when she'd realized Sara was jealous of her and Faith. Lucy might have noticed sooner but for the unlikeliness of it. At that age, Lucy looked like a scrawny boy. Faith, at thirteen, was already a lumbering six feet tall, with broad shoulders and childbearing hips.

But Sara was a knockout. Even in her late thirties, she had men falling all over themselves to fix her transmission or take her to Reggae on the River. But some of her boyfriends had started to give her daughters a second look. Lucy thought it was creepy, except when it gave her a secret thrill.

Sara started fishing for compliments in a way that diminished herself, like the first spots of mold on a marijuana bud. She'd strike up conversations with checkout clerks and gas-station attendants so she could throw out lines like, "Aren't my daughters gorgeous? And me, just an ugly old woman."

"You're pretty gorgeous yourself," was the common, if baffled, response.

The sisters burned with embarrassment. Lucy was also on fire with rage, which got worse when Sara started setting traps for her boyfriends, leaving them alone with her daughters to see what would happen. If she invited a guy over for dinner, she'd invent something she needed from the grocery store at the last minute and insist on making the trip alone.

"Did he do anything?" Sara would demand later. Lucy suspected that if something had happened, their mother wouldn't be concerned for her daughters, only outraged on her own behalf.

One lazy summer afternoon, their mother led her latest fling into the woods. The girls knew where the couple were heading: the clearing where Faith and Lucy used to make dandelion chains, chew on sour grass, and play house in a burned-out stump.

The sisters exchanged glances, watching them go. Then Faith did something that Lucy couldn't quite figure. She got their mom's rifle, which of course both girls knew how to shoot. She motioned for Lucy to follow. They giggled. This was a lark, the gun a prop—for what drama, Lucy wasn't sure.

They found Sara and her date, lying in the springy loam under the redwoods. The girls watched through the bushes as the man flipped their mother over roughly so he was on top, holding himself up with his arms.

The gun went off.

Sara screamed, and the man slid off her and into a defensive crouch. Lucy's head snapped back as if she herself had taken the shot. But it was Faith who stood stock-still with the gun on her shoulder, aimed into the branches above the couple.

Sara told the story for years, each time trying out new theories on who had shot at her and why. Never did she voice any suspicion that it might have been one of her own daughters. But something shifted that day. Sara seemed to regain her dignity. She became more reserved and dated less.

The girls never talked about what had happened, but sometimes Lucy would study Faith, wondering how her sister had known just what it would take to get their mother in line.

At dusk, a Black kid with blue hair appeared at Lucy's cabin door. "You don't remember." He smiled.

He was at least a decade younger than she was, with big arms and an easy manner that said the differences between them—age, race, upper-body strength—didn't matter. Not tonight. The moon was almost full, and the air felt like a vitamin cocktail. She'd gotten a good day's sleep.

"Remember, at the bar? We danced. You said you'd come to our party." He cocked his head, assessing, and Lucy suddenly felt old. "It's on the beach, but we have chairs."

"Well, if you have chairs..."

Turned out they had exactly two camp chairs, set back from a raging bonfire. Dancers wheeled around the blaze, oiled skin gleaming. A woman down by the water juggled flaming clubs. The guy who'd come for her at her cabin handed her off to a skinny man in a Speedo. He led her to a chair and then literally skipped away.

Lucy dug for a beer in a cooler but found only energy drinks and bottled water. Whatever was making their eyes bright, it wasn't alcohol. Smiles were stretched a little too wide. The partygoers shimmied and cartwheeled and cackled and just generally looked like they were all in on some big cosmic joke.

Splashing came from the water. A man was lying on a surfboard, paddling slow and steady, surfboard as transport rather than wave-riding device. When he steered his craft toward shore, Lucy felt a flare of danger, as if some ancient overlord had come through time to see who dared trespass on his domain. But the partiers ran down to welcome him, draping a colorful scarf around his wet shoulders and fitting a feathered mask onto his face.

The new arrival made straight for Lucy, claiming the other chair. He stretched out his legs, adjusting his mask so his eyes were wholly visible through the slots. When he trained those eyes on her, she felt a shiver of something she had the good sense not to label as sex.

"Hola." She extended her hand.

He gazed at her hand until she withdrew it. Barking a laugh, he held out a fist. By the time she realized she was supposed to do a fist bump, he'd dropped his hand to his side.

The newcomer scrunched down in his chair. A long hank of hair, pulled over his shoulder, dripped onto a taut belly that shone international brown in the firelight. He could be from almost anywhere, born brown or baked in the sun. They both watched the revelers for a while.

"So anyway," she said in English, hoping he'd follow suit.

More than follow, he led, like a skilled dancer. His English was good, if a little distorted by the mask he wore. Their conversation was the verbal equivalent of the partiers' acrobatics. They sprang from sandcastle competitions to Andy Goldworthy's ice sculptures to Burning Man to a praying mantis in Malaysia that disguised itself as an orchid. He knew as much about US politics as she did, and a lot more about politics in the rest of the world.

He told her how tourism was both the lifeblood of the Costa Rican economy and a malevolent force that broke down family ties and drove out locals. Lucy nodded earnestly, as if she herself was not part of that process. But something of what he said touched a nerve. She offered up a seeming non sequitur that was in fact an invitation to see newcomers in a new light.

"In 1890, in New York, there was this man who loved Shakespeare and wanted to introduce every bird mentioned in his plays into the US. He released sixty European starlings in Central Park. There weren't any starlings in the US before that. You know how many there are today? Two hundred million!"

"An invading army."

"An invasive species, to be sure. But now we couldn't imagine the US without them."

His face behind his mask was unreadable, but a small shrug seemed to signal the end to that particular subject.

Once they'd warmed up, the two of them talked at the same rapid clip. Even their pauses seemed in sync.

She'd known other people who seemed to have similar wiring when it came to rhythm and timing. Faith wasn't one of them, but Sara was.

Lucy recalled asking her mother, after they'd met some Dutch tourists at the local coffee place, "How old do you think those guys were?"

"Let me think," Sara said.

Sara thought and so did Lucy, picturing the men, how they'd talked and moved, what they wore.

"Ready," they both said at the same moment. They laughed, and even their laughs were of the same timbre. They didn't come up with the same ages for the Dutchmen, but the duration of their decision-making was identical.

A salty gust came off the ocean. The man was talking about how Gram Parson's friends stole his body to burn it in the desert, but botched the job because they were too high.

"I can't believe you've heard of Gram Parsons," Lucy said. They'd played a Parsons song at Sara's memorial, something about going down twenty thousand roads and all of them leading back to you. To her. To Sara.

Lucy shook it off. She didn't want to grieve right now.

"Edward Abbey's friends did better," he said.

"You know Edward Abbey too?" Lucy was glad to focus on something other than her mother. "They took him out to the desert, buried him in an unmarked grave."

"Like he wanted. God, I can't believe you've read Edward Abbey."

"He was one of my father's favorites." The man's voice almost broke.

"No way! What a coincidence. You are *not* going to believe this." She launched into the story of her parents meeting in Yosemite, each with their own copy of Abbey's *Desert Solitaire*. Then she remembered that the story her mother had told her about her parentage was almost certainly a lie.

"Except that it's all probably a bunch of crap," she said, not liking the whininess of her own voice. What had Martin said at lunch? "But like somebody told me recently, family is an accident you just might recover from."

He asked her to repeat that last part. She did, but he still didn't get it.

"Explícame," he said, reverting to Spanish. *Explain it to me.*

Lucy explained, mixing Spanish with English. When recognition showed in his eyes, she was happy, as if together they'd solved a particularly hard crossword puzzle.

"Yes," he said thoughtfully. "An accident."

It was then that he flipped his hair back, and Lucy noticed the plugs stretching his earlobes out of shape. It was the guy from the soccer game, who'd also been at the restaurant. Lucy had already assessed him as a little off, and half-suspected him of stealing the stuff in her bike basket. She remembered his name: Beto. This was the man she'd been spilling her guts to.

She scooted her chair away. "I know you."

He took off his feathered mask and set it in his lap, petting it like it was a tame bird.

The full view of his naked face was too much information at once. "I have to go home," she told him.

"You're a long way from home." His voice had changed, and his body seemed charged with a darker energy now.

"I have a connection to this place."

Beto opened his hands as if to say, *This very place? This beach?*

"The town," Lucy said. "Palmita."

Beto repeated the name of the town, giving it the amplitude of native Spanish pronunciation.

"That's what I said."

"Did you?" He tilted his head.

"I don't get you. I'm not sure you're even gettable." The made-up word would probably fly right over his head, but she didn't care.

"I'll get *you*," he said evenly.

Lucy wondered if he knew what he was saying. Studying the set of his jaw, she decided he did.

DAY THREE

MONDAY

CHAPTER 10

> Bromeliads cling to trees but live on air, snagging nutrients that drift by, collecting rain into little pools that become their own ecosystems, with decaying plants, protozoa, bugs, frogs, even crabs and snakes. How long before I figure out the creatures in the pool that is Palmita?
>
> —*Lucy's bug notes*

"You know that guy Beto?" Lucy asked.

Hilda looked up from draping a yoga mat over a wooden railing. In this climate, the mats got funky fast; they needed to air out. "Calaca's son."

Lucy let her heel hang off the step to the yoga studio, stretching the back of her leg. She wasn't sure what she wanted to know. Maybe she just wanted Hilda to agree that Beto was a weirdo. Maybe she wanted an ally. "I saw him last night on the beach. There was a party."

Hilda reached for a broom and started sweeping. "Did something happen?"

"He was wearing a mask. I didn't know who he was at first. He seemed different from when I first met him."

"He lost his father recently."

Lucy softened. She knew what it was to lose a parent.

"His father was not kind to him," Hilda continued. "He didn't treat him like a son." She stopped sweeping, folded her hands over the top of the broom handle, and looked at Lucy.

"Family is fucked," Lucy mused.

The landline in the reception area began to ring. Hilda dropped the broom and ran for it.

Alone now, Lucy shook her head at her tendency to get sidetracked. Who cared about Beto? If Palmita were a self-contained aquarium like those found in tank bromeliads high up in the canopy, Beto would be the mosquito larva that gets bumped off by a bigger sibling. She needed to look further up the food chain, to the frogs, crabs, and snakes that were top dogs in that mini-world.

In fact, she needed to look beyond Palmita to the larger ecosystem that included Bocas, where she could report the theft of her backpack, ask the police what they knew about Gabriel, and track down the lawyer whose name was on Gabriel's will: Gutiérrez. The lawyer was key; he'd know what she should do next to claim what was rightfully hers. She'd already wasted a day and a half of her eight precious days.

There were just two buses a day to Bocas, and Lucy had already missed them. She asked Hilda to call her a cab.

Hilda said she knew half a dozen Gutiérrezes. Chances were one of them was related to the guy Lucy was looking for. Norma Gutiérrez, for instance, worked at the Megasuper in Bocas.

Lucy sighed.

"You'll get the hang of it," Hilda said.

The hang of it being, apparently, that you had to do everything in person, and come at people sideways, through their relatives. The internet was a joke, cell reception spotty. Lucy had learned that people who could afford it had three or four phone lines, land and mobile, in case some of them gave out. But because they had so many lines, they couldn't realistically be expected to answer them all. The last phone book was from fifteen years ago, before anyone had cell phones.

What Lucy wasn't getting the hang of was that even if you were willing to spend a small fortune on a high-clearance taxi, sometimes they just couldn't be bothered to show up.

An hour slid by. Still no taxi. She sketched a little and read from the books above the front desk.

"Just start walking," Hilda said. "Someone's probably going into Bocas this afternoon."

Lucy set out. It felt good to have a mission. So what if everyone in Palmita seemed to think that reporting the theft was a waste of time? She was a tourist. An American. The police would want to keep the likes of her happy so she would spread the good word back home.

Was she a tourist, soon to be heading home? Her nonrefundable plane ticket said *yes*. That everything here was more complicated than she'd expected said *maybe not*.

Heat moved in slow waves across the road. An electric line overhead sang like a one-note bird. A cow on the side of the road had a face as long and narrow as a horse's. A flap of loose furred skin under its chin cried out to be stroked.

"I know you," Lucy said.

I know you, the cow's soft brown eyes echoed.

Back when Lucy played with Inés, they'd pretended they were a couple. Inés was Carlos, in love with Lucy, who was Samantha. An old fishing net was the wedding veil.

She coughed, startling the cow. Dust had made its way into her mouth, her nose, the corners of her eyes. She could even feel grit in her ears.

A high whine came from the Palmita direction. It sounded more like a leaf blower than a car. Over a rise, in a cloud of dust, came a giant grasshopper riding an outsized horsefly. On second glance, it was a man, all elbows and knees, on a motorcycle as skeletal as he was. He stopped in front of Lucy, planting his feet and pushing goggles up onto his forehead. Pale ovals around his eyes were the only clean part of his face.

"Sorry about the dust. But next week, we'll be nostalgic for it."

Lucy tilted her head as if to better understand.

"The rains are coming," he explained. "Remember me?"

Lucy looked closer. White teeth blazed in a drawn and dusty face. It was the old man from the café, the one who'd told her where to find Rafa.

"I don't think I ever introduced myself. Keith."

"Lucy."

When he learned she was heading to Bocas, he pulled a canvas hat and a bandanna from a deep pocket on the fisherman's vest he wore over a bare chest. Lucy tied the scarf on bandit-style, cinched the hat strap under her chin. She squinted into the sky as she climbed on behind.

Hanging on to Keith was like hugging a sapling in a hurricane. There were pegs for her feet, but her sandals kept slipping. No goggles or glasses meant she saw everything through eyes squinted nearly shut against the hot wind.

Trees flew by. A field. A glimpse of the sea. More trees. A stretch where they slowed to sidewind through sand. A rutted straightaway, then a metal bridge like driving over a raft of giant Legos. The river burbled below, cool relief just out of reach.

At one point, they sailed past a strangler fig tree that looked like the one that had marked the turnoff to Gabriel's place. Tomorrow, Lucy promised herself. Everything took so long here, even if occasionally you found yourself hurtling along at teeth-rattling speed.

When they approached the hill that had made the bus's brakes scream, Lucy thought for sure she'd have to get off and walk. But they got a running start and roared on up, carving around islands of broken concrete. She pressed her cheek to Keith's bony back and closed her eyes.

I will crawl on hands and knees through tropical fire ants and eat their queen, she vowed silently, *before I take a ride home with this guy*.

Just before Keith dropped her at a strip mall of three real estate offices and a surf shop, Lucy asked if he knew a lawyer named Gutiérrez.

"Related to Norma Gutiérrez?"

"Maybe."

"She was a clerk at the Megasuper."

"Was?"

"I think she married a guy from Puntarenas." Keith revved his engine. He was late for his AA meeting.

"Thanks for the ride," Lucy said. "Can you tell me how to get to the police station?"

"Out past the clinic."

"Where's the clinic?"

"A hundred meters north of the school."

"And the school?"

"Honey," he drawled. "It ain't New York. You'll find your way."

It wasn't New York, but it wasn't Palmita either. A dozen hotels encroached on a white-sand beach. Half-finished condos bristled with rebar and *For Sale* signs. An SUV with surf boards piled on top almost ran Lucy down. A few streets inland, she found the regular businesses—bank, hardware store, gas station, supermarket.

Keith had been right: Norma Gutiérrez no longer worked at the Megasuper. Lucy stuck around for the air-conditioning, browsing sunscreen and hair conditioner. She bought the overpriced toiletries, along with two bottles of water, one to drink and one to pour over her head.

It took her a while to find the police station, mostly because it looked like someone's house: a tin-roofed one-story building, its front porch made homey with wood and leather rocking chairs and geraniums blooming in an old tire.

A woman next door, hanging clothes on a line, motioned Lucy over.

"He'll be back soon," she said in Spanish. She made a gesture as if drinking from her own thumb. "He's at the meeting if you need him."

"What meeting?"

Again, the woman made the sign for drinking. Presumably the official was off having a liquid lunch.

The clinic was closed too. A sign said the doctor was in every Wednesday and every other Saturday. Pity the person who had a heart attack or machete accident on the wrong day.

At least the school was operational. It was recess. Kids in blue-and-white uniforms ran around or bounced balls off a mural with all the local fauna represented. Someone had scrawled *No al T.L.C.* in a speech bubble coming from the mouth of a goofy-looking sloth.

It was graffiti against the Tratado de Libre Comercio, the free trade agreement between the US and Central America that Lucy had read about. One economist said it was like a fight between a tiger and a tied-up mule.

A girl ran up to the chain-link fence separating the schoolyard from the street, her pleated skirt lifting with each stride. Threading fingers through wire, she shook the fence like she was in a cage.

Lucy laughed in recognition.

"¡Es mi última dia!" Pilar was jubilant. *It's my last day!*

"Vacation?"

"My dad says I don't have to go to school anymore."

"Why?"

"It's too far. It's dark when I get home."

"But you don't mind the dark, right? You're not even scared of the Mona Bruja."

Pilar opened her eyes wide.

A shrill whistle sounded. The teacher called out, and all the kids—Pilar, too—pivoted in her direction.

If I were that teacher, Lucy thought, I'd have a little talk with Pilar's parents.

"See you later!" Pilar shouted in English as she ran off.

Everyone Lucy spoke with knew Licenciado Gutiérrez. She chatted with a waitress, a pharmacist, and an old man in a battered orange vest, a member of the countrywide cadre of freelance parking attendants, the guachimán—a Spanglish take on the word "watchman" for the people who'd watch your car while it was parked on the street, accepting small tips for their trouble.

Most of the people she talked to even knew where Gutiérrez's office used to be. Where he was now, they couldn't say. Once someone moved to the capital, more than one person said, all bets were off. It was another country up there, full of crime and corruption and terrible traffic.

Though she could have used the ATM, Lucy waited in line at the bank to get money so she could chat up the teller. If anyone knew people's business, it would be someone who worked at the town's only bank. Turned out the woman knew Gutiérrez well. He had a mortgage he was still paying off—he'd gotten a good rate, less than 16 percent. He'd been a valued member of the community.

"Had been?"

He'd moved his family to San José so his kids could go to a good private school. The elementary grades were okay here, the teller said, but once kids got a little older, this place wasn't so good for them. Too many became *delinquentes*. Either that or nature guides.

People waiting in line laughed. Nobody seemed impatient that Lucy was taking her time with the teller.

Did anyone take over his office? Lucy asked. His clients?

The teller repeated what Lucy had asked to the rest of the bank. Everyone—even the security guard at the door holding a submachine gun—pondered the question.

"Parece que no," said the teller, speaking for all of them. *It seems not.*

One last thing, Lucy said. "Can you give me Licenciado Gutiérrez's number in San José?"

The woman regarded her severely. "Bank policy is to never share customer information."

People shook their heads at Lucy as she left.

One man, taking pity on her, called out, "His cousin Chuy works at Bar Avión."

CHAPTER 11

> E. O. Wilson puts things in perspective: "If all mankind were to disappear, the world would regenerate back to the rich state of equilibrium that existed ten thousand years ago. If insects were to vanish, the environment would collapse into chaos."
>
> —*Lucy's bug notes*

"CONSIDER THE COMMON GOLDFISH," said the loudest of the off-duty nature guides.

They were celebrating their release from a week of pointing out the obvious to tourists. They were drinking at Bar Avión, built around an old Fairchild C-123. In the 1980s, the camo-painted airplane brought US-backed covert aid to rightist rebels across the border in Nicaragua. Tourists rarely asked about the plane's history; they came for the novelty and the ocean view.

Part of the bar was the body of the plane, like the belly of a scrap-iron whale. Wings jutted from either side of the deck, the preferred place to watch the sun go down. Guides drank cheap here, in exchange for bringing tourists who paid full price.

"A small carp domesticated in China. They've spread far beyond their native habitat, but you can't really call them invasive."

"Because they never leave their bowls!"

"Those fish are pussies."

"The fight's been bred right out of them."

"It's humans who are the invaders," sighed the oldest of the crew. He drank coffee instead of beer, wanting to be sober for his wife and kids.

"My point," said the first speaker, "is that not every newcomer is invasive."

"Now we come to it."

"He likes his white girls. His wriggling little albino goldfish."

Lucy, seated nearby, didn't understand most of what the guides were saying. She was waiting for the bartender, Chuy Gutiérrez, to have time to talk to her.

When the guides mentioned insects, Lucy's comprehension improved.

"It's hard to get tourists to want to see anything but monkeys, sloths, and turtles. I point out a long line of leafcutter ants and they take a quick photo, wanting to move on. If I try to tell them how amazing they are—that they can strip a tree in twenty-four hours, and they're not only hunter-gatherers but also farmers—their eyes glaze over."

"Farmers?" another guide challenged. "That's pushing it a little."

"No way," the leafcutter fan countered. "What did they teach you at that guide school in San José? The habits of cockroaches and rats?"

"Pretty soon that's all we'll have left."

"So the leafcutter, they bring the leaves back to the nest, grow fungus on the leaves, and then feed that fungus to their larva."

"Fascinating." The naysayer rolled his eyes.

"I know, right?"

When the guides started yelling out the stupid things clients said to them, Lucy understood every word. They were mimicking English-speaking tourists.

"'I want to come back as a turtle!'" in a trembling falsetto.

"'When do they turn on the volcano?'"

"I *love* this island!"

A lull in the conversation caused the men to look around. Goldfish Guy chin-pointed toward a group out on the deck.

"The Thief of Hearts. Word is he may come on part time."

The others squinted into the sun to make out the long-haired man, but they already knew who their friend was talking about. The stand-offish Nicaraguan who didn't know his place.

"He's genius at finding birds."

"More genius at getting girls."

"There are already too many of us," said the guide eager to get home to his wife. "How long before half of us have to dress like monkeys while the other half points us out to the tourists?"

The guides glared at the long-haired man on the deck, as if he were to blame. "You can't trust a man who won't get drunk with you."

The coffee-drinking guide grimaced. The rest raised their bottles to toast.

"My cousin was learning to draw up wills." Chuy yelled to be heard over the blender. He clamped his hand tightly on the rubber lid as if a wild animal were inside, scrambling to escape the blades. "He thought it would be a good sideline."

"To what?" The blender had stopped suddenly and Lucy's voice boomed. "Sideline to what?" she repeated in a normal tone.

"Real estate. With all the land changing hands, everyone wants in on that."

Chuy said he'd broken contact with his lawyer cousin after the man routinely stiffed him on referral fees. "He'll do well in the city. The cutthroat son of a whore."

He loaded a tray with virgin coladas, Coca Lights, and cups of black coffee. "Got to tend to the non-drinkers."

"Funny place for them," Lucy observed.

"AA people are some of our best customers."

Lucy watched as the bartender delivered the drinks to the group on the deck. Wasn't that Keith, goggles pushed up onto his polished-wood skull? He must have wiped his face clean of road dust. On one side of Keith sat a local man in uniform. On the other, a man whose face Lucy couldn't see but whose shoulders—the muscled slope of them—reminded her of Rafa.

Rafa and his girl at the Palmita bar took on another possible layer of meaning, not just man coming for woman, but clean and sober coming for young and plastered.

It hadn't felt bad, being by-catch in Rafa's rescue net. But the man had a woman. Or a girl. A girl he had to chase down. A girl who dressed in foreigner drag, camouflaging herself among the tribe that could come and go as they pleased. A girl, in short, who wanted out.

What was that to Lucy? Nothing at all. Rafa was Gabriel's friend. She needed to talk to him about her alleged father.

The group on the deck grasped each other's hands and bowed their heads.

When the meeting broke up with fist bumps and high fives, Lucy went out on the deck to see if it was Keith.

"So you found your way." Keith smiled.

"More or less. The police station was closed."

Keith introduced her to the policeman who'd been sitting next to him at the meeting. He was a small, trim man with a tired face.

"Can I help you?" the officer asked.

She said she wanted to report a theft.

"Of what?" he asked pleasantly.

"My backpack, my phone—"

"Would you like to make a report?"

"That's what I said."

"But would you like to make an official report?'

"Isn't that what—"

"You are perfectly free to make an official report." His demeanor was accommodating, even gallant. "But sometimes we find it is better to address these minor infractions in a more casual fashion. In addition," the man went on, "it is difficult to solve crimes so far away. We had a truck, but it broke down. There is no money to fix it."

Keith nodded. "We're collecting money for repairs."

"So I shouldn't report this?"

Shrugs, nods, eyebrows up, mouths turned down.

Rafa approached. Lucy had been right in recognizing his shoulders. When he offered her a ride back to Palmita, she pretty much forgot about making any kind of report.

A lot of pop songs faded out, but not many faded in. That was even more true when the Beatles recorded "Eight Days a Week" in London in 1964. Half a century later and halfway across the world, the song's intro began with an almost imperceptible chiming, swelling to fill the cab of Rafa's pickup truck.

The music lifted something in Lucy. For all the frustrations over the last few days, this particular time and place and set of problems had a rightness about them. Though she'd already wasted three of her eight days, this was where she needed to be. She looked out the window at the velvety trees, breathing in the salt air.

Rafa loved the song's simplicity, like a dream of where people with regular jobs drove straight, well-paved roads. The kind of place Lucy, sitting beside him now, would go back to as soon as she had her fill of exotic confusion.

He was a Beatles fan and a student of false starts, having had so many of his own. Gabriel once told Rafa the Beatles tried at least six radically different introductions before settling on this one, which kind of crept up on you. Like Lucy was creeping up on Rafa.

"You're from Nicaragua," Lucy said.

One hand on the wheel, he turned to look at her, his chin raised in challenge. "So?"

"Nothing. Just that you're not from here, either."

His eyes were back on the road. "We came when I was young. I went to high school in San José. But to a lot of Costa Ricans, I will always be—" He stopped himself.

"I knew Nicaraguans where I grew up."

"Yeah?"

"Yeah," she said.

Rafa thought she was going to say more, but she didn't. "They don't love us here. They say we come across the border like an invasion of army ants. Take their jobs." He looked at her sideways. "Steal their women."

She laughed.

They were driving through a stretch of sandy gravel that swung close to the beach. Even over the growl of the engine, Rafa could hear the waves slamming down.

"How long," Lucy asked, "do you think it takes to feel at home in a new place?"

"Forever." He laughed, trying to pass it off as a joke. But there was heaviness in his voice.

"I need to tell you why I'm here."

"I think I know," Rafa said. "In fact, I think everyone knows. Gabriel wanted you to have his land."

"Does everyone here know my story, maybe even better than I do? Anyway, yes, Gabriel's will says he wants me to have his land. It seems strange, right?"

"It sounds like Gabriel. He gets ideas."

"Like that I was his daughter?"

"That wasn't just an idea, as far as I could tell. Of course, in the end, everything is just a story, right? It's about which story you want to believe."

Lucy looked out the window. "Was he a good man?"

"He was a friend."

"Tell me about him."

Rafa waited a beat. "At first, we didn't like each other. Not at all."

They came from different countries, classes, and generations. It was a surprise that two solitary, self-sufficient men came to trust each other and truly enjoy each other's company. "We went birding, then drank at the bar. Fanta for me, beer for him."

"Did other people like him?" She told Rafa she remembered a certain distance between Gabriel and the rest of Palmita, but that was a long time ago and may have had something to do with him being wholly absorbed by a visiting gringo family.

Rafa slowed to take a tight curve. "He was like a sea snake."

"What do you mean?"

"Most snakes rub up against trees or rocks to shed their skin. Sea snakes only have water to work with, so they have to be their own hard surface. Tie themselves in knots and then pull themselves through."

Lucy nodded, but Rafa wasn't sure she understood.

"No one in Palmita pushed back hard enough for Gabriel to define himself against," he said.

"So he tied himself in knots, tried to pull through?"

"Exactly."

She was quiet for a moment. "Do I look like him?"

Rafa made a show of studying Lucy.

"It's just that, with the man they *said* was my father—not Gabriel—my mother said that me not looking like him, well, it got under his skin. My mother was kind of saying, I think, that that was one of the reasons he left." Lucy rushed on. "Now I know that guy wasn't my dad, but still, I wonder if, back then, if I'd looked different, more like my sister, prettier maybe, then—"

"You're very pretty!"

Lucy looked taken aback.

Not as taken aback as Rafa was. What was he doing, feeling protective of a woman he hardly knew?

He parked at Hilda's and then reached across Lucy to pull a worn paperback from the glove compartment: Edward Abbey's *Desert Solitaire*.

"It was Gabriel's. It meant a lot to him. Or it did before he got rid of his gringo stuff. He went through phases. Had a sort of love/hate relationship with the US."

"And me, my family, us being from the US, did he have a love/hate relationship with us?"

Rafa put his hand on the book, which now lay in her lap. It was a strangely intimate gesture, and Lucy looked as if she was trying not to squirm.

"I think he could probably separate the two," Rafa continued, "but who knows? Even when he was hating the US, he would still tell stories about his trip there. Red rocks in strange shapes. There was a word—"

"Arches? Hoodoos?"

He took his hand away. "Yeah, maybe. Sometimes I forget what I read in the books and what Gabriel told me. But he was still talking about that trip, even just before he died."

Lucy froze.

Rafa knew immediately that he'd made a mistake. He also felt an almost unbearable tenderness towards Lucy. How could that damned Gabriel die before Lucy had a chance—just a moment, even—to be his daughter?

"God, I'm sorry. I thought you just didn't know *how*—"

Lucy held up her hand. "Wait." She opened the car door, leaned out, and vomited. "Sorry."

"No, *I'm* sorry. I must have misread—"

She sat back in her seat, wiping her mouth on the back of her hand. "So, how did he die?"

Rafa sighed.

"Weren't you just about to tell me?"

Rafa shifted in his seat. "The thing is, I'm not sure it's for me to tell."

"What do you mean? I thought you were the one who knew Gabriel best. Why wouldn't it be your story to tell?"

"It's complicated. But I'll tell you what. I can show you his house, tomorrow, show you what he left behind. But like I said, the how and why of it, well, that's not for me to say."

"Who *can* say?"

"You deserve to know more. You *will* know more. But I can't be the one to tell you. At least, not until I clear it with—"

"This other person who apparently owns the story."

He sighed. "I've made promises."

She slumped in the seat. "Okay. I get it." But Rafa could see that she didn't, not really.

Lucy's cabin door was ajar, the light on inside. She slowly pushed the door all the way open, the hinges squawking. The room was empty. Moths circled the bulb. She checked and double-checked her stuff and found that only one thing was missing: the cut-glass doorknob she'd brought from home, which she'd set out on the windowsill to catch the light. What a strange thing to steal. It meant something to her. But of what value could it be to anyone else?

DAY FOUR

TUESDAY

CHAPTER 12

> Moths and butterflies have false eye spots to scare away predators. Other bugs masquerade as twigs, thorns, leaves, bark, and flowers. "Be yourself" is not good advice when you're about to be eaten.
>
> —*Lucy's bug notes*

WHEN HIS GRANDFATHER had entrusted Beto with the bones, he passed off the heavy burlap sack like a giant dirt-encrusted hot potato. Only now, years later, did Beto understand the potential in that grisly burden.

His bare foot resting against the sack, Beto thumbed through a paper he'd downloaded to his phone. Someone at a university in Texas had written a dissertation on the Chorotega. Beto knew how pathetic it was that he, descended from the Chorotega, had to look to some foreign academic to learn about his own people. But you used the tools at hand to reclaim the past. In towns a few hundred miles north, potters descended from pre-Columbian tribes known for their ceramics had lost the thread of technique and design over the centuries. Then they got their hands on an old book that had sketches of the pots of their ancestors found in archeological digs. The modern potters began to recreate the ancient designs. Tourists now paid top dollar for these genuine native crafts.

Beto was looking for information on skull and teeth alterations, and on burial rites, but kept getting distracted. *The Chorotega wrote by means of hieroglyphs in books made of deerskin,* he read, *using red and black ink; in these they also painted maps of their estates.* So even before the Spaniards had arrived, the people of this peninsula kept records of who owned what. Beto wondered what the inheritance laws had been back then.

A few pages later: *Their sense of ownership over property was not deeply rooted. A sort of fraternal communion prevailed.*

You couldn't have it both ways, could you? Having a clear idea of who owned what, but also having a fraternal communion prevail?

Beto found what he was looking for: drawings and diagrams of how the Chorotega altered their teeth and skulls.

He pulled a partially smashed skull out of the bag. It might be old Didi Sanchez. He'd heard the stories: The man's wife had killed him with a shovel in a fit of jealous rage. Didi would be the first to get the Chorotega treatment: teeth notched for status and beauty. The Chorotega did the alterations while the subject was still alive, but better late than never. It was far too late to elongate the skull, however. That deforming beautification had to be done when the person was an infant, with a malleable skull.

Beto's plan was to arrange the doctored bones into secondary burials, what the Chorotega did with bones once the muscles and sinews had released them. They'd make a nest of ribs and long bones, placing the skull on top like a bowling ball on top of a stack of neatly folded clothes. He'd seen the dioramas in the anthropology museum in the capital.

Next, he'd seed the cemetery island with these burials, wait for wind and weather to erase signs of newness and then alert the museum to the find. If he said that grave robbers were at work, they'd come quickly. Palmita would have a direct line to its past and might even become an archeological destination for tourists. That class of visitor would be better, more respectful, than the current surfing and backpacking crowd.

Beto had read that a people is alive if they remember their language and how to bury their dead. While he worked the bones, he chanted the one Chorotega verb conjugation he knew. He'd found it on the internet.

Neje sumu. *He is.*

Cis mi muh. *We are.*

Cejo. *I am.*

Somehow it was easier to declare himself to himself in a dead language.

The bag of bones came from when Don Diego was trying to sell some of his land. He had dug up the cemetery island, part of his family's estate, because it was illegal to build on graves and developers were looking to build. What better place for high-end condos than a breeze-kissed island separated, most of the time, from the mainland, with all its poverty and over-tourism? It was a ready-made gated community. They'd probably build some Disneyland-like vaulted bridge to the mainland so they wouldn't have to time the tides.

Don Diego had paid off the families of the disinterred, promising to rebury the bones in a new mainland plot. He fenced off an area, put up concrete headstones, and threw a collective memorial that lasted four drunken days and resulted in one marriage and countless children. He never, however, got around to reburying the actual bones.

When the developers lost interest and Gabriel made an offer, he was outraged to learn that Don Diego had desecrated the cemetery. And for what? Gabriel had demanded. The hope of some cash that Don Diego would blow on a new pickup and six months of drinks all around?

"If you'd pay a fair price," Don Diego told Gabriel. "I could have two pickup trucks. One for me, and one for Beto. My grandson," he growled, as if Gabriel didn't know. "Your son, you *hijo de puta*. You know, it's as possible to miss someone right in front of you as it is to miss someone who leaves."

"What are you on about, old man?"

Don Diego shook his head. It was a losing battle, trying to get Gabriel to love Beto or even acknowledge him as his own.

After years of maintaining he'd done nothing wrong in digging up the cemetery and selling the land, Don Diego began to privately nurse the idea of reclaiming the island as a cemetery and putting the bones back where they belonged.

He had turned the bones over to Beto for safekeeping and then forgot he'd done so. Don Diego's big plan, his guilt and shame and desire to make things right again, had boiled down in his age-addled brain to the necessity of a new arch. The entryway would dignify the rock outcropping and signal that all was well in Palmita. Don Diego would collect money for the building of the arch.

Don Diego had plans for the cemetery island, when he could remember them, and now Beto did, too. Both thought their plans would save the town. Palmita could stop masquerading as a tourist haven—which had never quite worked, anyway—and become its true self.

How would Beto's fake Chorotega burials save Palmita? It was part of a larger scheme. Step one, purge the place of Martin. He'd convinced Isa to help him with that. She was useful, now that she had a job at the Rancho Dulce Vista. Next, he'd bring the town back to itself. Way back. Back in time.

Notching teeth was hard work. Beto shattered a jaw before he got the hang of it. There was some cocaine left from Martin. He snorted a little and kept working. Then he snorted some more. His plan grew more ambitious. Soon he was carving names of families in town onto the long bones.

The drug sent purpose coursing through him. He, outcast genius, would single-handedly connect the present to the past.

When the cocaine wore off and he crashed, he was mortified by what he'd done. He rapped his own knuckles with a bone in a fit of self-disgust. Just how stupid could he be? No anthropologist would believe the Chorotega would put Spanish names on their bones, not even after they'd been conquered. That would be like him getting Martin's name tattooed on his forehead.

* * *

Isa plunged her hand into a big bag of birdseed. It slumped against the wall like a drunk in an open-air shed out near the Rancho's animal cages. Isa usually avoided the area. She didn't like looking at the sad monkey, the moldy sloth, and the rainbow-billed toucan chained to its perch.

She was sweating through her new uniform, digging for a zip-top bag Beto had assured her would be shoved deep in the birdseed. It was Martin's secret hiding place, Beto said, where he hid important documents. She was supposed to be cleaning Villas 4 and 5. If she got caught, she'd be fired and maybe taken to the police station in Bocas, where Don Martin had special pull, having paid for the station's new roof.

If she didn't bring Beto what he wanted, he'd tell Rafa she was working for Martin. She had planned to tell Rafa. Eventually. She just wasn't ready to risk blowing the best opportunity she'd ever had.

She wasn't anywhere near where she was supposed to be. The eagle-eyed head maid liked to check on new hires, and Martin himself, Deysi had warned, had a habit of turning up where you least expected him. The monkey let out a half-hearted roar that trailed off in a whimper. He was no longer part of any troop, and no amount of hooting would change that.

"Cálmate, hermanito," Isa said under her breath. *Calm down, little brother.* The animals seemed only half-alive. If she opened the doors to the cages and unchained the bird's leg, how long before they figured out they were free to go?

Isa herself was trying to figure out the same thing. The money she earned here could give her options, though the man drove a hard bargain, deducting for the cost of the uniform and charging new hires a training fee. She'd heard rumors of foreigners arriving for a promised job and having their passports held until they worked off their supposed debt. She didn't want to believe it. But even after filling in four times and twice working her own shift (her own shift!), Isa was still in the hole.

But she loved it up here on the hill. It was like landing a job inside a fairy tale. The pink, white, and gold carousel horse at the bottom of the drive signaled entry into a gilded world. Isa smiled up at it every time she arrived, exhilarated by the beautiful creature caught mid-prance, its eyes rolled back in ecstasy.

Of course, it was a slightly different matter, being the maid in a storybook. Everything had to be perfect but guests weren't supposed to see the effort. There were special ways to cut each kind of fruit and different insecticides for different bugs. Bedspreads had to be pulled taut—no wrinkles—and fresh flower petals strewn in an exact pattern. Martin even coached Isa on how to talk to the guests—with a smile that said nothing was off limits and no request would be denied.

"I'm not like other bosses," Martin told her, "who tell employees not to fraternize with the guests."

Already Isa had fraternized with a group of guests who were the most remarkable people she'd ever met. So beautiful and talented and rich, but also so down-to-earth, as if they were no better than the girl cleaning their toilets. They'd dressed her up in their clothes and taken her dancing. She'd felt like she was in disguise, in a good way, though her dad told her that when insects or birds or animals disguised themselves, it was usually out of fear. If that were true for humans as well, what was she afraid of? That she'd never be more than she was right now, a light-brown girl in a starched white maid's uniform, another sort of disguise.

The dancing night hadn't ended well. Next time she'd suggest they go into Bocas, where fewer people knew her, and her father would be less likely to show up.

Isa's world was opening up. She didn't want that door to slam shut.

Her fingers found plastic among the hard spill of seed. She pulled out the bag, shook it off. Inside was a dark-blue booklet with gold lettering. A passport. She stared. She'd never had ID of any kind. She'd never been anywhere. For a moment she imagined that she'd open the booklet and see her own face, only prettier and older, with her name below and all sorts of stamps and seals proclaiming a life well lived and a world well-traveled.

At first, Isa didn't recognize the person in the photo. He had long hair and a wild look in his eye. Then she saw that it must be Martin, back when he had all his hair. He looked almost handsome.

On second glance, maybe it wasn't him. The name printed below the photo was not his.

Isa saw a flash of white through the leaves. She had just seconds to shove the passport into her pocket.

It was Deysi. "What are you doing?" she demanded in Spanish.

Isa hated lying to her best friend. "I thought this was where they kept the insecticide."

"I get you a job and this is how you repay me?"

Isa knew Deysi was really mad that she hadn't been invited to hang out with the people who'd taken Isa to the bar. "I'm sorry."

Deysi continued berating her as if she hadn't heard.

The toucan looked from one girl to the other. He knew a pecking order when he saw one.

CHAPTER 13

> Male bowerbirds build intricate stick structures—bowers—where they sing and dance to attract a mate, making sure their moves show off the bower's decoration: bright berries and seeds, cleverly arranged leaves, or found objects like buttons, beach glass, and colorful bits of plastic.
>
> —*Lucy's bug & bird notes*

LUCY RECOGNIZED GABRIEL'S HOUSE, but couldn't quite fit her memories into this modest one-story with a tin roof. She yanked at the padlock on the front door. Back home, Sara looped locks through the latches on outbuildings, never clicking them shut because the keys were long gone. From a distance, the place appeared secure.

But the lock on this house held. Plywood nailed over the windows had warped, splaying away from the exterior as if shying away from what lay inside: a big load of nothing. No one lived here anymore. She could feel absence crouching in the shadows.

Why had Rafa wanted to show her this place? To prove that Gabriel was truly gone, and wouldn't be back?

Around the back, a cement patio was crumbling at the edges. It looked like rodents or insects had tunneled underneath. On a waist-high shelf nailed between two supporting pillars, someone or something had deposited beetle carapaces, burnished brown pods the size and shape of human ears, and miniature plastic animals that looked like they'd been chewed on.

She and Faith had kept shells and other washed-up treasures on that shelf. Lucy remembered swinging in a hammock out here when it was too hot to do anything else, pushing off a polished wood beam with her bare foot. Sometimes they dragged a table and chairs out to the yard to eat in the open, mindful of bugs crawling up their legs. Back then, they could see the water from here. Now, overgrown hibiscus bushes and pochote trees with spiked trunks blocked the view.

The will had mentioned three structures that were supposed to be part of her inheritance. She'd pictured dilapidated sheds. Was this structure, this house, now hers? Having so recently accepted that Gabriel was dead, Lucy didn't feel ready to accept what he'd accumulated in life. It felt more of a burden than a gift.

Chuy at the bar had told her that with unoccupied property here, squatters could move in, gaining legal rights the longer they stayed. Documenting the improvements they made helped their case. Absentee owners often hired caretakers to guard against squatters, but that could backfire: The caretakers themselves might squat the property, claim it as their own.

Such a lot of effort to claim and hold on to a place! Faith had made a point of telling Lucy how much she'd spent on improving the family home in California. Lucy didn't know the law of her own land any better than she knew the law here. If she were to fight for the house back home, how would she make her case?

The thought of it made Lucy tired. And hungry. Rafa was late, and Lucy hadn't had breakfast.

From the side of the house came a sound like nails being wrenched from wood.

Lucy rounded a corner to see someone tugging at a loose sheet of plywood. "Hey!"

The person froze.

Lucy approached, only because the intruder wasn't very big. When Lucy saw who it was, she laughed. "Are you following me?" she asked Pilar.

"Are you following *me*?" Pilar was indignant. She said she came every week to make sure everything was okay. "And to do my homework. It's quiet here." She held the board back so Lucy could scramble through a low window, then followed her inside.

Through the soles of her sandals, Lucy felt the cool tile floor. The tropical hardwood paneling on the ceiling gleamed, even in the dim light. Gabriel used to knock a broom handle on the wood to scare away the iguana that wanted to nest under the roof.

"There's a lot to do." Pilar counted off on her fingers. "Check for cobwebs, wasps making nests, mold."

Lucy nodded encouragingly.

"Crabs come up through the drain," Pilar continued, "then can't get out."

Lucy remembered how small crabs would peek out of the open shower drain and then skitter across her feet and out the open door.

Equatorial homemaking was different from its northerly equivalent, but the idea was the same. Stake your claim. Carve out a space for yourself in the existing web of life. Could Lucy do that here? Did she want to?

Lucy took in the neatly made bed, the chairs tucked under the table, the tidy kitchen. She pulled a book from the shelf, blowing dust off its top.

"I clean as much as I can." Pilar was defensive.

"You do a great job. Books just like dust. That's a fact." It was a slim paperback called *Bird Behavior*. On the inside front cover, Gabriel had written his name and a message: *Birds are smarter than we are*. Lucy thought the same about insects. She tucked the book in her back pocket, elated at the perfect fit.

"I used to live here," she told Pilar, in part to account for her taking the book.

"Really? I don't remember that."

Lucy chuckled. "It was before you were born."

"I did hear that Don Gabriel was once *casado*." *Casado* meant married, whether officially or not. Literally, it translated as "housed." Lucy wondered if Gabriel had played house with other women and children.

Pilar looked around. "I heard Don Gabriel tell Calaca once that he'd outgrown this house. But how could that be? It's huge, especially for one person."

"A lot to keep up," Lucy agreed, though to her the place felt cramped, far smaller than it had back when they used to stay here. "Hey. Speaking of crabs. Do you know about hermit crabs?"

Pilar shook her head.

"They're crabs that don't have their own shells. They borrow shells that other crabs don't need anymore."

"Kind of like I'm borrowing this place because Don Gabriel doesn't need it anymore."

"Right! And do you know what else?" Lucy was in full teacher mode now. "Sometimes they get together for a house exchange. Each crab leaves the shell that has gotten too small for it, and it takes the next-size-up shell."

Pilar thought for a moment. "What about the biggest crab? Where does she go?"

Lucy was saved from having to invent an answer when a crash sounded outside. Pilar put a hand on Lucy's arm, shushing her, though Lucy hadn't made a sound.

The sun was bright outside the boarded-up house. Whoever had been there was gone, and they'd taken Pilar's bike with them. The girl described what she'd lost in loving detail. The multicolored handlebar tassels. The banana seat repaired with silver duct tape. The rust she sanded off when she should have been helping her mother with dinner.

"I think I know who took it." Pilar grabbed Lucy's hand and pulled her down a path that paralleled the water. Bushes raked their legs. The air smelled of rotting seaweed and tasted of salt. The waves weren't booming like they sometimes did. The sound now was more intimate, like someone chewing with their mouth open.

Lucy noticed a ceramic mask that curved neatly around a sapling. The mask's cheeks were slashed with paint; chunks of shell were stuck in its earlobes. Nails had been driven through the eye sockets. *Creepy.*

They pushed through a curtain of what looked like oversized beads. On closer inspection, they turned out to be shells alternating with mango pits. In a clearing were large assemblages of sticks, nets, and beach trash. A fishbone mobile swayed in the breeze.

Pilar led Lucy towards a wooden shack on stilts. The girl vaulted up the stairs and banged on the front door.

"Ladrón!" she called, as if *thief* were a proper name. While Pilar kept banging on the door, Lucy cupped her hands to peer through a dusty window. Inside was an unmade single bed and a table dark with heaped shapes.

"Calaca says Beto can't help himself but I—" Pilar kicked the door. "Think—" Another kick. "He *can*!" She stomped, and the whole place shook.

Spent, the girl slumped. "My parents are going to kill me. They're always telling me to keep an eye on my bike. And I'm late." She started to cry in a choked way that told Lucy crying wasn't something the girl often did. "I'm so stupid!"

Lucy put an arm around Pilar and hugged her close. "You are very far from stupid," she soothed. "You are as smart as anyone I know, and you're a very good girl."

Lucy herself was crying now, for Pilar and because she wished someone—someone named Mom—had said those simple words to her when Lucy was a girl. Even just once.

"You go home," Lucy said. "I'll find your bike. Tell me how to get to your house. I'll bring it to you."

It took Lucy a while, but she did find Pilar's bike, a few hundred yards from Beto's shack, leaning against one of about a dozen poles of varying heights. Together the poles formed a circle; on top of each was a bicycle seat, creating a kind of perverse and inaccessible merry-go-round. One of the seats—dirty white, with red trim and rusted springs—looked like the one swiped from the bike Lucy had ridden to the soccer game.

The tide was coming in fast. Soon the rocky spit connecting the cemetery island to the mainland would be underwater. But Beto lingered, kicking at the rubble of sledgehammered headstones, wondering if he could salvage his idea of faking a Chorotega burial site. Buzzards hunched in the treetops and hop-flew along the rocky perimeter. They were always there, waiting for the dead to return.

Or, rather, the rest of the dead. Beto glanced at a rise of newly disturbed rubble. It hadn't been easy, chipping out a cavity in the rocky soil. He'd had to enlist Rafa for muscle and moral support.

The sea had spit Gabriel out like so much trash. He was Beto's now, as he had never been in life. Beto didn't know if he wanted to share, especially not with some gringa who blew into town like she owned the place.

Lucy was walking Pilar's bike along the beach path when she spotted her mother, whitewater riffles at Sara's feet. Lucy let the bike fall to the ground. She squeezed her eyes shut and then opened them again. Sara kept coming. Lucy should be afraid, but all she felt was love—a love that didn't wash away the anger or hurt, but neither was it tainted by those feelings. A love that came from a different and deeper source.

Sara walked on water, thousands of miles south of where she'd lived and died. Her hair streamed out as the ocean gleamed like beaten bronze. The night when Lucy had thought she'd seen her mother's eyes in the bushes, Lucy had been silly with fatigue. Now, it was the full light of day and she'd had a decent night's sleep.

Over the apparition's shoulder, Lucy caught site of the cemetery island, remembering a funeral she'd once witnessed, a single-file procession, coffin hoisted on men's shoulders, women bringing up the rear with armloads of gladioli. They'd crossed the rocky, narrow land bridge between mainland and island when the tide was low. She remembered how, as the tide rose, some people would risk sloshing along the slippery spit, knee-deep in water. They looked like they were walking on water.

She realized now that the figure was not her mother after all, but a slender man. His long hair lifted in the wind. Ear plugs swayed as he walked.

"Ladrón!" she shouted into the calls of gulls.

Beto stopped. Water covered his feet and lapped against his shins. Lucy had a sudden memory of picking her way over to the island herself, long ago, her friend whipping them up into an almost erotic frenzy with tales of being stranded where ghosts far outnumbered the living.

There was nothing pleasurable about the rage Lucy felt now. She wanted to throttle the thieving bastard. His biggest offense was not stealing Pilar's bike or her backpack, but stealing her hope that Sara might be here for one last visit. To explain, maybe, or to help Lucy bear her absence. It was easier to be angry at Beto than to admit to her own hopeless hope.

She was having much the same response to Beto that most townspeople, even his own father, had. Just three people had escaped the miasma of collective blaming: Rafa, an outsider sympathetic to other outsiders; Martin, who had loved the boy in his own way; and his own mother, Calaca.

When Beto not only kept coming but picked up his pace, Lucy's anger ebbed and fear trickled down her spine. But it was important to hold her ground, to take a stand here, as Gabriel had had to do. She picked up Pilar's bike. It could be a shield, or a weapon if necessary.

He was there before she could second-guess her decision, stopping a few yards from her on the path. "That's my bike," he said.

"The hell it is."

Beto snorted a laugh. Lucy wondered if maybe he appreciated her standing up to him. When he came closer, she abandoned that idea and took a step back, dragging the bike with her.

Not looking at her, he pulled a phone out of his pocket. He thumbed madly. After a final stab he looked up. "Hecho," he said. *Done.*

"What's done?"

"All your people. They're gone." The phone he held was Lucy's. "I think I got all your contacts. None of them can help you now. You have a lot of friends." He stared her down. "A lot of family."

A breeze hit the back of Lucy's sweaty neck, giving her a chill. "I don't have anybody anymore."

"Boo-fucking-hoo." He held the phone loosely now, in one hand.

Letting the bike clatter to the ground, Lucy lunged for it. He sidestepped her advance and then lobbed the phone into the water, out past the shore break. "Say *adios* to your *amigos*."

"You fuck."

When he brushed by her on the path, she froze. He continued on toward his hut, not once looking back.

Pilar's mother had bad teeth and a pregnant waddle, though she wasn't, for the moment, pregnant. Pilar's father had a drunk's mean and rheumy eyes. They stared, unsmiling, as Lucy approached their house, wheeling Pilar's bike. The couple made no move to quiet the madly barking dog tethered by a thin piece of twine.

Coming out of the house's dark interior, Pilar shushed the mongrel, petting its scabbed head. "My bike!" she cried happily.

Her parents waved her back inside, but she stayed on the cement porch long enough to tell them her friend Lucy was una maestra simpatica de afuera, *a nice teacher from outside,* presumably of the country, but at this point Lucy wondered just how far outside her own better judgment she had strayed.

Wielding her best Spanish, Lucy told the sullen pair what a pleasure it was to meet them, and that Pilar seemed to be a very intelligent girl who, with the proper schooling, could go far. She knew enough not to share her half-formed fantasy of adopting the girl and taking her back to where she would have a better chance of continuing her studies. Lucy knew her impulse even had a name: white savior complex. Knowing what something is called doesn't mean you won't fall into that trap.

Lucy wished someone had done the same for her when she was a girl, recognized her potential in a way her own family hadn't. There had been one teacher who came to the house to ask Sara to change her mind about allowing Lucy to join the after-school science club. Sara had been rude, in part because the young, very pretty teacher was dating a man Sara used to date.

"She gets all the science she needs right here." Sara had gestured to the woods and stubbly fields. And in fact, for a while, Sara had homeschooled her girls. Drilling them on the chemical makeup of marijuana plant fertilizer was science. Shouting at radio talk-show hosts was social studies. When she realized her girls had no idea how elections worked and thought Washington, DC, was just up the coast, past Oregon, Sara finally let Lucy and Faith go to real school.

"How do you know our daughter?" Pilar's mother demanded. "Why do you have her bicycle?"

Lucy shifted her weight from one foot to the other. She couldn't tell the story of the bike without revealing Pilar's refuge in Gabriel's house. "We met on the bus."

More glares.

"I know it's a long way to Bocas. But I can say that your daughter—"

"Why aren't you taking care of your own children?"

Lucy knew the woman meant children she'd given birth to, but she thought then of her students, missing them fiercely. They were each so very particular and so dear. It was like having a brood from dozens of different fathers.

"Are you at the Rancho Vista Dulce?"

"No," Lucy said. "Hilda's Cabins."

The mother and father exchanged glances. "But you know Don Martin at the Rancho."

Lucy shrugged.

Pilar's father shambled down off the porch, coming toward her. Lucy braced herself, but he only took Pilar's bike out of her hands, walking it around the back of the house.

Pilar's mother raised her chin. "Give Don Martin our regards," she said, giving a rude flick of her hand. When Lucy didn't move, she shooed again, and shouted, "¡Vete de aquí!" *Get out of here!*

CHAPTER 14

> Picture a tiny sparrow feeding a chick four times its size. The chick is a cuckoo, but the sparrow parent doesn't know that. Cuckoos sneak their eggs into other birds' nests, let them raise the chicks. Not everyone's cut out for parenting.
>
> — *Lucy's bug & bird notes*

CALACA DIDN'T SERVE BEER, but she did have ice-cold Fanta Orange. Lucy had worked up a thirst, facing off with Beto and alienating Pilar's parents. Neon bubbles never tasted so good. She took in half the bottle on the first pull. She wasn't surprised that Beto wasn't at his usual table—he'd been heading for his hut when Lucy saw him.

She thought about mentioning that encounter to Calaca, but didn't want to make the same mistake she'd made at Pilar's house—telling the parents all about their own child.

It was hard to believe that Beto was Calaca's son. She was so grounded and straightforward; he seemed slippery and unhinged. Maybe she'd raised a child who wasn't hers.

In the animal world, mothers could be tricked into raising another's offspring. You saw it in fish, insects, and birds. A five-ounce cowbird mom might sneak its egg into the nest of a tiny phoebe weighing half an ounce. The cowbird was then free from the energy-sapping duties of parenting, but could rest assured that its genes were still being passed along. From an evolutionary standpoint, the duped mothers were wasting resources on alien infiltrators. Why the phoebe mother didn't catch on—or didn't mind—when one of her brood swelled to ten times her size was one of the mysteries of motherhood.

When she first learned about brood parasitism, Lucy had wondered if she herself was a nest invader. Maybe Sara had sniffed out her alienness.

Setting out jars of spicy homemade relish on each table, Calaca swabbed the flowered table coverings though they were already clean.

"I met Pilar's parents."

Calaca looked up from what she was doing.

Lucy explained in Spanish what had happened. She wasn't sure why she felt close enough to this woman to tell the story. She spoke in snatches, in part because her legs itched terribly from insect bites and the salt crust of seawater. She kept scratching, digging in her nails, but any relief was short-lived.

"Like I said, that's not your business," Calaca said in Spanish, as if they were continuing a previous conversation.

Lucy sighed.

"You never had kids?"

"No."

Calaca waited, but Lucy had long ago stopped apologizing and explaining.

"You used to want kids."

Calaca had looked familiar when Lucy had first met her, but when she couldn't place her, she'd stopped trying.

"Or maybe it was coconuts you liked?" Calaca said.

The scene came back sharp and pungent, full of the smell of sun-warmed weeds. Back when Lucy had played with her friend Inés, a coconut was their love child, left with a Brahmin cow when they needed time to themselves.

Could Calaca be Inés? This woman looked almost old enough to be Lucy's mother.

She took a sip of her Fanta. "Inés?"

Calaca circled her rag over the same spot again and again. When she looked up, her smile was like the fast-motion blooming of a rose. Lucy thought she saw the wiry, mischievous girl in the hefty woman. Still, she wasn't convinced. Maybe the real Inés had told Calaca their stories.

Lucy narrowed her eyes. "What were our names?"

"I was Inés," Calaca said. "They started calling me Calaca, *Skeleton*, when I got fat." She said "fat" with pride, as if her previous, slimmer incarnation had been a less evolved version of her now fully realized self. "And you were Luz," she went on. "For that first summer, at least."

"No," Lucy said. "I mean our names when we—played."

Calaca grinned. "You were Samantha. I was Carlos, a Sandinista on the run after stealing Daniel Ortega's beret-wearing girlfriend."

A quarter of a century collapsed as the two women looked at each other. Lucy couldn't know what Calaca was thinking, but Lucy was remembering how the older girl's mouth had tasted. They'd been on a bluff above the river, spying on two people below who were clamped together on a flat rock, limbs waving like the legs of pinned bugs. The girls tried the position out for themselves, Inés on top.

Blood rose in Lucy's face, and the itchiness on her legs flared.

All the same, she was relieved to have found someone from back when she'd come here as a kid. Not just someone. Inés! Her ally. Once, she'd defended Lucy when a shopkeeper accused her of stealing a popsicle from the outdoor fridge. The girls had shoplifted there before, but not this time. Inés had stood with hands on hips, yelling, until the man backed down and even apologized.

"Remember the popsicle?" Lucy said.

"And I got him to say *he* was sorry!" Calaca sat in the chair closest to Lucy. She smelled of sweet onions, the slightly sour rag in her pocket, and the rich human scent of unwashed hair.

Lucy wasn't about to ask if her friend remembered when they played Pareja, *Couple,* mock-fighting so they could make up. But it came to Lucy suddenly that here was someone she could ask about the summers they'd visited. She couldn't ask Sara—ever again—or Gabriel. The way things were with Faith, Lucy wondered whether that last tie to their common past had been snipped as well.

"Remember Faith, my sister?"

"Of course."

"Remember how Faith looked so much like our mother?"

"All you gringos look the same to me." Calaca let out the throaty, almost masculine cough of a laugh that she'd had even as a girl. "Your mom didn't like me." She wasn't accusatory, just thoughtful.

Lucy leaned back in her wooden chair, contemplating the remaining inch of soda in the shapely bottle. "I think you're right. I don't know why, exactly."

"I do! Because Gabriel did. Like me, that is."

Lucy looked at her.

"He liked you, too."

Lucy's eyes opened wide.

"Not like that!" Calaca said. "Not with you, anyway." She allowed herself a small, private smile.

"What do you mean? Did you and Gabriel—"

"You remember how hot he was?"

"Hot? Ew."

"What's that word you taught me back then? Foxy?"

"You were just a girl."

"No, no," Calaca said. "It wasn't until after you left. But I think it kind of started—"

"Wait." Lucy leaned forward in her chair. "How old were you?"

"Almost sixteen by then."

"Almost sixteen." Lucy shook her head in disbelief.

"The age of consent here is fifteen. At least, that's what Gabriel told me." Calaca giggled softly. "I couldn't keep waiting for you to come back." She fluttered her lashes in the way she used to, mock-flirting that was actually the real thing.

Without realizing it, Lucy had kept her friend in her heart for years, measuring other friendships by the yardstick of this one, with its elaborate storytelling, its secret sweaty fumblings, and its backdrop of tropical languor.

"How is your mom?" Calaca was apparently done with the subject of Gabriel.

Lucy drank the last of her soda, warm now. "Dead." Suddenly her face broke open, laughter stretching her mouth to the breaking point.

Calaca tried to control herself but soon she was laughing too. The women laughed as girls did, feeding off each other's helpless hilarity, fully committed. They had to get up from their chairs to give it full access to their bodies, so it could make its way through and leave them spent, wet-faced, collapsed in each other's arms.

"I'm so sorry," Calaca murmured into Lucy's shoulder, but that platitude, however genuinely meant, sent them into a new round of hysterics.

"¡Hija!" *Daughter.* It was Calaca's father, Don Diego. They hadn't noticed him come in. The two women stepped away from each other.

"¡Los caballos!" he shouted. *The horses.* Don Diego seemed to see Lucy for the first time. He pulled limp sheets of paper from his pocket. "¿Donación para la entrada?" He was soliciting again for the new cemetery gate.

"Papá," Calaca soothed. "She already gave a donation, remember?"

Don Diego fumbled with the papers, trying to stuff them back into his pocket without folding them. When Calaca reached for the papers, Don Diego batted her hand away and made as if to strike her. Calaca's hands came up to protect her face.

"Chica estupida," he spat. *Stupid girl.*

Calaca glanced at Lucy, embarrassed and defiant. "What about the horses, Papá?" Her voice held an extra measure of love. She wanted no one's pity.

Don Diego looked angry, then lost.

Calaca turned to Lucy. In Calaca's face was all they had once been to each other, but also a sense that her heart was not entirely open to her old friend. "The horses need to run. Want to go for a ride?"

As a girl, Lucy had been horse-crazy. She got her first taste of the mania in Palmita. Back home in California, she helped out at a ranch where they let her ride after she mucked out stalls. Her last ride—more than twenty years ago—had been on Plummet, a high-strung gelding boarding at the ranch while his owners went through a messy divorce. The horse sulked and lashed out like an abandoned child, only his tantrums destroyed fences and sent riders—Lucy included—flying. Before that, on her last visit to Palmita, Lucy rode behind Inés—Calaca—on a mare whose gallop was so smooth, it was like the three of them were one big surge of animal joy.

Approaching the barn now, Lucy smelled the tang of horse sweat under the waxy scent of leather cleaner. Bridles and old blankets hung from the rafters. Dust motes showed in the light filtering between planks.

Calaca told her that when her father sold off his land, he kept a barn and a few horses so he'd still qualify as a *caballero*, which literally meant *horseman* but had come to mean *gentleman*. He owned two scrappy *criollo* geldings, with barrel chests and short legs, whose bloodlines ran back to the horses Spaniards had brought to the New World. One of the horses kicked his stall and snorted with impatience.

Lucy recognized him. "Bobo."

"How do you know his name?'

"I was on the bus when you were chasing him."

The other horse was a palomino with a tangled mane and wild blue eyes. "Meet Mister." Calaca pronounced it *me-stare*.

"Mr. What?"

"Just Mister." Calaca took a bridle down from its hook. The horses pranced like dogs shown a leash. Lucy thought about what she'd just learned about Calaca and Gabriel. Turned out Sara had been right to mistrust the girl. Lucy was loath to admit it, but she was a little jealous. She'd been possessive of Gabriel back then, and even more so of her best friend.

Calaca saddled the horses and then slipped a bridle over the palomino's nose. Only it wasn't a bridle—it was a halter, a few flimsy straps around the horse's muzzle. You couldn't control a horse with just a halter.

"Don't worry." Calaca slapped Lucy's behind like she'd slap a horse's flank. "The horses know where to go."

They mounted, and despite the simple halter, Mister was an easy ride. They took a path that led steeply up. Overhanging branches made the riders bend low over the horses' necks. Even now, at the end of dry season, there were still pockets that smelled of loamy damp. One enormous tree was dotted with delicate orchids and blade-leafed bromeliads like a tropical Christmas tree with living ornaments.

"This hill was too steep to clear," Calaca said.

"Lucky hill."

At the top, they turned their horses around to face a vista that hit Lucy like a branch to the chest. It reminded her of the aerial view she'd seen on the computer before she booked her ticket: trees like broccoli crowns, sloping down to where waves lined up like an endless swath of blue corduroy.

The way down was a dirt road, closed to cars because big hunks of earth had fallen away during the last rains. The animals were surefooted and alert. It wasn't until they were back on the flat, on a narrow beach of firm sand, that they let the animals truly run. At the height of their gallop, with all four legs off the ground, the horses were wild again, their Old-World bloodlines left far behind.

In mid-gallop, Lucy herself felt a sense of suspension between time and place. Memories of riding with Inés when they were girls lay like transparent wings over the body of the present moment and the women they had become. She gazed at Calaca's broad back, swaying in response to her horse's movements, wondering what it would be like to do now what they'd done back then.

Calaca stopped her horse, waiting for Lucy to come alongside.

"I should get back," Calaca said, as if for her, this epic ride had been just another thing to check off a list. "But I think we have time for a swim."

They dismounted, but instead of heading into the water, Calaca took the saddles off the horses and gave Lucy a leg back up.

Taking the horses in the water was like launching four-legged boats. Lucy's horse splashed in until he was shoulder deep and then commenced what felt like a dog paddle writ large. Lucy's stomach dropped as the beast's muscles worked in this new weightless medium, with no ground to meet the running hooves. The horse was warm under her even as water circled her waist like a swirl of cool silk.

Calaca, submerged from the hips down, called back over her shoulder.

"Okay?"

Lucy pried one hand from Mister's mane to give a thumbs-up. Before she knew it, the horses were scrambling back out onto the beach.

"Something to write home about?" Calaca was proud of knowing the English colloquialism.

"Or even call." Lucy agreed, picturing her phone plopping into the water. Had that been just this morning? "That is, if I still had a phone."

They dismounted. Mister's flesh twitched, trying to flick away water. Lucy followed Calaca's lead, brushing water off her horse's back and then laying the blanket and saddle back on and cinching the girth.

"Someone took your phone?" Calaca said, trying to sound casual. "In Bocas, no doubt. The place is full of *delinquentes*. You'd think their parents would have more control."

Lucy tried to wring out her shorts while they were still on her.

"So was it in Bocas?"

"It was here," Lucy said. "After I played soccer on the beach."

They mounted the horses and rode at a walk. Finally, Calaca asked, "Who was at the soccer game?"

Lucy wavered. What good would it do for a mother to have one more reason to be ashamed of her son? On the other hand, who was Lucy to decide what Calaca should and shouldn't know? She hesitated, but Calaca snapped, "You don't have kids." There was a curl of accusation in Calaca's tone, like a back arching.

"No."

"I can't believe you, talking to Pilar's parents like you did."

Lucy kept her gaze between the horse's ears, alert to the sudden change in the air. "I know. It was a bad idea."

"A stupid idea. Insulting."

Lucy looked at Calaca, whose face was pinched now, her features bunched together.

"People like you," Calaca muttered.

"People like me?" Lucy's ire was rising.

"If you're not a mother, you can't possibly—"

"What? Have an opinion?"

Calaca jerked on the reins. Bobo stopped in his tracks. Mister stopped too. The women were close now, their legs almost touching. "I can't stand some outsider accusing my son. How would you feel if your own father denied you in favor of some gringa he could barely remember?" Calaca's horse shared her agitation; he lifted his head and snorted.

"Wait," Lucy said. "Who is Beto's father?"

"You poke your face in everyone's business, but you don't know your own?"

"How is Beto's father my business?" Lucy's mind revved but didn't get anywhere. Then it dropped into gear, a dull *clunk* that she felt in her gut. Her horse stood stock still as if he, too, had just realized something.

"I told you about Gabriel. I thought you'd figured it out."

"So Beto is—"

"Your brother."

Lucy slumped in the saddle. Her feet slipped out of the stirrups. How could it be that after looking into every face in Palmita for family resemblance, it turned out the village thief was a blood relation?

Funny thing was, Lucy used to long for a brother. She'd imagined him as a lifeline in the sloshy sea of estrogen created by a mother and two teenaged sisters in close quarters. She'd harbored the idea of man as savior even though everything in her life contradicted that dream. Sara had a taste for guys who were good-natured do-nothings, out-of-work fisherman or loggers, stoned surfers who paddled out only if conditions were perfect, which was pretty much never on their rocky coast.

Lucy hadn't longed for a father, or a stepdad, but the idea of a brother had secretly taken hold. But not like this. Not Beto, for chrissakes.

"He'd be my *half*-brother," Lucy corrected. "Assuming Gabriel is even my father." Wait. If Gabriel was her father, and he'd been with Calaca, would that make Calaca Lucy's stepmother? Oh, God.

"He was pretty sure you were his daughter. Anyway, he's gone. Your brother is still here."

"How could we be related? We have nothing in common."

Calaca waited a beat. "You both like to steal."

"I don't steal! How can you compare—"

Before Lucy could finish, Calaca brought her open hand down on Mister's flank, letting out a high *iyeee!* that set the horse in motion. Lucy's head snapped back. She clutched at the mane and gripped with her knees. It was too late to thread her feet back into the stirrups, so her legs bounced crazily.

Calaca called out again, and the horse stopped short, planting its front feet. Lucy flew over the horse's lowered head.

Someone had once told her how to fall. To her surprise, the advice came to her. Relax. Duck and roll. She felt a jolt to her shoulder and arm, a crackle of leaves on her cheek. Her knees bent and rose as if for a sideways somersault, then settled back down. Thank God for a small seepage of water that made the ditch into a stew of grass shoots and decaying leaves. It was as soft a landing as she could have hoped for.

From where she lay, Lucy looked back at where Mister still stood. Calaca approached, letting her horse amble leisurely. She reached for Mister's reins as she passed the horse. When she got to where Lucy lay, she looked down with a face that badly wanted to break into a grin.

Lucy shifted in her bed of dirt and leaves. It didn't feel like anything was broken.

Calaca dismounted. Held out a hand.
Lucy sat up. And grasped it.

CHAPTER 15

> Army ants have no fixed home. Each night, they build a shelter of themselves, linking limbs and jaws to form a lacework of bodies that supports more bodies. Come dawn they let go, and keep traveling.
>
> — *Lucy's bug & bird notes*

AT THE MINI-SUPER she headed for the back. Her body throbbed and her brain seethed. What was she supposed to do with the idea of Beto as her half-brother? Calaca had laid out a scenario that would be fair and proper, she said, with Lucy acknowledging her brother even as their father had not.

Lucy had been half-hoping for something similar from Faith: that her sister would enforce some sort of equity in the face of their mother's unfairness, divide Sara's assets even if Sara hadn't specified that.

Now the shoe was on the other foot.

The open refrigerator case huffed cold. This was the same market she'd been sent to as a girl to get fresh eggs and a bag of rice. Now the place was stocked with packaged snacks and imported beer. She closed her fist around a bottle of Duval Ale.

Up front, the clerk was talking to someone in English.

"I've been the adult for far too long," Lucy heard a woman tell the clerk. "This is *my* time."

"Where are you from?" the clerk asked.

"Hawaii."

"Why leave paradise?" the clerk flirted. His good English was testament to the fact that tourists had indeed discovered Palmita.

"No place is paradise," the woman said, "when you really know it."

"Mom," came a young boy's voice. "Let's go."

"I hear you about the paradise thing," Lucy called, coming up the aisle.

The woman, accompanied by two teenaged girls and a boy around ten, didn't look up. People who found this out-of-the-way town often became possessive, looking askance at other visitors. Or not looking at all.

Lucy tried again. "Where are you staying?"

The woman still didn't acknowledge Lucy. Her daughters followed suit. Only the young boy dared a glance at Lucy. His expression said either *Please don't judge them* or *Get me out of here*.

Chuy, the bartender at the Avión, must have taken pity on Lucy and called his lawyer cousin in San José. The lawyer had left a message for Lucy at Hilda's.

Make a claim on the land, read the message. *Everyone else has. Possession is 9/10 of the law.* There was a phone number, and something about now charging by the hour rather than the day.

"What does that mean?" Lucy asked Hilda. "Why would I have to make a claim on land that's supposed to be mine?"

Hilda had something else on her mind. "I need to tell you about Martin. First of all, his claims about sustainability are pure—"

"Don't worry," Lucy said. "I'm happy at your place."

"That has nothing to do with it! You need to understand. He doesn't have friends. He has underlings, and people who owe him favors. He dumps raw sewage into the sea. He destroys—"

"Hilda!" It was as if she were shaking the woman awake from a nightmare. "The message. From the lawyer."

Hilda busied herself with a stack of papers. "I guess the lawyer raised his prices now that he's in the city."

"No," Lucy said. "The part about everyone else making a claim."

Hilda looked Lucy up and down. "What happened to you?"

Bruises bloomed along Lucy's arm, and there were probably a few on her face. "Who would make a claim on my land?"

"Your land," Hilda echoed, grabbing Lucy's wrist, trying to pull her outside.

Lucy shook her off. "Ow! What are you doing?"

"I want you to see. To really look at the land. To take a handful of it. Smell it. It's all so abstract for you."

"It's not abstract," Lucy protested. She ran her hand lightly up her aching arm. "In fact, the reality of it is hitting me pretty hard."

"Remember what I told you about my uncle's preserve, which became part of the national park?"

"I guess."

Hilda retold the tale of Gabriel buying land from Don Diego for a song, and Diego throwing in pieces—the island cemetery, part of the national park—that weren't his to sell.

The only thing new was that now, Lucy knew who Don Diego was. When Hilda had told her this story earlier, he'd been a faceless character in a story that didn't have anything to do with her. "Ancient history." Lucy shrugged.

"My uncle founded the preserve, which is now the park. He charged me with protecting it. Then Don Diego moved the fence, claiming some of the park as his own. When he sold that land—"

"You already told me."

Hilda shook her head. "You need to understand. Why I did it."

"Did what?"

Hilda hesitated. "Made a claim. A small part of the land. To return it to the national park."

"How small a part?"

"Don Diego moved the fence. So, you see, ancient history, as you call it—"

Lucy stepped closer to Hilda. "How small a part of my land did you make a claim on?"

Hilda took a step back. "Less than half. And like I said, I'm not the only one."

Lucy couldn't believe it. "All this time, you were lying—"

Hilda seemed to gain several inches in height. "Lying? I owe you nothing!" she thundered. "Who the hell are you to this place? To the story of this place? It began before you were born and will go on long after you're gone."

Rising ire won the day. Lucy squared off against the taller woman, raising her chin. "My father says I'm a part of the story. It was his will, literally, that I come and claim his land."

Hilda gave an exasperated sigh. "Vamos a ver," she said in her heavily accented Spanish. *We'll see.*

Perched on a rock in the shade on the side of the dirt road, Lucy watched a beetle the size of her big toe stiff-leg its way through patches of light and shadow. She'd left Hilda's in a huff, the drama of her departure dulled by having to ask if she could leave her suitcase. She'd stuffed a few possessions in a plastic bag and took off.

The beetle looked as hapless as Lucy felt, trundling from shade to brutal sun and back again, vulnerable to car tires, birds, and its own foolishness.

Doing research for her bug blog a few months back, she'd stumbled upon a tiny beetle in Costa Rica that rode army ants like cavalrymen rode horses. When the million-ant army bulldozed through the jungle, devouring everything in its path, scraps flew—perfect leftovers for little beetles. They couldn't keep up with the ants' relentless march, so they latched onto an ant's waist and held on tight, detaching when they needed to feed and then hopping aboard again for the next leg of the trip. The ants were true nomads: They swarmed the world and made camp with their own bodies. The tiny beetles were freeloaders, just along for the ride.

Hilda and a lot of other people had implied that Lucy was a hanger-on. Was it true? Was she clinging to Palmita's chitinous waist, hitching rides she didn't deserve and gorging on scraps she hadn't earned?

She could get places under her own power, dammit. Lucy was fine with walking all the way to the Rancho but needed a few minutes in the shade to recoup. The sun was molten, streaming out over the road and edging into her shade, like a sped-up film. The insect chorus merged with the heat, crossing her sensory wires and making it seem as if the buzzing itself caused sweat to bead on her forehead and behind her knees. For a moment it was hard to say whether something was inside or outside of her. Was that pulsating hum, for instance, only in her head?

Sara had kept honeybees for a while. Lucy remembered sweating in the full protective outfit as she tried to sync her thoughts to the hive's vibrations. She got the idea when Sara told them about bee therapy. You went into a chamber with bees all around, though they couldn't get at you. The oscillating vibrations were supposed to calm you down. Lucy did indeed feel better after spending time with the bees.

During those years, Sara called their household the Magic Queendom, a three-monarch domain flying high on estrogen; no drones need apply. Sara was homeschooling them at the time. What Lucy remembered best from the lessons were that bees apparently made a whooping sound, inaudible to humans, the bee equivalent of a surprised gasp. That, and the fact that Saint Bernard had excommunicated a swarm of bees whose buzzing kept him from his work.

Lucy and Faith had loved that story. They'd gone around excommunicating everything in sight, from mosquitos to dirty dishes. Later, Lucy herself had been excommunicated from the Magic Queendom.

A van came into sight, gleaming white against the rutted road. There was a carousel horse on the driver's-side door. As before, Martin drove at a snail's pace to save his van's shocks. A tinted window came down, squeaking along its rubber seal. Cool air poured out.

It wasn't Martin behind the wheel. The driver wore a police uniform.

"Señora," the man said.

"Señor," Lucy greeted the policeman from the AA meeting. The one who had told her that her minor problems could be taken care of in a casual fashion. Did her problems still qualify as minor?

"¿Le llevo?" *Do you need a ride?*

Riding beside him in air-conditioned comfort, her bag rustling in the footwell, Lucy tried to tell him about Hilda and the lawyer, but although his English had been good when they spoke at the bar, the policeman now pretended not to understand her. He suggested, in painfully slow and clear Spanish, that she come to the station so they could have a translator present. It might take a week or two to locate an official translator, he said.

"Martin might be able to help," he added in perfect English. He dropped her at the Rancho.

Martin half-listened to Lucy's tale of woe as he gave orders to his staff. They backed out of his presence, as if he were their monarch. Lucy thought she saw Isa, dressed in a white uniform, carrying a stack of bed linens. The girl looked much younger and more tentative than she had on the soccer field.

"You can stay in Number 3 for now," Martin said.

"Thank you," Lucy said with relief. "I've got a lot to figure out."

"Another group arrives Saturday."

Saturday was the day before Lucy was scheduled to fly home. "If I haven't figured it out by then," she added, "I'm in trouble."

"I can offer a local's discount. Talk to the girl at the front desk."

A discount on stratospheric was still out of range. Lucy grimaced.

"Or—we could do a trade."

Lucy stiffened. Apparently, there was no free ride, unless you're a beetle yee-hawing it up on an army ant. But when he told her what her end of the bargain would be, she had to smile. She was to help Martin do a favor for Rafa, but keep it quiet so as not to insult Rafa's pride. Martin also offered to call his own lawyer and talk to him about Lucy's "complications."

"In the meantime, why don't you get settled? Make yourself at home."

The very air up here was better than down below, Lucy noted. Cooler and fresher. Things were definitely looking up.

CHAPTER 16

> When birds find a new mate, there's a steep learning curve in figuring out how to sing with the new partner. But some birds have such fine control over their voice box that they can produce two sounds at once, essentially singing duets with themselves.
>
> —*Lucy's bug & bird notes*

"You'll be tempted to touch." Rafa looked around the tour group, his gaze resting a beat longer on Lucy. "Maybe grab a tree to help you get up a hill, or a vine to see if it holds your weight. Please don't. Trees can have spines, or a colony of biting ants. A vine might not be a vine. There's a snake called the Vine Snake that looks exactly like—"

"A vine." Yvette nodded. A small army of barrettes made a valiant effort to hold back the girl's springy hair. She and her brother Max were here with their father, Ned, a Jamaica-born man who now lived in Toronto and saw his kids twice a year. He was desperate that they have not just a good but an unforgettably great time. A night hike in the tropics fitted the bill.

A last-minute booking had saved this tour from cancellation—four hikers was Rafa's minimum. Flustered when Lucy turned out to be his fourth, he mumbled an apology for standing her up that morning.

"No problem," she said, though of course there had been a fistful of problems, from Pilar's stolen bike to Beto lobbing her phone into the surf. She hoped there'd be time later to talk, but she had to remember not to tell Rafa that Martin had signed her up for the hike. Lucy didn't want to wound Rafa's pride by revealing Martin's role in producing more customers.

Rafa being the hike leader gave Lucy permission to look at him for as long as she wanted, and look she did. She was starting to have a thing about the slope of his shoulders and the callouses on his beat-up hands.

They were at the trailhead, in the buggy beams of the truck's headlights. Rafa passed out headlamps and binoculars. "Don't look directly at someone, or the light from your headlamp will temporarily blind them."

"The mosquitos here are fierce." Ned looked down as instructed.

"These are *mariposas del noche*—night butterflies, or moths. Not many mosquitos this time of night." Rafa turned to the kids. "Did you know that only female mosquitos drink blood? They need to keep up their strength so they can lay their eggs."

"Gross," Max said appreciatively. His headlamp beam swept the dark woods.

Without the headlamps, the woods would have been inky black. Rafa led the way, and Lucy brought up the rear, a habit from chaperoning school field trips.

What they lost in the visual they gained in the aural. The closer to the equator, the greater density of animal life and the richer the soundscape. The night forest was alive with keening, dripping, and rustling.

Rafa stopped after ten minutes of walking and pointed. Headlamp beams converged on a hard-shelled hump at ground level. At Rafa's whispered command, they moved their beams a little to the side of the creature so they could still see it, but it wouldn't be blinded by the light. Lucy felt the thrill of encountering another living being in a form she didn't immediately recognize. The armadillo—so that's what it was!—snouted around in the undergrowth. It looked up for one long moment, then went back to its work.

Armadillos were special, Rafa told them, in that they didn't have eyeshine, which meant color reflecting back from their eyes at night. Lucy remembered the blazing orange eyes she'd seen in the forest on her walk into town a few nights back. A kinkajou or La Mona Bruja, if Pilar was correct. Lucy's mom, if Lucy's gut was right.

Rafa pointed at a dark blob in a tree. Eventually they all spotted it: an animal that looked like a moth-eaten toupee someone had tossed into the crook of a tree. They stayed for a while, hoping it would move. At last, it did, just enough to give a glimpse of faint red eyeshine and a small, smiling face.

"Sloth," Rafa stage-whispered.

The group walked and walked, and then walked some more. The air was damp and the ground slippery. For fifteen minutes, the only wildlife they saw was a walking stick insect, like a skinny pencil with legs. Its coloration was exactly like the lichen-spotted branch it rested on.

After another few minutes of walking, Rafa stopped, waited for everyone to catch up. His headlight illuminated what appeared to be a big tree root. Part of it humped up out of the damp ground; the rest was buried under leaves and dirt. Then the root moved. Everyone but Rafa drew back. They watched as the boa burrowed muscularly under leaf litter. They could follow its progress—away from them, thank God—by watching for movement in the fallen leaves.

After that, Max and Yvette weren't so eager. Their father's brown face shone with sweat. He'd rolled up his sleeves and pants legs; scratches crisscrossed the exposed skin. At one point, Ned dropped back to where Lucy was.

"I'm losing confidence in our guide," he said. "My kids are really tired. The guy's your friend, right?"

Lucy shrugged but made her way up to Rafa. "Are we heading back?" She kept her voice low.

"Hear that?" Rafa called. They all listened. Eventually, they picked out a four-part whistling call.

"Rare to hear it at night. It's a red-eyed vireo. Little bird. Probably just passing through."

"If it's singing, it's a male," Ned told his kids. "The males sing to defend their territory and attract mates."

"Hmmm," Rafa said.

"What?" Ned said testily. His headlamp shone directly in Rafa's face.

Rafa turned to avoid the glare. "That may be true up north, in temperate regions. But we're in the tropics, where both sexes sing."

"Both sexes sing," was maybe the most erotic phrase Lucy had ever heard, but then she had a penchant for animal lore and jargon. In the bird book she'd borrowed from Gabriel's house, the author described birdsong with words like trill, jangle, chatter, and screech. When words failed, he spoke in bird language: the bare-throated heron's *wowrrh*, the limpkin's *krrAAOOoow*, or the tropical kingbird's *bibididi*. Each bird had not one but many songs and calls, depending on whether they were warning, wooing, or just belting it out for the hell of it.

The white-throated magpie jay, which, with the book's help, she'd identified as the bird that landed on her lunch up at the Rancho, could have a loud, raspy scold or a sweet serenade.

"Can you do that bird's call?" Lucy said softly, as if asking him for a kiss.

Rafa whistled a multi-part call that ended on an upswing, then repeated a similar phrase that ended on a down-slur. It was as if he'd asked a question and then answered it.

"Wow." Yvette was impressed.

"Wow," Lucy echoed.

Rafa whistled out the upswing part of the call again. After a moment, an unseen bird answered. "It's like we're having a conversation."

"So cool," Max said, looking up at Rafa with wide eyes. Ned frowned; he'd wanted his kids to remember him as the hero of this adventure.

"So is *that* a female?" Ned goaded. "I guess since we're down where the girl birds sing, we should know what we're hearing."

"I don't know about this particular bird. But female birds sing in other parts of the world, too," Rafa said. "You just have to listen." He palmed his headlamp before beaming a smile at Lucy.

Oh, to have someone flirt by offering up fun nature facts! He sure had Lucy's number.

Ned couldn't let it go. "All I've read says it's the males who sing."

"All you've read has a bias toward temperate regions," Rafa replied. "Which happens to include the US and Europe. Even birders can be biased."

"He talks to *me* about bias?" Ned said to no one in particular.

Rafa and Ned looked at each other long and hard. The threat of violence seemed to hang in the air, but then Rafa turned away. "I'll take us the shortest way back," he said. "I know everyone's worn out."

He led them down a steep descent. Openwork concrete blocks had been fashioned into stairs, but most were buried in mud or had broken into sharp fragments. They all slipped and slid, their shoes making long gashes in the mud, the beams from their headlights jerking wildly. Ned took his kids' binoculars from their necks and strung them around his own. They were all doing what Rafa had warned them against—grasping at roots and vines and saplings to help keep their balance.

The worst spot was a wooden footbridge across a muddy creek, its cross pieces mostly rotten, no handrails. Ned carried Max over and then came back for Yvette.

"This is bullshit," Ned said more than once. His kids were too tired to be thrilled that their father was swearing.

The drive back to Palmita was quiet. Through the clouds, they could see the promise of dawn on the horizon. Rafa drove slowly, easing the tires in and out of potholes and gullies so as not to wake the kids, who'd fallen asleep in a heap, draped over their stone-faced father's lap.

Back at Rafa's office, Ned was fuming. "You endangered my children. You'll be hearing from my lawyer."

"I'm sorry the hike wasn't what you expected," Rafa said. His tone was sincere but his face told a more complicated story.

Ned seemed to be assessing whether to escalate the conflict. A look at Rafa's set face and muscled shoulders made him decide against it. The kids waved at Lucy on their way out. Making sure their father was already out the door, they waved at Rafa too.

Car doors slammed. An engine turned over.

"It was a hard hike," Rafa allowed. "Thanks for helping out."

Outside, Ned gunned the rental car engine. Gravel spit as he peeled out.

"It's good that you didn't get into it with Ned," Lucy said, relieved.

Rafa looked surprised. "Why would I do that? He was just worried about his kids."

"I thought you wouldn't be able to hold back."

"I always hold back. Where kids are involved, anyway."

"You'd make a good dad." She hadn't meant to say it aloud.

"Thanks. I try."

Of course. The man probably had offspring scattered like weeds.

"You have kids." It was more of a statement than a question.

"You met my daughter. At the soccer field. Isa."

"Your daughter?" Lucy's head felt fizzy. So the soccer game girl who'd kicked the ball in Lucy's face *wasn't* Rafa's girlfriend.

"She takes after her mother."

The fizz went flat. No doubt the little woman stayed home to cook and clean while her husband and daughter were out playing soccer and just generally having lives.

"She died a few months after Isa was born." Rafa's voice held sorrow, and still, after all these years, a trace of incredulity. Lucy knew the feeling. In the face of her mother's death, Lucy's primary state was still numb disbelief.

But upon hearing that Rafa was a single dad, Lucy's buzz was back. Intact families were like sealed boxes; broken ones let light and other people in through the cracks.

Rafa grabbed his keys from the counter. "Want to go for a swim? Wash that hike off?"

The moon shone down on a broad and shallow river that was the visual equivalent of birdsong. Water trilled and warbled over the rocks. Night-blooming something-or-other gave off a heady scent.

"After the rains, the river gets wild," Rafa told her. "Right now, it's shallow, so we're going to have to head upriver for a place deep enough to swim."

Lucy scanned the banks. Bushes crowded down as if wanting to be the first one in. "Is there a trail?"

"We go up the middle."

The rock under the water was mostly flat and not slippery. Rafa told her it was all of one piece, that the river had sanded it down over the years. If the river were to dry up, the sculpted rock would be its own sort of river, its running measured in millennia.

Twenty minutes of knee-deep sloshing brought them to a big rock at the edge of a swimming hole. Rafa peeled off his shirt and launched himself in a shallow dive. When he stood, the water came to his chest. He motioned her in.

The force of the dive took her underwear to her knees and pulled her tank top up around her armpits. She found the bottom of the pool with her feet, adjusting her clothing underwater. The current was gentle but insistent. A leaf spun past.

In Spanish, fresh water is *agua dulce*—sweet water, as opposed to the savory ocean with its freight of salt. When Lucy ducked her head underwater, the river tasted like a sip from a cold metal canteen.

Rafa was breast-stroking toward her.

Yes, she thought. When he swam past her and climbed up onto the rock, her stomach contracted in disappointment.

"Like it?" Rafa squeezed water out of a hank of hair pulled over his shoulder.

Lucy took in the rush of the water and the call of early-rising birds. The air was heavy with scent but light with promise. "God, yes."

Getting out of the pool was harder than getting in. She felt around for hand- and footholds.

Rafa reached down a hand, and she took it, bracing her foot against the rock. In one silky show of strength, he lifted her out of the water and pulled her to him. She was so close, she couldn't see him but she smelled him, animal and mineral both. His pelvis ground against hers as he pulled her closer, one hand clamped to her ass. His other hand tilted her head back so he could see her face.

When he kissed her, it wasn't the passionate pressure she expected, a match for the hard crush of their lower bodies. It was soft and tentative, and more intimate than anything she could have imagined. Because she *had* imagined this, but in her mind, it hadn't been this delicate, or this thrilling. It was fire crackling over water, the sparks staying lit even as they hit the surface and spun away downstream.

In the truck cab, wrapped in a towel against the predawn chill, Rafa laughed at her story of being thrown from Calaca's horse. Lucy laughed too. "I think our little 'swim' is going to leave me sore in other places." She smiled. Suddenly everything that had happened to her in Palmita shimmered with a rose-gold light.

They talked about leatherback turtles swimming 10,000 miles a year and capuchin monkeys holding grudges. Lucy fanned out some fun bug facts; Rafa countered with cool bird behavior, like that when mating pairs learned to duet, their brains actually synced up.

Rafa wanted to know about the animals where Lucy grew up. She told him the story about raccoons messing with their dogs and getting into the greenhouse. Her mom borrowed a Havahart trap from a neighbor, the kind where you catch the animal live and release it somewhere else, hoping they don't find their way back. One morning, the trap was so chock-full of something furry, they couldn't tell what it was. Then they saw the round ears and the short tail. It was a bear cub.

"Of course, where there's a cub, there's a mom," Lucy said. "If you get the cub out of there, the mother follows. We got the cage in the back of the truck—don't ask me how. Went up a fire road into the national forest. We're doing about ten miles an hour when the mama comes out of the trees. You know the word *galumph*?" Seated in the cab of Rafa's truck, she tried to mime a *galumph*.

Rafa's smile was so big, it squinched his eyes almost shut.

"So mama bear's galumphing after us. She's gaining. My mom guns it. When we're up the road and can't see the bear mom, we try to get the baby out of the trap. Mom's yelling, *Poke the fucker!* We used a broomstick to poke him into the back of the trap so we could get enough space to open the door. Finally, we get the door open.

"Me and my sister are laughing and my mom's yelling and finally, when mama bear's about twenty feet away, the cub shakes off the trap and jumps down from the bed of the truck."

This story makes it seem like we're all one big happy family. "Mom floored it. Got us out of there." She went quiet then, remembering. "It was Mom who said it, on our way back home."

"Said what?"

"Who knew how hard it'd be to have a fucking heart?" Lucy's eyes stung and she blinked hard, surprised at how much emotion the words held. Would it be okay to cry? She stole a glance at Rafa. She had a sudden urge to call him sweetheart, but knew it was too soon. What she could do was honor his telling her about Isa's mom by sharing that her own mother had recently died. She told him in the simplest terms she could muster, because words always got it wrong. She was rewarded by a big damp hug that lasted a long time and soothed her like she hadn't been soothed in years. She made a murmuring sound of satisfaction, and he echoed it, as if they were birds cooing to each other.

Rafa didn't say, "I'm sorry." It was as if the words would just create distance between them.

After a long while, Lucy pulled away.

"Now you," she said. "Tell me something."

Rafa thought for a while. "Ever heard of the Great American Interchange?"

"Isn't that what we just did?" She smiled.

"I'm talking millions of years back. North and South America are two separate continents. Volcanoes erupt and plates shift. A land bridge forms. Today's Central America."

His tone had changed and the towel around her felt suddenly clammy.

"The bridge let animals from the south head north, and vice versa."

She reached out to touch his arm. "So you and I, we meet on—"

"Deer and bears and cats and rats come south. They do okay. But the animals going north, not so good. Giant ground sloths, terror birds—"

"Terror birds?" Lucy shuddered, remembering the bird that swooped in when she was having lunch by the pool at the Rancho.

Rafa stared out the steamed-up windshield as if he could see through the condensation. "Huge, meat-eating, flightless birds. Apex predators down south, but they couldn't make it in the gringo world."

Lucy swiped at the fogged glass, looking for signs of how this day would turn out.

"It's more complicated these days," he allowed. He was so matter-of-fact now. "We Nicaraguans migrate south to Costa Rica to find jobs and a government that almost works. And the animals, they're just moving toward water and away from heat."

He turned to face her. She thought he was going to make a flirty joke, tell her that he himself moved toward heat rather than away from it. Her lips parted in anticipation.

"As the cloud forest shrinks, Resplendent Quetzals are moving higher into the mountains."

Lucy grunted, both in sympathy for those having to push into new territory to survive and in frustration that Rafa hadn't gone in for the kiss.

"Come on," Lucy said.

His dark brows shot up.

"What about *your* story?"

Rafa hesitated. "That *is* my story."

In fact, he longed to tell Lucy more. To breathe the hot wind of confession into her neck. He'd been a bad man, drinking and getting in fights, losing jobs to his quick temper. He left Isa home alone when she was very young. It killed him to think of all that could have gone wrong, and he promised himself he would reform. AA helped. He had left his drinking and carousing behind. Or at least the drinking. Now he bedded only tourists, so he'd never have to run into them again. He hadn't had a proper partner since Isa's mother Elise died.

He attributed his philandering in part to not knowing how people kept more than one big love in their hearts at once. He loved Isa more than he'd ever loved Elise. Was that strange? He'd mourned Isa's mom, but his grief was selfish, at least in part. He felt abandoned and couldn't imagine how he would raise a child on his own. Eventually he had figured it out. All it took was everything he had, and more.

All it took was letting your child be the landscape you lived in.

Rafa remembered Gabriel's warning. *You're a man, not just a dad.* His friend had seen it: The dad part of Rafa deepened while the man stayed shallow. Truth be told, Rafa was lonely as fuck. And here was a woman, right next to him, who made the back of his neck prickle.

Rafa let out a long slow breath. "I like you." He didn't look at her but his voice was like a tender gaze.

Lucy was transported back to grade school. That lacerating joy of someone you like liking you back. Outside the truck window, surf boomed a slow, distant heartbeat that undergirded everything. She breathed in the smell of the dark earth and all that grew from it.

"Me too," she mumbled, then, louder. "I like you too." She scooted over until their thighs were touching.

Rafa turned the key in the ignition, and the engine roared to life. They drove along in contented silence for several minutes. Then Rafa slowed the truck, eased into a pullout, cut the engine.

"You asked me about my story."

Lucy pressed her back into the side door, folding one leg under her. Her eyes gleamed with anticipation.

He told her about growing up poor in a San José shantytown and about his mother's Canadian boyfriend, who paid for him to go to a fancy private school. Rafa liked his classes but was always an outsider, ashamed when his mother came to pick him up, her skin even darker than his.

"Don't let anyone tell you that the people here aren't racist. And my mom, she said, *Sí, como no* after someone thanked her, instead of *con gusto*." He looked at Lucy to see if she understood.

She didn't.

"Only Nicaraguans say *Sí, como no*, which means, 'Yes, of course.' Ticos—Costa Ricans—say *con gusto*. With pleasure. Like there's just so goddamned much pleasure in this country that it spills out all over the place."

"I get it," Lucy said. "Your mom spoke like a Nicaraguan."

"I'm embarrassed now that I was embarrassed by her back then. But pretty soon it didn't matter because her boyfriend took off, and she couldn't afford the private-school tuition on her own." They went back to the rough riverside town in Nicaragua where he'd grown up. Neither of them fit in anymore. They had called his mom a *puta*, a whore, and called Rafa a *playo*, which in that town so close to the border meant both "gay" and "Costa Rican."

"We came back to Costa Rica, but I hardly remember that second time." The first time, he said, he remembered the smell of diesel fuel, and how when he came by boat into Lake Nicaragua, it looked as huge and dark as an ocean. They hugged the lakeshore, eventually pulling into a swampy area and clambering out onto mudflats. The captain handed Rafa's mother their bundles, and was gone. They stood listening until they couldn't hear the boat engine anymore.

"The not-so-great Central American Interchange," Rafa summed up.

Lucy put a hand on his arm. His story made her think of what she herself had left behind, but also of how she'd had a choice and Rafa hadn't. "Thanks for telling me. And I'm really sorry." It was insufficient, but she didn't know what else to say.

"No worries," Rafa said, laughing bleakly.

They sat without talking. The air was warming up, and the light of the rising sun edged the dark trees in gold.

"Hey," Lucy said after a while. "What happened to you this morning? Or rather, yesterday morning." She told him about going after

Pilar's stolen bike and about what Calaca told her about Beto being Lucy's brother. "It's hard to believe that fuck might be a blood relative."

Rafa seemed unfazed by the news that had so stunned Lucy. "You have to know how to handle him."

"I doubt he's even related to me. It's all probably a big—"

"If you aren't related," Rafa said sharply, "then it's *you* who isn't related to *him*."

"Isn't that what I said?" The mood between them had turned on a dime.

"Forget it," he said, his face shutting down.

What had happened to liking each other, to the stories they'd just shared? To birdsong and duets?

For some reason, Lucy thought again of the tourist on the bus in San Francisco. Of strangers and locals, who stays and who goes. Was Rafa a stranger? Or was she the stranger and always would be?

"At least you got your pack back."

She shook her head. "It was in Beto's place. Which was locked."

"Let's go get it," Rafa said, as if to make up for being short with her.

The sun was up now, the sky a clean blue. It looked like it was going to be a beautiful day.

"The big rains are coming," Rafa said, shifting into third gear on a straightaway. Someone had told Lucy that this wasn't a Third World but a third-*gear* country. The backroads never let you shift any higher. They drove past Rafa's tour office.

"I might get out of guiding," he said. "Move to the capital."

Though she'd just arrived in Palmita and didn't know if she would stay, the idea of Rafa leaving hit her hard. It drummed up previous abandonments, like a hard rain muddies the waters. Her memories of loss had geological layers: the bedrock of childhood self-blame, the volcanic strata of adolescence rage, and the sediment of adult practicality, a gradual hardening of her heart against the fact that in the end, everybody leaves.

"There's nothing for Isa here," Rafa continued.

"She doesn't like her job?" Lucy was distracted, wondering how she could end things with Rafa even before they'd really begun. Yes, everybody left. Unless you left first.

Rafa stamped down on the clutch but forgot to shift. The car hurtled along, the engine unengaged. "What job?"

"At the Rancho."

"She doesn't work at the Rancho. She knows to stay away from Martin."

"Maybe it wasn't her."

"It was her," he said, almost to himself.

"Is it so awful that she wants to make a little money for herself?"

His foot slipped off the clutch and the truck seized. Their bodies snapped back.

"Sorry," Rafa said.

"Is Martin so terrible? He wanted you to have more business. He signed me up for your hike. He wants local businesses to do well."

"Martin signed you up?" Rafa looked as if he was working through a math problem. "He knows I would have cancelled the hike without one more client. What time did you see Isa?"

"I don't know if it was Isa."

"What time?"

"Late afternoon, maybe five. Why?"

Rafa executed a frantic three-point turn, almost knocking down a fence post. "I'll drop you at Hilda's. Actually, could you walk the rest of the way? It's not far."

He stopped the car for her to get out.

"What's so urgent?" It was as if she was being unceremoniously dumped after an evening that had had its share of magic, like a cloud of yellow butterflies all suddenly dying in midair and plummeting to the ground.

"I think my daughter's in trouble," he said. "I don't have time to explain."

He drove off. Only then did Lucy remember that she wasn't staying at Hilda's anymore.

DAY FIVE

WEDNESDAY

CHAPTER 17

> Rafa teased me that insect lovers look down while birders look up, and did I always want to be the downcast one? What I should have said is that it's easy to love a pretty little songbird or some keel-billed toucan. It takes more imagination to fall for a potato bug.
>
> —*Lucy's bug & bird notes*

As much as Rafa thought and talked about the Rancho Vista Dulce, he'd been there just a handful of times. Once for the grand opening, back when everyone thought Martin was the answer to Palmita's prayers, and a few times to pick up guests for a nature tour. But he remembered the steep grade of the driveway, how you had to gun it to get a running start. At the top of the drive, Rafa's parking job boxed in two rental SUVs. He wasn't planning to stay long.

Breezing by white-shirted staff cranking up their morning smiles, Rafa found Martin out by the pool, reading a Costa Rican tabloid while enjoying his usual power breakfast: black coffee and a skinned chicken leg, cold from the fridge.

"Where's Isa?" Rafa demanded.

"Good morning," Martin said, as if he hadn't heard the question. "What can I do for you?"

"Where's my daughter?"

Martin folded the paper. "I have no idea."

"Doesn't she work here?"

"She would like to," Martin said. "Right now, she's on probation." He made "probation" sound like some bizarre sex act.

Rafa came closer. "Stay away from my daughter."

Martin scraped his chair back to move out from under Rafa's shadow. "*She* came to *me*. And anyway, she's not my type." He stood, coffee in hand. "The guests seem to like her."

"You are this close"—Rafa held thumb and forefinger an inch apart—"to big trouble."

"How close?" Martin taunted. "How big?" He signaled to a workman nearby. "Get this *payaso* out of here," he said when the uniformed man approached. "He's trespassing and threatening the safety of our guests."

The man took Rafa by the arm, and Rafa let him. They recognized each other from town, and Rafa knew the man relied on this job. Out of Martin's sight, the man dropped Rafa's arm. "What's the matter, *compadre*?"

"Have you seen my daughter?"

"Her shift ended last night. I think she got a ride to Bocas with some gringos. They were going to spend the night in Bocas and fly out this morning."

"Fly out?" Rafa's stomach fell, picturing Isa on a plane. It would be her first time. He'd been too protective, denied her so many things.

"The gringos are flying out," the man clarified. "I don't think Isa was going with them."

Rafa slumped in relief. "But she went with them to Bocas?"

"I think so."

Rafa pictured Isa in Bocas, in one of those clubs where the bartender also sells cocaine and who knew what else. Rafa was all too familiar with those kinds of places. Then she'd go with one of the gringos to their overpriced motel room.

"I'm sorry, Don Rafa," the man said.

"No, no." Rafa shook his head. "It's not your fault." He pulled the man into a bear hug so he wouldn't see the tears in Rafa's eyes.

* * *

Alone on the beach, Lucy sat with knees drawn up, gazing across the water at the cemetery island. The sky was the color of a late-stage bruise. Waves sloshed over the island's narrow land bridge and rolled toward the beach. She thought about what she should have asked Rafa when he wouldn't tell her how Gabriel died: Where was her father now? Because even dead people had to go somewhere.

She pictured the route from her San Francisco apartment to her job. She often took the bus because it was hard to find parking near the school. But if she went toward the water, sometimes there were spaces. She could navigate that city like a pro, her car tires like sticky housefly feet on the crazy hills, parallel parking on steep grades. She missed knowing where she was and where she could park.

A week ago, Lucy had been sitting in her own apartment, in the taloned grip of an idea: to go in search of a branch of her family that might give her something other than grief.

Look how that had turned out.

What if she took off right now? Found a way back to the capital, got an earlier flight home. Borrowed money to hire someone to fight this fight for her. Or not. Did she really want a stake in a town where the one thing people seemed to agree on was that she didn't belong?

She lay back on the damp sand, fingers laced under her head. Sleep came like a kidnapper, a chloroformed cloth to the mouth.

Lucy awoke to heavy, scattered drops splattering her face and blooming dark on her shirt. In her dream, she'd been looking up from a new grave, shovel marks like fresh scars on the sides of the hole.

The rain came now in arterial spurts. On her feet in an instant, she headed for the shelter of the trees. It was like being pursued by some apex predator, evolved to be everywhere at once.

Through a glassy sheet of moving water, she saw two other figures running for the same cover. When they converged in a protected spot under an enormous strangler fig tree, Lucy recognized them: Beto, flipping his long, wet hair back like someone in a shampoo ad, and the boy she'd seen with his rude mother and teenaged sisters at the mini-super.

Beto saw it was Lucy. "No!" he barked, as if she'd tracked him down and was bombarding him with demands. He motioned with his chin to the boy, and they took off running, diving back into the downpour.

Drenched to the skin and winded by her run, she bent over, hands on knees. But watching Beto disappear down the path, she knew she had to follow.

Beto pushed through squalls like they were bedsheets hanging on a line. Lucy ran with her hand held in a salute, as if that would keep the driving rain out of her face. The boy seemed to have taken a different route.

"¡Ladrón!" Lucy shouted. The Spanish word for *thief* felt righteous and substantial in her mouth. "¡Hermana!" he shot back, as if *sister* were as bad as *thief*.

Suddenly the boy was in front of her. She almost ran into him, slipping in the mud and then righting herself. "Go!" she shouted, as if they were all fleeing the same threat.

They were on a different path to Beto's than the one Lucy and Pilar had used, but this one also had a flurry of mobiles made of bones and beach trash, now battered by the rain and dancing in the wind.

They spilled out into a clearing, and there was Beto's hut. He took his front stairs in one leap, and was in and back out again in an instant. On his porch, framed by the open door, he swung a pack and let it fly. "Take it!"

Lucy caught her backpack by the strap just before it hit the ground.

She stood in the rain, leaves stuck to her calves and mud streaking her legs. From his porch, Beto waved her off. His shoulders jerked upward and it sounded like he was choking on his own tongue. He was crying.

"You," he wailed. "You are the thief!"

The rain stopped even more suddenly than it had started. There was an eerie quiet, punctuated by the occasional hollow, explosive sound of a big drop hitting a broad leaf. Steam rose from the ground.

She looked up at Beto. From the moment they'd met, she'd shared the town's view of him as a pariah, tainted by his father's rejection and his alliance with Martin. But for Lucy, it was a point of pride to value creatures that made other people's skin crawl, like spiders and centipedes. Most people hated them out of fear, and because they didn't know just how complicated and cool their lives were.

If she could pet a tarantula, why couldn't she see the softer side of Beto? She hadn't known he existed before she'd made this journey, but maybe she'd come all this way to find *him*, the missing part of a puzzle made up of half-siblings and half-truths.

They should at least be collaborators, putting Gabriel to rest for good. Not for his sake, but for their own—to somehow make themselves whole again. Such a shift seemed both essential and impossible.

She sat on the rain-wet front steps, making a show of checking the contents of her backpack. It looked like everything was there—money, sketchbook, and the key to the room at Hilda's. Of course she'd never get her phone back. No doubt it was on the seafloor, half-buried in sand, its glass face winking up through the murk when the light hit it right.

Beto pointedly ignored Lucy, and out of solidarity, the boy did the same. The two worked well together, hardly having to speak. Beto spread a tarp in a clearing where there were no trees to drip down on them, then began to pull odds and ends from the space under the raised hut, handing them to the boy, who lugged them to the tarp. The boy was stronger than he looked. He hauled bucketloads of shells, pieces of broken surfboard, sticks, snarls of wire, and a clod-encrusted burlap bag.

The sun blazed, drying Lucy's skin and making her hair and clothes steam. The warmth felt good after the pelting rain. She paged through her sketchbook, stopping at the drawing of Palmita she'd made on the bus ride here. She'd gotten a lot right, like the way the road curved just before you saw buildings. But the physical contours of the place didn't begin to get at the tangle of human connection and motive she had begun to discover. If she were to sketch the human web, it would blot out the landscape itself.

"Anyway," she began.

Beto flinched at the sound of her voice.

"No harm done," Lucy continued.

Beto looked up sharply.

Lucy hardly knew what she was saying. She wanted to make a few harmless noises, to ease into other, more important noises.

Beto went back to work with renewed vigor. He and the boy dragged column-like frames of rebar from under the shack, their sharp ends leaving grooves in the mud.

"Are you making something?" Lucy asked, trying to keep her voice light.

"You have your stuff," Beto said, lashing two of the rebar frames together. "Now go. Or, since you know Spanish so well, ¡Lárgate de aquí!"

"Rafa sent me."

Beto stopped what he was doing.

"He said you could tell me about Uncle—about Gabriel." She cleared her throat. "Our father."

The phrase seemed to do both of them in. Their shoulders sagged; their heads hung. The curve of their dejection looked remarkably similar.

Beto recovered first. "What about him?"

What a miracle that here was someone who might actually be able to tell her what she wanted to know. More than Rafa, who'd been in Palmita less than a decade.

"To start," Lucy said, "I want to know where to pay my respects."

"Your respects?"

Maybe Beto didn't know the English phrase. Lucy remembered their conversation at the beach bonfire, before she'd known their connection. She'd figured out how to explain the thing about family being an accident you could recover from. But could you really? Recover, that is. And did Gabriel deserve their respect?

"Where he is," she said quietly. "Where he's—"

"He's nowhere," Beto said. "That's what happens when you're dead." He tossed out the last word as if flinging salt in her eye. "Anyway, what does it matter? He can't accept your—what did you call them? Your respects."

Lucy thought about her mother again. She was glad to have been in on the decision of what to do afterwards, where to scatter the ashes. It had been emotional and contentious, but it had also helped Lucy make the loss her own. To keep half sane and centered, you had to claim people in life, then claim them again in death.

"I know. And I know I'm too late for, well, anything. But can't we—"

"No," Beto said. "*We* can't."

Lucy closed her eyes. The sun was hot, and too bright.

"*We* are busy," he said, nodding at the boy.

She felt soaked in emotion and also hollow, a wet cloth over an empty bowl.

"Busy," the boy echoed, trying for Beto's tone.

"You owe me a phone," Lucy said wearily.

Brushing by her on the steps, Beto went into his house, coming back out with a cardboard box full of cell phones.

He rattled the contents under her nose. "Choose."

CHAPTER 18

> **From Jim Harrison's poem, "Returning to Earth"**
> It is very hard to give birds advice
> They are already members of eternity
>
> — *Lucy's bug & bird notes*

Lucy's clothes dried in the time it took to walk from Beto's hut into town. She sipped coffee as the store owner fiddled with an ancient CD player, choosing songs to mark the first rains of the season. Up now was The Grateful Dead's "Box of Rain."

How Sara had loved that song. As a teenager, Lucy had told her it was a funeral march for aging hippies. Lucy had always meant to amend her assessment, to tell Sara that, really, the song wasn't half bad.

Lucy was killing time at the store where she'd first met Keith. They'd packed in even more stuff since her first visit. Tucked between a pyramid of motor oil cans and a rack of beach towels was a new cardboard display of sunscreen. The tables were so engulfed by merchandise that they felt like private booths.

It was a good place to regroup. Lucy longed for a day or two when nothing much happened. She was spilling out all over the place, letting too much in.

The owner approached her table. Hadn't Keith called him Chanchito? Little Pig. He asked if Lucy wanted anything else.

Lucy shook her head.

"How is your mom?" he asked in Spanish, crossing his burly arms. He wore glasses with heavy plastic frames, one arm mended with duct tape. "Is she coming down too?"

It was as if her thoughts had seeped out of her head and into the humid air, there for all to see.

"I'm on my own this time."

"She was beautiful. Is she still beautiful?"

"Yes." Lucy wanted this moment to last: The man picturing her mother, young and beautiful and alive, even if it turned out he was thinking of someone else. Because Sara hadn't been here in decades.

"She liked this song." He nodded along to the beat for a moment.

Lucy shook her head in wonder. So he really did remember Sara.

"Bringing two girls down here alone, that couldn't have been easy," he said.

"She had Gabriel."

He raised an eyebrow. "A lot of people had Gabriel. But your mother didn't complain. She just made sure you girls were happy."

"I *was* happy," Lucy said, her eyes misting up. "I didn't know that she wasn't."

"Well, I wouldn't say that. She had friends. She made people laugh, even though her Spanish wasn't very good. Yours is better."

"Gracias," Lucy said, knowing it didn't take much to have Spanish better than Sara's. "Why do you think she brought us here?" It was an odd question to ask a virtual stranger, but he didn't hesitate in his reply.

"She wanted you girls to learn Spanish. And she wanted you to see that how people lived in the US wasn't the only way to live."

Lucy was astonished. That the man remembered Sara, yes, but even more, that Sara had had such a well-articulated rationale for bringing them here. Lucy had always explained their coming to Palmita as Sara chasing after a man.

"What about your sister?" Chanchito asked. "What was her name?"

"Faith." Lucy flashed on a scene, or rather, a feeling: holding Faith close so she wouldn't fall off the narrow couch back home, their bodies like flimsy paper plates you can't separate.

"She didn't like it here as much as you did."

Lucy had often run off without Faith, but she'd assumed her sister had her own friends and adventures.

"We never saw her on a horse," he continued. "And I remember she was afraid of the waves."

Lucy had a hard time picturing Faith afraid of anything. But then again, Faith had chosen to stay close to home, where she knew what was around every bend.

"She was little." Lucy felt protective. "Maybe I should have stayed with her more." She wondered how she and her sister had come to a point where they argued about everything.

He shrugged.

"I guess I should pay the bill."

"No charge," he said. "In honor of your mother."

The sudden knowledge of what he had to do was like an axe finding the right tree. Martin was the tree. Beto was the axe that would bring him crashing down.

It was hard to piece the archway together on his own. Thankfully, the boy had helped get the components ready for assembly. Beto had borrowed his mother's *quadriciclo* to drag the bigger pieces to the chosen spot.

Lucy waltzing into town had made him crazy, but it was she who had brought him to this point. She was maddening, claiming connection to Palmita without the very steep downside of having had to endure the place for any length of time. But when Beto saw all her friends on her phone, he was impressed she'd left them behind to come here. Ties could be broken. Better yet, chopped to bits.

All these years, Beto had been denying the obvious. Not just that his father would never claim him, but that Martin owned him, body and soul. Admitting that was both horrible and wonderful. Wonderful because truth—no matter how awful—brings clarity. Knowing what he had to do made him finally feel at home in his own body. It gave him a dignity that he'd never had. There would be no more skulking or apologizing while he still walked this Earth.

Which might not be for much longer. Even if Martin didn't get him, the town might string him up. Martin brought a lot of money in; people might well choose to continue to see Beto himself as the source of infection.

His plan was perfect, but he was well aware he might not survive it. Making up for that small glitch was the satisfaction that the plan also solved the problem of what to do with the bones he'd carved up. How to make that misstep into a leap forward, into something surprising, yet inevitable. Something that once pointed out could never be unseen. The installation was a bridge to eternity. Birds and butterflies would circle it after the Earth had purged itself of people.

His grandfather had the right idea: an archway to mark the entrance to the island. A way to make the townspeople see it as a real place again, not just a junk heap of broken gravestones where people did drugs and dumped trash.

The archway was like a frame on a painting. It said, pay attention. What's inside is valuable.

Where grandfather and grandson differed was in what they wanted people to pay attention to. Don Diego wanted the island to once again be a cemetery. Beto was more interested in the living part of town. Palmita had no real center anymore, and it certainly had no entrance. No ENTERING PALMITA sign. The road went past a couple of houses and fields, then rounded the bend to a cluster of buildings that might or might not be a town. Beto wanted to frame Palmita. Make it coherent and united, not as easy to sell off piecemeal or plow under for some outsider's grand plan.

He climbed up one side of the column and then the other, to lash on the final curved top piece. Back on the ground, he surveyed his work. The archway had turned out even better than he'd imagined. Bones wired to the rebar made it look like a sort of skeleton. But it wasn't, to Beto's eye, morbid or ghoulish. The arch looked both sturdy and soaring, and the names carved in the bones—*Luna, Mora, Madrigal, Calderón*—brought history out of the ground and into the open.

Yes, there had been Chorotega here centuries back, but theirs was not the only history that Palmita had buried. Just fifty years ago, this place had been intact, self-sufficient. They grew and caught what they ate and luxuries came by boat. Beto knew the town couldn't go back to that. But it couldn't hurt to remind people that this place had once been its own kingdom rather than some lesser satellite in the tourist universe.

He wove vines in and out to soften the effect of the bones, and hung bromeliads and orchids that blazed blood red and creamy white. Seeds and shells and shards of CDs were like encrustations of jewels. At the top of the arch and in a clear plastic sleeve, Beto hung a blowup of the passport Isa had brought him, with Martin's true name. Then a blowup of an old article Beto had found online: *Florida Man Wanted for Child Abuse*, with the same photo as the one in Martin's old passport.

The hardest things for Beto to put up were the yellowing snapshots of himself more than a decade back. His young body in a variety of clinches with Martin and with long-forgotten guests of a place that had seemed to Beto like a glittering city on the hill. Beto didn't mourn the acts committed to film. What he mourned was the boy he'd been, a boy in love with Martin and the guests like emissaries from other planets. But most of all, he'd been a boy in love with himself, his own smooth body and its talent for making others want it. He remembered the surprise and delight of that. He had thought, Finalmente, soy yo. *Finally, I am me.*

Everyone in town had suspected, rather lazily, that something seamy went on at the Rancho. Now they would have the proof, whether they wanted it or not. Yes, someone could climb up and pluck off the offending photocopies and printouts. That was why those same images were now plastered across the Rancho Vista Dulce's website, along with the words "pedophile," "human trafficker," and "cheat" in

Spanish, English, French, Italian, and German. It had been easy to make the changes. The password for the remote files was still Frisky60.

After he was done, Beto had switched the default email address and changed the password to something no one would ever guess: Cis_Mi_Muh, Chorotega for *We are*. He'd never written the words anywhere, but lately he'd be repeating them over and over in his head, wondering if he had the pronunciation right.

All day, Martin wondered why so many of his employees were lingering at the computer terminals in the reception area. Usually, they wouldn't have dared. He shouted that they should watch porn on their own time if they wanted to keep their jobs.

It was the front-desk girl who motioned him over to see. Her dark eyes were wide. When Martin approached, she backed away, almost tripping over a basket of clean towels.

He stood in front of the screen for a long time, his face immobile, his mind racing. Finally, he looked up. "Take the day off," he said to the girl, who had been afraid to move.

"What about the guests?"

Martin didn't answer. He was trying to get into the back end of the Rancho's website, but his password wasn't working.

For the first time ever, Martin drove the Rancho's white van with no regard for its shocks. The tires spit coffee-colored sludge as the van bounced along toward what one of Martin's informants had called a *problemita*, a little problem that nonetheless might be serious enough to warrant the big man's attention.

Martin hadn't been able to fix his website or take it down. He knew he'd never come back from this attack on his character, but he wasn't going to run away with his tail between his legs just yet. That every accusation plastered across the Rancho's site was true made not a bit of difference to him. Wasn't the whole messy world held in check by the suppression of useless truths? Up until now, he'd provided just the right mix of incentive and threat to keep people—Beto included—from stating the obvious about him and his place in Palmita.

Rounding the bend, he saw the fruits of his miscalculation. A junk-strewn archway loomed, Martin's mugshot-like passport photo, from back before he was Martin, blown up and given pride of place at the top. Beto must have gotten the enlargements at the copy shop in Bocas. The image took him back to when he was a younger man, the age gap between him and his boys not yet so wide. Still, the authorities had come down hard on him. If he hadn't skipped bail, Martin would have gone to prison, where his predilection would have gotten him beat up or worse. Palmita was a godsend. He ditched his name but maintained his habits, hardly raising an eyebrow as long as he picked boys who had already in some sense been thrown away.

Martin knew who'd slapped together this archway, just as he knew who had hacked the website. A small part of him felt admiration, even pride, that his boy Beto had finally made something happen. A bigger part felt a cold rage.

Going for the archway's right pillar might put the van in the ditch. He aimed for the left, picking up speed. When he hit, it sounded like a pileup on the highway. The pillar crumpled but didn't come down. What did rain down were magpie bits that sparkled and drifted and clunked: CD shards, seed pods, plastic-shrouded photos, wilting flowers dripping rainwater, and—could it be?—bones. The blown-up passport photo shook but stayed put, while what looked like a skull bounced hard off the windshield, a crack bursting out in a star pattern.

Fear shot up Martin's spine. This was not just a prank. Beto had gone off the deep end.

A dark figure appeared in the rearview mirror. It was Beto, walking toward him. It looked as if the boy was smiling. Martin jammed it into reverse and hit the gas. The van careened back, toward Beto, whose stride never slackened, even as he saw what was coming. Beto had done what he set out to do. Nothing could change that now.

CHAPTER 19

> **Lifespans**
>
> Mayfly: 24 hours
> Female adult American cockroach: 440 days
> (Cockroaches can live a week without their heads.)
> Spiders: 2 years (In captivity, they can live 20.)
> Cicada: 17 years
> Sara Gale: 56
> Termite queen: 60 years
> Beto:
> Lucy:
>
> — Lucy's bug & bird notes

Lucy headed for the Rancho on foot. The air was easier to breathe now, having discharged its heavy freight of rain. Water dripped from leaves and clung to the waxy red blooms of wild ginger growing along the road. Even the twisted wire fence looked better after the rain, each barb with its own jewel-like drop.

She couldn't see the ocean from the road, but heard it booming, along with the rocks that tumbled over each other in the surf, like someone grinding their teeth. Rounding a bend, Lucy caught a glimpse of a car up ahead. On second look it was a white van, not moving, splattered with mud, but with what looked like the Rancho's carousel-horse logo visible on the side. Maybe she could catch a ride.

When she got within shouting distance, she saw a spindly dark structure spanning the road, with all sorts of junk hanging off it and scattered on the ground nearby. Then she saw a man holding another man in his arms. The man being held was slack, his head dangling to one side, but Lucy thought she saw his foot jerk.

Lucy slipped behind a bush, watching as the man, about Martin's height and build, pushed the man he was carrying through the side door of the van. The slam of the door made Lucy jump. The man stopped, looking around, and Lucy saw his face. It *was* Martin. He went to the driver's side, got in, and drove off. She held still until she could no longer hear the engine, then held still some more.

The sun came out from behind a cloud. The structure spanning the road up ahead winked and glittered, reflecting the light. It reminded Lucy of the archway her hometown used to put up back home during the holidays. Pine boughs and Christmas lights.

Up close, the archway looked less built than woven, threaded with seashells, sun-bleached vertebrae, and beach trash. The decorations would have been right at home in Beto's compound, but nothing around his shack had the scale or presence of this structure. It looked like a scrap heap standing on is hind legs, but it was oddly coherent, even beautiful.

Did the arch have something to do with why Beto had been shoved into the van? Because now, Lucy was sure it had been Beto. Playing the scene in her head, she recognized his long hair, hanging sideways, and the long legs, bent where Martin held them under the knees, carrying Beto as if he were a sleeping child, at least until he flung him through the open side door of the van.

It was a couple of miles back to Palmita. She ran, slowed to a walk when she got tired, then settled into a slow jog.

"Calaca?" Lucy called as she burst into the open-air restaurant. But only Calaca's father was there, shuffling papers at his usual table.

"Señor." Lucy approached. "I'm looking for your daughter."

"That cow." His jowls shook as he giggled like a child.

If this was what fathers were, maybe it was better to not have one.

He motioned her to his table. "I've prepared the papers."

"I need to—"

"First, we drink. Then we talk business." From a sideboard, he grabbed a bottle and a couple of glasses, pouring two healthy portions of something clear and viscous.

"Don Diego," she pleaded. "Your grandson is in trouble. Beto."

He handed her a glass, drinking his own off in one gulp. "Now you," he said, leaning close. His breath was one part poor dental hygiene, two parts burning field. Lucy took a sip, then gasped, spilling the rest down her front.

"Guaro." He laughed. "Makes bad things good, and good things better."

Lucy put down her glass. "Beto needs help. It's serious."

"Yes," Don Diego agreed.

"I mean right now."

"Twenty hectares." He stabbed a finger at a paper laid out on the table. "Half of it beachfront. Reforestation in progress, so the buyer gets that grant from the government. Bordering a national park, so good hunting. A small island, suitable for development. No, it was never used as a cemetery. That's a nasty rumor."

"Don Diego."

"My price is firm."

"Sorry, I have to—"

"Your bastard of a father was a thief, just like his son."

At any other time, Lucy would have tried to learn more about the transaction that he couldn't get over and about Gabriel, the buyer, her bastard of a father.

"If Calaca comes back, please tell her that Beto is in big trouble." She tried to keep the message simple. "He's probably up at the Rancho."

The old man waved her away. "We lost Beto a long time ago."

"So why didn't you help him back then?"

Don Diego stood up straight, which took visible effort, as if bone and muscle had hardened into a stoop. "Why didn't *you*?"

The old man was obviously confusing time periods, but for a moment, Lucy wondered how things would have been different, not just for her but for Beto, had Sara not stood in the way of Gabriel and Lucy having a relationship. Father and daughter might have known each other as flawed individuals rather than idealized versions of what they couldn't have.

Maybe then Gabriel wouldn't have valued his absent daughter over his all-too-present son, and Beto wouldn't be the town punching bag who fled to the slimeball on the hill, the man who'd just tossed him like a sack of dirty laundry into the side door of a van.

Forget the perhapsing. She didn't have time for that right now.

"I do have one condition." Don Diego was back to his negotiations. "Or, should I say, request. I would ask that my daughter, my grandson, and I be allowed to stay on after the sale. Perhaps in a caretaking capacity?"

Lucy looked at him.

"The restaurant is a good earner, and of course you would have a stake in that. And Beto's little house takes up very little room."

Lucy was not the buyer of times past, but she was most certainly the present claimant. She hadn't considered that her inheritance might include not only Gabriel's house but Calaca's restaurant and Beto's shack.

"I'll give that some thought," she told the old man.

"It's not your fault he didn't want to live."

"Who?" Lucy asked.

"Gabriel."

Now was her chance to learn what Rafa hadn't had time to tell her and she hadn't had the chance to ask Beto. Despite her hurry, she paused. "How did Gabriel die?"

Don Diego fixed her with a penetrating look. "He went for a swim."

Lucy nodded, encouraging him to say more.

"He was a good swimmer. But not good enough. They think I don't know."

"Who?"

"They think I'm a crazy old man," he said, as she stood before him, hungry for more details. "But really, I'm not that old."

Lucy wanted to ask him so much more, but she'd have to wait. Right now she needed to find help. She jogged from Calaca's to the café where she'd met Keith. It was closed. So was Rafa's tour office. The only thing open was the bar.

People stared as she came in, then looked away. Lucy was sweaty and streaked with mud. She stank of the guaro she'd spilled on her shirt. Scrapes from falling off Calaca's horse made her look as if she'd been roughed up—an aphrodisiac for the wrong sort of man.

Yelling to be heard over the soccer game on TV, she told the four or five men there that she was looking for Calaca. That Beto was in trouble and needed help. No one looked familiar, not even the bartender.

"Sí." A few of the men nodded. "Claro." *Yes, of course.*

"You know where Calaca is?"

"Yes."

"Where is she?"

"Yes," the men said, sly smiles forming on their faces.

Lucy knew they were messing with her but thought she might break through, get some information. "Do you know Rafa? The nature guide?"

"Yes."

"Where is Rafa?"

"Yes!" they shouted in unison, erupting into laughter.

The bartender, with gray wooly hair and a broad nose, took pity on Lucy, waving her over. He turned the sound down on the TV. She told him what she'd seen—Martin shoving a limp Beto into the Rancho's van. By the end of her story, other men had come closer to listen.

"A matter for the police," said one. His breath smelled like cigarettes floating in stale beer.

"We could call them," Lucy agreed, backing away slightly.

"No cell phone service," the bartender said. "And no land line."

"The police don't answer their phone, anyway. Too lazy," another man said, and everyone laughed.

"We could go to the Rancho, find Beto," Lucy said.

"Don Martin has private security," the bartender said. "And he and Beto are—friends. Maybe they had a misunderstanding. Between, you know, *friends*."

The men exchanged glances.

Another man approached. He seemed fairly sober. "I could drive you to Bocas, to the police. You could make a report."

Bocas was hours away. And did she want to take a ride with someone she didn't know? But if she refused the ride, how would she help Beto?

"Thank you," she told the man. "That would be very generous of you."

"I'll just finish my beer," he said. "Unless"—he held the bottle out—"you want to finish it for me."

The other men found this hilarious.

"I'll call a taxi," Lucy said.

"No phone," the bartender reminded her.

"And no taxi!"

Ten minutes later, the man who'd offered her a ride finished his beer. He just had to drop off a few friends on the way. Lucy knew this was normal—giving rides to neighbors who didn't have vehicles or were too drunk to drive. She locked eyes with the bartender as if to ask, *Is all of this okay?* The bartender nodded encouragingly.

The man's vehicle was a car, not a pickup or SUV like most people drove out here. Its clearance was so low that he crept along at about five miles an hour to avoid bottoming out. He was going the wrong way, explaining that his friends lived in the other direction. He'd said before that they lived on the way.

"I need to go back," she said. "The bartender—"

"Are you in love with him?" a man in the backseat singsonged.

"Are you in love with me?" another man wanted to know.

"She's in love with all of us," a third snickered.

"It'll only take a minute to take my friends home," the driver said.

"Then you and me—"

From the back seat came a couple of hard-edged wisecracks that Lucy didn't understand. The driver sped up, swerving around potholes filled with muddy water.

An arm came from the back seat, reaching for something on the dash, brushing her breast, then coming to rest in her lap, as if that were its natural and rightful home. She pushed it off, swearing. Then two burly arms snaked from behind, pinning her arms to her sides in the bucket seat. She could smell the man's yeasty breath.

"Let me go."

The arms came up under her breasts, as if to weigh them.

"What the fuck!"

The man let her go, laughing. "Calm down," someone said lazily.

"Let me out." Lucy tried to control her voice.

No one said anything. The car didn't slow.

Lucy looked at the driver, then craned around to gaze at the men in the back seat. No one would meet her eye.

When she reached between the two front seats, the driver tried to bat away her hand, but it was too late. Yanking the emergency brake up hard, Lucy braced as the car lurched and then spun. The men in the back slammed against one side, *thunk*, then the other. The car heaved to a stop just short of a big tree. Lucy got her door open, stumbled out, and took off running.

She ran and ran, away from Palmita, away from her own bad judgment, through puddles and gravel and mud, towards a blood-red sun setting over distant trees.

The fact that no one was chasing her wasn't what made Lucy slow down. Up ahead, a stream cut across the road. The water was reddish, with serrated waves. It gave off a sound that reminded Lucy of cable cars clicking up the steep San Francisco hills.

The stream turned out to be a slow-motion flood of crabs, scrabbling over each other on their seasonal trek from their burrows to the sea. The supply of hand-sized crustaceans looked to be endless; they came from a field, flowing across the road and into the last stand of trees before the beach.

She watched their progress, though *they* seemed the wrong pronoun, with so many creatures acting as one. She taught her students about swarms, flocks, and herds, explaining that such groupings were most often for protection. But she had to admit it was unnerving, this groupthink, if thinking played any part in it.

If she lay down in the crabs' path, would she be just another rise in the landscape, or would her warmth and scent signal food? They might start in on her with a thousand pairs of pincers. Insignificant things, cooperating, could do significant damage.

Like drunk men—clumsy, but in league, capable of doing anything they wanted to a woman on her own, out of her depth, with no tribe to back her up. So many groupings, doing their group stuff, and she, Lucy, alone.

She couldn't go back the way she'd come. The men might still be there, in a stalled car on the side of the road. Going forward would take her into the dark heart of the undeveloped national park. She decided to follow the crabs, to wherever it was they thought they had to go. Because after failing to find help for Beto and putting herself into a stupid situation, Lucy had absolutely nowhere to go.

The crabs were a softly clicking presence down the beach when Lucy shed her clothes. She waded in. Fist-sized stones tumbled over each other and knocked into her ankles. Past the debris line of yellow foam and small branches, she launched into a breaststroke, swimming towards the horizon, a blurry line between different shades of dark blue. Maybe if she swam far enough out, that line would snap into focus, as would what she needed to do next.

But the line just got blurrier, the water colder, her muscles weaker. Lucy turned on her back, opening her arms. Floating, she watched the cloud-streaked sky, steel gray on blue-black. In her peripheral vision, she saw her own hair waving like the arms of an octopus. A deep, hiccupping breath allowed seawater to slop into her mouth. She coughed and sputtered, coming out of her float to look back toward land.

The view was almost entirely water now, sloshing gently and sometimes not so gently, like when a swell smacked squarely into the side of her head, as if it had come all the way across the ocean for just that purpose.

It took all of her self-control to steady her breath and start back in with a slow, measured crawl, alternating that stroke with breaststroke and the occasional break to tread water and see the progress she'd made. She'd drifted south, and no longer recognized the beach she was heading toward. The trees there were taller, the strip of sand narrower.

When she hit a cold patch, her very tired brain thought that meant she was almost to shore. But the colder water was a current, and a strong one. The force of it was at first comforting, as if Lucy could now stop fighting and let the water take over. But then she realized she was being swept rather quickly away from land.

She'd heard you weren't supposed to fight a riptide. But wait, that couldn't be right. If you didn't fight, it would take you farther and farther out.

With energy born of panic, she swam hard toward the shore. Soon she was utterly spent. When she stopped swimming, the current carried her back out. Her limbs felt numb, her brain a floating thing just out of reach.

Why fight it? Maybe this was exactly where she was meant to be. Her mother was gone. Her father was gone. Her sister was far away and not so sisterly anymore. Her unconscious brother had been carted away in a van. Lucy remained oddly calm as the current carried her. Maybe she wanted to be gone too. To go after all the people who'd left her behind.

In an eternity that probably lasted fifteen seconds, she considered how she wasn't really a fighter. People often mistook her detachment for strength. But she just chose not to compete—for the good jobs, the decent men, and her mother's love—because she knew in her bones that she would never be anyone's first choice. Sometimes she even hastened things to their end because she couldn't stand the suspense.

DAY SIX

THURSDAY

CHAPTER 20

> A bug might lash itself to a stem, with silk spun out of its own body, to survive the coming storm.
>
> — *Lucy's bug & bird notes*

The villa was ready for guests, the tile floor mopped, the towels folded into swans. The window was open a crack for ventilation but not far enough to let in the rain, which, judging from the clouds, would be rolling in again soon.

Beto was still breathing but hadn't yet opened his eyes. Blood that had foamed pink in his mouth was now crusted on his cheek. Martin had turned Beto on his side so he wouldn't choke. He wanted the boy to be okay, just not before he'd figured out what to do next.

Martin pictured the town coming for him, people no longer willing to endure the indignities he'd inflicted. Silvio would get him back for being made to inform against his neighbors, Maria for years of jokes about her rotten teeth and tiny brain. That was the least of it. He'd done so many people wrong. Or worse, helped them in ways they couldn't admit to, getting a son out of jail, arranging a daughter's abortion, paying officials to look the other way. The web he'd woven was tightening, with him at the center.

He needed his passport, cash, the passwords to his accounts, a change of clothes, and a thirty-day supply of his expensive nutritional supplements. He almost relished the idea of starting over in some new quasi-paradise. Law enforcement here could be lax, but recently a mania had arisen to at least appear to be going after foreign men who messed with underage locals. He'd have to be careful. He wouldn't get on a plane; he wouldn't rent a car. He'd drive the dented van on back roads to somewhere he could catch a bus.

Built on stilts, the villa had a crawl space underneath where a body would be out of sight. At some point, when he was safely away, Martin would call and tell someone where to find the boy. And when Beto woke up, he'd get a nice surprise, the equivalent of a gold watch after years of devoted—if sometimes sullen—service. Something that would convince him not to come after Martin, not to follow Martin to the ends of the earth to make him pay, once and for all.

Rafa awoke to the boom of breakers and a whiff of raw sewage on the breeze. The beachside hotels in Bocas must be pumping their tanks into the Pacific, trusting that health inspectors wouldn't be up this early.

Curled up on a hard bench, cheek against wood, he opened his eyes to a massive head with lurid peachy-pink skin and eyeholes rimmed with painted-on lashes—one of the papier-mâché heads used in the town's yearly festival.

Rafa's own head felt almost as big. His tongue was like matted monkey fur, and his gold tooth was cold, as if he'd been sleeping with his mouth open to the night. His arms and legs felt twice their usual weight. Even his hair felt heavy.

A murmured conversation came through the wall. Rafa thought he recognized the voice of José, his AA buddy, the policeman on Martin's payroll who nevertheless occasionally tried to do the right thing. Rafa put his ear to the wall.

"I picked him up last night," José was saying. "You don't have to worry about him."

It was all coming back. Rafa had gone to every bar in Bocas, searching for Isa. One bartender, a pal from his drinking days, had slyly urged him to have a *tragito* or two. Reminded Rafa how much fun they'd had before he got all uptight. Rafa had been easy to convince that life was better when alcohol smoothed over the snags and rough spots. That he'd been more charming, more easygoing. Women had liked him, a lot. Men, too, because what do men do together except drink?

What finally got him to accept a drink was that he couldn't stand himself anymore. He was sick to his stomach with shame. He pictured himself roaring up to Martin's, posturing and demanding and then letting himself be led away by the watchman like the weak dog that he was.

Someone was at the door. Rafa wasn't in a cell, but a room with bars on the windows, not to keep people in but to keep the papier-mâché heads safe from thieves or pranksters who thought they'd be great props for a drunken romp.

The door opened, and Isa came in, the door closing behind her.

Rafa stood up, unsteady. "Mi amor."

Isa went to him. "Papá." She buried her head in his shoulder. "I'm sorry, Papá."

"I'm the one who's sorry." He pulled back so he could get a look at her. "Are you alright?"

"I'm fine, Papá. I'm sorry I worried you."

It was starting to dawn on Isa that her father's reach and authority had their limits. He couldn't always protect her, especially when she went behind his back and against her own best interests. She would have to learn how to take care of herself, and him.

"Where were you?" Rafa demanded.

"I got a ride back from Palmita last night."

"Who drove you? How'd you get back here?"

Isa tried to distract her father by telling him about Beto—the gate, the website, and now, no one knowing where he was. She saw he wasn't taking it in. He looked worn out and sad. For the first time, Isa thought about how lonely he must have been since her mother died. Isa had been made motherless, yes, but he'd lost a wife, and hadn't had a real girlfriend since. Isa had probably played a role in that.

"Don't worry, Papá. I'll help Calaca find him. She's called a meeting to get people to help her look. I have to get back for it." Isa hoped her father would see that she was stepping up, or trying to.

"Okay." Rafa sighed. "I'll get José to let me out, then I'll get someone to drive me."

"Yes, Papá," said Isa, but it was clear she was humoring him. When she knocked on the door to be let out, Rafa sat down heavily on the wooden bench. "Can you tell José to bring me some water, *mi vida*?"

No one answered Isa's knock, but when she tried the door, it was open.

José the policeman sat behind his battered metal desk, fiddling with the insides of a flashlight. He looked up. "You're not taking your father home?"

"He needs to stay here."

By gossip and instinct, Isa knew all about José: devoted husband with only one other woman on the side, middling policeman, AA member in good standing, expert at tap dancing around the brute fact of Martin's influence over him. No doubt, part of why José picked up Rafa was to keep him out of Martin's way. That he was now willing to let Rafa go meant—something. Isa wasn't quite sure what. Maybe that Martin had already finished what he started.

Please, she pleaded silently, don't let what he finished be Beto.

"If you say so," José said.

"He needs some water." Isa's gaze darted around the room. It looked more like a family living room than a police station. Handcuffs lay on the shelf next to a framed graduation photo, and there was a gun on a crocheted doily near the television.

José nodded and studied Isa. "I'll get you some water, too."

When he came back, Isa was on the verge of tears. "It's my fault." Her voice broke. "I wouldn't listen."

"What's your fault? Sit down, *m'hija*. Take a moment."

Isa tried to explain, keeping the more embarrassing details to herself. For years, she said, Rafa and Beto had warned her against Martin.

For years, she'd brushed off their concerns, sure that Beto was jealous and her father just wasn't ready for her to grow up.

The blood rose to her face as she remembered the Rancho's job interview. Martin said she'd filled out the application brilliantly but that some things couldn't be assessed on paper. It was important to know the full range of her talents. The phrase made Isa's mouth go dry. She had stood very still, waiting, willing herself not to wet her dry lips with her tongue.

To bolster her courage, she had pictured the carousel horse at the bottom of the driveway. She thought of it as a magical beast marking the entrance to an enchanted realm, where different rules applied. It gleamed pink and white and gold up there on its pedestal, eyes rolled back in ecstasy. Martin once compared her to the horse, saying that she, too, would one day sprout wings and fly.

She managed to dodge the bullet of having to demonstrate her talents. Martin had even respected her insistence on keeping her underwear on when he took the photos to clip to her application. Later, she and Daisy laughed, making fun of the old man for thinking he was the one in charge.

Now, at the police station, Isa shuddered at how she'd fooled herself. Yes, she was like the carousel horse, but not in the ways she'd imagined. Her father wanted her up on a pedestal like the horse on its pole, childishly radiant and untouchable. Martin wanted her to be a gleaming but inanimate amusement park ride for his guests. Other boys and men in town would be happy to pull her down into the mud until there was no trace of gleam left on her. What were her chances of outrunning all of that, of tearing up the earth in a jubilant, solitary gallop?

"I'm an idiot," Isa said softly.

José shrugged. "There's only so much a person can do."

Isa wondered if he was thinking of his own situation. People expected him to stand up to Martin, but even Isa knew that the best José could do was work around him. She would do better.

Back in Palmita, Calaca learned of her son's strange gate, his hacking of the Rancho website, and his disappearance. She didn't know about Martin throwing Beto into the van, but instinct told her Beto was in trouble and Martin was to blame. She'd been up most of the night. How could she sleep? She had to do the work of keeping him in this world, like a traveler tensing to keep the plane aloft.

At the same time, and especially when her eyes closed in exhaustion, she pictured Beto's funeral. Not planning it—that would be too deliberate. Oddly, there was solace in picturing a well-run event, even if it commemorated the worst thing imaginable.

They'd have big centerpieces of tuberoses and gladioli, then women would gather up the flowers and head for the cemetery island. Men would shoulder the coffin, their Sunday pants rolled to the knee; even at low tide, waves might wash across the land bridge to the island. Calaca would wear her navy-blue dress and use the last of that expensive foundation that hid the blotches on her face.

It would be the first burial on the island in a long time, or at least the first public one. Beto hadn't been able to keep from her the secret of Gabriel swimming out to sea, washing back in, and being buried on the island.

Son would join father under a thin layer of rocky soil on an island that might, if Lucy did the right thing, be returned to the town's collective ownership. They'd return the bodies Calaca's father had dug up to their original graves, with better views and a nice sea breeze. The town would be whole again.

Calaca shuddered. Her dark daydream had taken on a life of its own. It made Beto into some sort of martyr. And if his own mother could think this way, what was the rest of the town thinking?

She made herself more coffee, dripping the water through a stained, sock-like cloth filter and into Beto's favorite mug. She needed to be vigilant. It would take a doubling down of will to counteract her daydream, and to keep her flawed and beautiful son alive in this imperfect world.

CHAPTER 21

> Most birds have two alarm calls. One tells the flock to flee. The other is a mobbing call: "Let's harass this intruder so they'll wish they were never born!" Mobbing behavior includes dive-bombing, loud squawking, and defecating on the threat.
>
> — *Lucy's bug & bird notes*

It was midmorning before Lucy saw Palmita up ahead. Her hair was lank, her eyes glazed, her skin mottled with insect bites. She'd walked a long way, naked, keeping off the road, empty of thought. Closer to town, she swiped an oversized shirt off a clothesline. Brambles and stones pushed into her bare feet. But something had shifted in her out in the water, and she felt immune to small nuisances. She was saving her energy for the big trouble, a dull-eyed animal plodding along until it has to turn and fight for its life.

There was a crowd at Calaca's restaurant. A homemade banner read TERRITORIO CHOROTEGA OCUPADO. *Occupied Chorotega Territory.*

Lucy was so thirsty, she couldn't think straight. She wanted a bottle of Fanta Orange more than she'd wanted anything in her life. She made her way inside, past small groups of people in animated conversation, passing around photos, clippings, and copies of the inside pages of a passport. They were artifacts, shaken loose from Beto's archway.

"It's him," said a man with a copy of the passport in his hands. "It's Don Martin."

"Can't be," said another. "He put my cousin through school."

"The police have someone in custody!" A man with slick-backed hair, who Hilda had once pointed out to Lucy as one of Martin's henchmen, jumped up on a chair to address the crowd. Conversation stopped as all eyes turned his way.

"And the police never get it wrong," someone said, drawing a laugh or two.

At the cooler now, Lucy grabbed a bottle of Fanta, pried the cap off with a bottle opener nailed to a beam, and drank in long gulps, her head thrown back. When her gaze leveled out again, it was as if the loose crowd had tightened into a big, angry knot. There were people on all sides.

"Think about it," the man on the chair urged. A hank of gelled hair had come loose, and it bobbed as he spoke, a single antenna trying to sense what the crowd was in the mood to believe. "It makes sense. Rafa—"

"Nothing makes sense," a woman called out.

"Don Rafa is part of this town," said another woman. She had high Indian cheekbones and a pink Pura Vida T-shirt. *Pure life.* The Costa Rican motto. Who had told Lucy that the phrase was less descriptive than aspirational?

"He's Nicaraguan," the man on the chair countered. "An invader."

The crowd's low drone rose in pitch, like a beehive hit with a stick.

"Why all this about Rafa?" Lucy shouted in Spanish, surprising herself. "The problem is Martin. He threw Beto into—"

"She thinks she's in charge," a man called out. Lucy looked over to see the driver of the car from the night before.

"Calls herself the governor," said another man, who Lucy thought she recognized from the soccer game, where she'd been wearing her *My Governor Can Beat Up Your Governor* T-shirt.

"She's here for the land."

"She wants to steal our dead!" Don Diego's voice was as thin as a paper cut. He brandished his sheaf of papers like it was a torch to light the way.

"Don Diego," someone placated.

"I can't find my bones," he lamented, crumpling as if he himself had been deboned.

"Martin has Beto!" Lucy shouted. No one was listening.

An angry murmur started at the edges of the crowd, lapping inward. A high whine broke through. "The gringa is here to steal our children!" It was Pilar's mother.

Lucy scoffed. That wasn't the right response.

There were shouts about land and theft and children and how outsiders were destroying the town and had to be stopped. Now.

Keeping her face neutral, Lucy tried to extricate herself from the sea of people. "Excuse me," she said quietly, pulling down her shirt so it wouldn't fly up and reveal she had nothing on underneath. The driver from the car last night was close now, his cologne an olfactory red flag. The crowd at large had its own scent: the iron tang of blood about to be spilled.

"¡Hermanos y hermanas!" Hilda called from out on the road. *Brothers and sisters!* Her Spanish was as singsong as her English. Everyone turned to regard the tall woman with gray-blond pigtails. "We are a community of love!"

Her claim was met by a collective growl of discontent.

"Community?" Calaca thundered as she came from the kitchen, wiping her hands on a dishtowel. The scarlet macaw, perched on a rafter nearby, half-opened its wings as if readying to do battle.

Lucy tried to catch Calaca's eye. Surely her old friend would stand up for her. But Calaca's gaze slid right past Lucy.

"All I want," Hilda said, "is for our town—"

"Whose town?" Calaca boomed. The macaw squawked in agreement. Lucy saw now that it was tied by one foot to the beam.

Hilda stood even taller. "I'm the only one who ever stands up to him. To Martin. Things would be different if any of you had ever once done the same!"

"Lies!" Calaca pushed at the people around her, as if to get to where Hilda stood.

Lucy wove her way through the closely packed crowd, glad people's attention was elsewhere. Everyone's breath seemed tainted with the same bitterness, from deep inside and long ago.

At the edge of the crowd, the air felt different. Less used up.

Hilda took Lucy's arm and the two women left the melee behind, going as fast as they could without breaking into a run.

Lucy kept looking over her shoulder.

Hilda said, "Don't worry. They are not coming after you."

"Coming after *us*, you mean."

Hilda's plastic clogs scuffed the pebbly mud. "I am an established member of this community."

Lucy didn't say anything. If Hilda wanted to pretend the two of them hadn't just been tarred with the same brush, that was her business.

Puddles on the road reflected a tumultuous sky. The watery light seemed to come from everywhere and nowhere. Rocks and trees and fence posts looked as if they'd been granted a fourth dimension.

Not Hilda. She was a paper cutout bobbing along the road, her gait as cartoonish as her accent. Lucy could almost taste the heavy sky, the flavor of dread. A big tree up ahead seethed, dark green edged with black, the border humming. Lucy glanced at Hilda to see if she noticed.

The tree erupted, the black hem unravelling upward. Birds. Black dots wheeled into the sky, disappearing into velvety folds of blue-gray.

Lucy remembered Rafa admonishing her to look up, not down at the ground for bugs. But these palsied scribbles on the sky didn't exactly inspire joy.

"What now?" Lucy said, as much to the birds and the sky as to the woman walking beside her.

From up the road came the growl of car engines and a high whine like a motorcycle. The concentration of sound was ominous in a town where hours could go by without a single vehicle passing.

Hilda's hand shook as she tried to open the door to the motel office. Finally, the key found its mark. The two women rushed in just as the entourage rounded the bend: a couple of pickup trucks creeping along, accompanied by quads, dirt bikes, and bicycles. A man on horseback led the way.

Hilda closed the door, turning the bolt gently, as if she didn't want anyone to hear.

"I need pants," Lucy whispered.

Hilda looked at her as if she were crazy, but reached under the counter and brought out a pair of long khaki shorts.

"And shoes."

Hilda looked down at Lucy's battered bare feet. She chin-pointed to a pair of Crocs near the doorway.

A deafening crash shook the room, and the women all but jumped into each other's arms. Hilda disentangled first, even as the pounding moved to the thin wooden door.

At some point—it seemed a lifetime ago—Hilda had told Lucy that her office was a converted shipping container, retired from ocean duty and bought from a nearby port. She'd cut holes in the metal for a window and a door. The container had seen the world. Would its tomb-like interior be the last thing Lucy saw? The crowd sounded as if it were about to break down the door. They'd surge in, then suck back out like a riptide, Lucy and Hilda caught in the current.

"They're probably heading for Bocas." Hilda tried to sound reasonable, and indeed, the pounding stopped in the middle of her pronouncement. She switched on a lamp, which cast a circle of light on the floor. A scattering of insect wings winked back their iridescence. "To the police station."

Lucy looked at her. "Because they'd never bother an established member of the community."

"Oh, shut up." Hilda was still shaken.

"Why did you run?" came a muffled shout from outside. "Only criminals run!"

"We did not run!" Hilda called out.

Silence, then a coaxing voice from outside. "Open the door. We just want to talk."

Hilda seemed to consider this. Lucy put a hand on the woman's arm and shook her head.

The posse settled in. They banged on the door, more lackadaisical now, then talked amongst themselves, then banged some more.

Hilda reached behind the counter for a phone and stabbed at the plastic keys. The landline. Why hadn't Lucy thought of that? More to the point, why hadn't Hilda?

"Now you're going to make a call?"

"I thought they would go away."

She listened as Hilda described in low tones how an American and a Swedish citizen were in trouble.

She hung up.

"Now who's a member of the community?" Lucy said.

"I called the police. In Bocas. They said they were concerned."

"I hope they're concerned enough to do something."

Lucy wondered why both of them kept saying *they* when it was one man they were talking about. Officer José. More than an hour away, and apparently in Martin's pocket.

The banging stopped, but they could hear the crowd still milling around. The front porch creaked under their weight. Lucy thought she heard Calaca's voice out near the road, but it was hard to hear what she was saying with Hilda muttering angrily.

"Twenty years of making nice," Hilda grumbled. "Of cooperation. Flattery. Groveling. Keeping my mouth shut. Most of the time, anyway." Hilda shot Lucy a hard look. "All shot to hell, trying to save *you*!"

The crowd outside seemed to hold its breath.

Hilda jerked a piece of paper from the fax machine tray, brandishing it as if it were evidence of Lucy's malfeasance.

"What's that?"

"For you. From the lawyer, I think," Hilda said. "Wait." She put her ear against the wall to listen. Lucy did the same. Outside, they heard Calaca yelling. Others were telling her to cool down. Calaca retorted that the real fight was up the hill, and who was with her? She was going to find her son, if she had to do it all on her own.

A sudden downpour made it impossible to hear anything else.

Looking back, Lucy would wonder why they decided she should go for help. Why not just stay put, wait it out? Maybe it had to do with the rain, which sent most of the posse running for shelter, under trees or into cars.

She slipped through a trap door at the far end of the room that led to an under-floor storage area. Muddy ground sloped away from the bottom of the container. Nobody was out in the downpour, though there might still be people under the front porch's overhang. A horse was tied to a tree a way off from the main group of vehicles.

Somehow, Lucy got to the horse without anyone seeing her. It plodded after her, head down against the rain, as she led it through a stand of trees and into an open field. She pulled herself up and squeezed with her legs.

The horse went from standstill to gallop in a few short seconds. The Crocs flew off her feet.

Rain came down hard and heavy. Part of its heft was sound, like a river pushing through a dam. It stung her face and her arms, and plastered her clothes to her body in a matter of seconds. Bending low over the horse's neck, Lucy aimed the crown of her head at the driving rain. The horse smelled of mud, wet hair, old leather.

Heeya! she cried out into the watery roar, though the horse was already running at full speed.

CHAPTER 22

> When an ant nest needs defending, its eldest residents—with the least long-term utility remaining to them—become the most suicidally aggressive. E. O. Wilson wrote: "Where humans send their young men to war, ants send their old ladies."
>
> — *Lucy's bug & bird notes*

SHE FOUND THE ROAD AGAIN. Up ahead, a muffled crunch.

Lucy slipped off the horse. She led the animal along, keeping to the trees. Rounding a bend, she saw a pickup truck backing into the pole that held the Rancho's mascot: the carousel horse. The truck's bumper made contact with a sickening crunch. The horse atop the pole swayed, then listed to one side. Lucy peered through a screen of leaves to see if it would fall. When it didn't, the truck made ready for another try.

Isa was at the wheel of Rafa's truck.

From the sidelines came, "¡Mi hija! We don't have time for this!" It was Calaca, astride her quad, hair and clothes dripping, thick brown legs splattered with mud.

Isa ignored Calaca, throwing the truck into reverse again, backing up fast, and hitting the pole even harder this time. The metal-on-metal crunch made Lucy jump. The wooden horse, white and pink against the storm-gray sky, started to topple in Calaca's direction.

"¡Hijo de puta!" Calaca cried, gunning her quad out of the way. The wooden horse slammed down a few feet from where Calaca had been. Its muzzle dug into mud; its rump shook with the impact.

Isa wasn't finished. She backed over the poor horse, again and again, until it was nothing but candy-colored splinters pressed into the mud.

As Lucy led her horse toward this scene of destruction, Isa let out a victory whoop.

Calaca shook her head; then, noticing movement in the trees, went on high alert.

"Isa!" she warned.

Isa, with her younger eyes, immediately recognized the figure approaching. Destructive glee still coursing through her, Isa called out, almost cheerfully. "What the fuck are *you* doing here?"

The rain let up. Its absence made for a breath-held kind of quiet. The three women—Isa half out of the truck cab, Calaca straddling her fat-tired quad, a machete tucked into the side of the vehicle, Lucy on foot, the horse on a lead behind her—took each other's measure.

"Beto could be up there," Calaca said. "He could be hurt."

The three women closed the gap between them. They stood facing each other in the mud. Together, they made a plan. A loose-limbed, wild-eyed, crazy kind of plan, but still: a plan.

Lucy's job was to ride—yes, ride—into the Rancho's open-air lobby. If Martin or any of his guards were there, a woman on horseback was sure to distract them while Isa and Calaca searched the grounds for Beto.

Lucy liked her role in the plan. She'd never had the good fortune of riding a horse into a room.

But the lobby, it turned out, was filled with people and suitcases. A new crop of guests had arrived an hour ago with no one to check them in. Already disoriented, what they saw when Lucy appeared was a looming figure coming out of the rain. Big chested, with long skinny legs. Hooves rang out on the red tile floor. Horse and rider looked as if they'd been held underwater and were just now fighting their way back to the surface.

"Where's Martin?" Lucy shouted.

The people stared. Finally, a solid older woman who'd made her way behind the counter called, "Is he the pedophile?" She'd been gazing at the computer terminal that Beto had hacked.

"Fuck!" Lucy shouted. "Does everyone but me know everything that's going on in this fucking town?" Her shouting spooked the horse. She had to pull hard on the reins to control it. The horse reared up; she clung to its neck.

The horse's front hooves came back down with such force that they cracked the tile floor. The animal skittered into the center of the room. People backpedaled and suitcases toppled. Wild-eyed, the horse galloped out into the rain again, skidded in the mud, then unceremoniously dumped Lucy into a waist-high clump of pink-and-red hibiscus.

Calaca was having better luck, at least until a figure scuttled across the muddy path. Her machete shot up into striking position. She lowered it again as the creature—wet spiky fur around a wizened face—disappeared into the bushes. She was used to seeing monkeys in the trees, not on the ground. The bedraggled thing was dragging a chain, but it looked for a moment as if the chain were chasing the monkey.

She'd checked five of the six villas: all empty. Each time, disappointment battled relief. She wanted to find her son, but was afraid of the state she'd find him in. If she'd ever wished to be free of Beto, that wish was gone. If he was okay, she promised she would—well, she didn't know what more she could do for Beto. Maybe try to understand his need to make ugly art out of seeds and bones and garbage.

The sixth and last villa was off on its own—bigger, more private, with the best view. A few days ago, the view had been picture-postcard static. Now it was all roiling blacks and blues, scudding clouds and angry squalls.

Calaca saw footprints in the mud. Big ones. She glanced over her shoulder, hoping to see Isa or Lucy, but she was alone. Gripping the machete, she kept going.

When she saw someone dragging a body from under Villa number 6, it was as if her worst nightmare had been realized. The body was the right size for Beto; the man doing the dragging had to be Martin. Calaca let loose an anguished cry.

She cursed and sobbed and threw herself at the man, who sidestepped her advance, knocking the weapon from her hand. It wasn't Martin. It was a tall, white man in a red baseball cap. He looked as if he'd once had military bearing but now couldn't be bothered to throw his shoulders that far back. Calaca had never seen him before.

"I heard him," the man said. "I was doing a walk-through. What the hell is this place? Can you check us in?"

When Beto opened his eyes, he saw his mother's face, distorted into a howl to end all howls. Smiling weakly, he muttered something that hadn't passed his lips in a very long time.

Mamá.

DAY SEVEN

FRIDAY

CHAPTER 23

> **From Lea Page's poem, "Accidental"**
> Those who stray beyond their normal range are called
> Accidentals. They take a wrong migratory turn or blow in
> On a storm. Sometimes they hitch a ride—we drove a U-Haul.
> Depending on your frame of reference, we are all accidental
> On this land. Show me the map that says I don't belong.
> —*Lucy's bug & bird notes*

LIGHT TRANSFORMED THE GLASS of amber liquid into molten gold. Beside it on the nightstand was a damp square of paper, folded over and over again to fit in a pocket: the fax Hilda had given her.

Lucy reached for it, groaned from the pain in her shoulder, then fell back into bed.

"That paper was in your pocket."

With difficulty, Lucy turned her head to see a woman sitting at her bedside. They were in one of the Rancho's villas. The woman had a friendly middle-aged face and a smile that flickered like a bulb going bad. Lucy tried to prop herself on her elbow, but the skin there felt like several layers had been sanded off. She collapsed back to a horizontal position. The ceiling was narrow planks of hardwood, gleaming golden brown and russet red, with knotholes here and there that urged Lucy to fall upward and into them.

"You took a tumble." The woman's voice was as layered and honeyed as baklava. "Don't worry. Someone caught your horse."

Memories came like slaps of wet wind. Hooves ringing out on a tile floor. People backpedaling with terror on their faces. A fall into a wet bush with shrieking green leaves and shoutingly pink flowers.

The woman picked up the glass of gold. "Your friend brought you more of this. I'm not sure how she got the first glass down you. I told her she should wait until you were completely awake."

Lucy recognized her now. She'd been behind the front desk when Lucy rode into the lobby. "My friend?"

"I think she said her name was Calico."

"Calaca," Lucy corrected. Slowly, testing out each move, she squinched herself into a seated position, her back against the headboard. She took the glass and hazarded a sip, making a face at the bitterness.

"It smells weird, so I can only imagine how it tastes."

"Unh." The sound vibrated in Lucy's mouth and made her ears itch.

"We didn't know what to do. None of us have cars. Not that we'd know where to take you even if we did."

"I'm okay," Lucy said, though she felt as far from okay as green was from orange. Speaking of orange, the color of the wood on the ceiling now crackled like a campfire. The birdsong outside was shrill, and the air around this nice woman looked somehow quilted, as if she traveled inside her own elaborately stitched cocoon.

"I'm glad," the cocoon woman said.

"I'm glad too," Lucy echoed. The word "glad" was green, wasn't it?

"Your friend was worried about a concussion. Can you touch your right index finger to your nose?"

Her right index finger was galaxies away from her nose, but *presto!* She did what was asked. Then she couldn't stop giggling.

"Maybe I should get your friend."

"You know what I really want? A cold drink. In a bottle."

The woman nodded, scrutinizing her. "I'll see what I can find."

With the woman gone, the room expanded. Lucy shrank to the size of a peanut, then backfilled her way into her old self and beyond, to where she was too big, like Alice crouching so her head wouldn't hit the ceiling after she'd found the bottle that said, *Drink me.*

The glass on the nightstand quietly urged the same.

The sun shifted, and a beam targeted her left hand. The warmth was utterly marvelous. A breeze stirred the tree outside the window, and the light on her hand dappled and spread. What a beautiful arm. Odd that she'd never noticed before.

The glass on the nightstand pleaded: *Drink me.*

Lucy drank. She laughed mid-swallow and some of it came out her nose. What had Calaca told her about her home brews? That there was a potion for every problem, even if secondary effects could be hard to manage.

Okay. Stop. Breathe. You've done drugs before. You can manage this. So manage it.

How?

Sleep. Everything out there is too much. At least close your eyes.

Not yet! came a squawk from the doorway.

When had the door opened? She remembered the woman closing it on her way out. But now she saw through the door to the deck, with its railing of polished wood.

Something vegetal clung to the railing. Scaly vines that ended in thorns. Some sort of heavy curved pod—yellow, apple green, orange, and sky blue—weighing it down.

The pod split open with a bullfrog croak.

Except it wasn't a frog. It was a bird, with a beak so oversized it must be like carrying around a love that had outlived its object. Like Lucy's love for Gabriel, born when she was a girl, buried in the backyard of her heart, then exhumed to see if it could live in the adult world of paperwork and disappointment. It still weighed her down like—

Craaack! The toucan told her to stop her wallowing. If I can live with this bill, it said, you can live with your love. And what's all this about Gabriel? Aren't you forgetting someone?

Lucy breathed in the sticky green scent of Sara's marijuana. *Mom! Is that you?*

The bird bobbed its head.

Mom. Lucy's voice was soft but certain.

Sara spread her wings, unclenched her talons, and lifted her cumbersome bill and body into the air.

"Come back!"

Calaca appeared in the doorway. "I'm here."

Lucy watched as her mother flew away.

"Who am I?" Lucy demanded of Calaca. It was a test, to see if Calaca was real or an apparition.

Calaca sat down on the edge of the bed and took Lucy's hand. A hand that minutes—or was it hours?—ago had been beautifully dappled and sun-warmed. Now it looked old, with visible veins and the beginnings of what must be age spots.

"You're cold," Calaca said in Spanish.

"Do you speak English?" Lucy was still testing her. She wondered now if the other woman—the one who went to get her a drink—was also a figment of her imagination, like Sara the toucan.

"Jes."

A yes by any other name is still a yes.

Lucy gazed at her friend as if for the first time. Calaca was—what was the word for it? Splendid. Verrrry splendid. If Spanish could roll its *rrrr*s, why not English, too? Calaca's skin glowed a deep, multilayered brown, though brown was too small a word for it. The color of Calaca's skin was tall and proud. Her eyes were deep. So sweet. So warm. And her hair! It sprung from her forehead like its own animal.

"Sort of," Calaca clarified, smiling.

What teeth the woman had! What full and wantable lips! Nothing in Lucy's life had ever come close to the whatever-it-was they'd had when they were girls. What they were back then. How their bodies were part of the ever-changing landscape, mud and dust and surf and trees and monkeys and Luz and Inés.

"Inés."

"It's been so long since anyone called me that."

"She's back. You're back," Lucy said.

"And you're back."

Lucy wanted to cry. Wait, she already was crying. "I love you," she said to Inés, and to Calaca too. She loved the girl back then and she loved the woman holding her aging hand. What they'd done years ago, the kissing and rubbing and riding horses and shoplifting, was not practice for something that came later. It wasn't a substitute for the real thing, which in her case was supposed to be adult love directed at a man. It had been its own creature, like Calaca's springy hair, like the bird that had been so itself while also being Sara.

"I love you too," Calaca said shyly.

Had they told each other that back when they were girls? No, they'd just lived it. They might have thought it was something else, something bigger that they swam in every day: the wet and messy gorgeousness of this exact place. Maybe it had been something bigger. Maybe it still was. Thank God Sara had brought them all here.

"I love my mother."

"Sí, mi amor," Calaca soothed, stroking her hand.

"Did I tell you she died?"

"Sí, mi amor. You did."

Lucy remembered now. The two of them hadn't been able to stop laughing. She'd laughed in part so she wouldn't cry. Now she would. Many years passed as she cried for Sara and Faith and Inés and herself and everyone else who'd lost someone or was about to.

She wiped her eyes. "What about Beto?"

"He's good," Calaca said, as if she couldn't quite believe it.

"And Isa?"

"She's okay too."

"Martin?"

"Se fue." *He's gone.* The relief in Calaca's voice was its own weather, rain to rinse the town of Martin and all he stood for.

Lucy wanted to be a part of that, of everything, and right now. But when she tried to get out of bed, she was reminded that every part of her body hurt.

Calaca shushed her and made her lie back down. She glanced at the empty glass on the nightstand.

"Luz! Did you drink all of that?"

"Jes," Lucy gently mocked Calaca's accent. She'd always wanted to be like Inés. Calaca wasn't a bad role model either, what with her splendidness.

Calaca shook her head. "That's strong—"

"Medicine?" Lucy finished her sentence.

"You are probably feeling a little—strange."

"Strangely good, *mi amor*."

Calaca laughed in spite of herself.

Lucy glanced at the empty glass, and her eyes fell on the folded packet of paper next to it on the nightstand. "Could you hand me that?"

With care, Lucy opened the damp packet, trying not to tear the thin paper where it had been folded. It was the fax Hilda had handed to her when they'd been holed up in the office that was a shipping container. From the lawyer, Hilda had said.

But when Lucy tried to read, the letters swam all over the page. Maybe she really did have a head injury.

"Want me to read it to you, Luz?"

"Please."

"But then you have to promise me you'll try to sleep."

"Sí, mi amor." Lucy must be coming down from the homebrew, because she suddenly knew that soon, Luz and Inés would be back to Lucy and Calaca, their prickly and complicated adult selves, each with a different history and agenda. But for a few moments longer, they could be the girls they once were, part of something larger that both of them seemed to have misplaced along the way.

The woman who'd gone to get Lucy a drink was back. She hadn't found any beverages but had rediscovered her entitlement. "No drinks," she said peevishly. "No food. No help." She glared at Calaca. "I take it you work here?"

Calaca returned her gaze but didn't say anything.

"She doesn't work here," Lucy said.

"This is totally unacceptable," the woman declared.

"Yes," Lucy agreed.

"Jes," Calaca said.

The woman got the message and left them alone.

Lucy sat up in bed, Calaca in a chair nearby. A stiff breeze came through the open window, shaking the flimsy paper Calaca held with both hands.

"Careful!" Lucy said.

"I know."

The women exchanged a rueful glance. They were already on the downslope of their love fest. There was still a deep familiarity, but notes of irritation were creeping in, like with an old married couple. They'd lived an entire relationship in the space of a few minutes, thanks to Calaca's homebrew.

"You can start reading."

"Give me a minute." Calaca shifted in her chair, scanning the document. "So what's this supposed to be?"

"A fax from the lawyer. The one who drew up Gabriel's will."

Calaca sighed heavily. "You want me to help you take what's not yours?"

"Just read it."

"'My will is that—'"

"Wait. It can't just be another copy of Gabriel's will."

With exaggerated patience, Calaca started over. "'My will is that you girls,'" she read clearly and with a strong accent. "Then it's just a list. With, what do you call them in English? Little circles, to make a list?"

"Bullet points."

"'Give Travis the truck,'" Calaca read.

How would Gabriel know about Travis, Faith's son?

"'He needs to feel in control of his comings and—'" Calaca hesitated. "'Goins.'"

"What?"

"Goins. G-o-i-n-g-s."

"Goings."

Calaca held out the paper. "You read it."

Lucy didn't want to be alone with whatever this was. "Sorry. I'm just, I don't get what this is." But all of a sudden, she knew. This was Sara's will, not Gabriel's. Or not a will, but a letter. The one Faith had mentioned in her email.

"Fuck," Lucy said.

"Like I said, you can read it if I'm doing such a bad job."

"Please. Read it to me. Slowly. I have to get my head around this."

Calaca read. "'Fix the downstairs sink, for chris aches.'"

"Crissakes," Lucy said. "Like 'for Christ's sake.'" It really was from Sara. That was her favorite word.

Calaca shrugged and continued. "'Know that everything is going to be okay.'" She paused. "This isn't Gabriel's will."

"It's from my mother. Sara."

Calaca continued, "'Know that I love you girls like crazy, each the same, or not the same but each with my whole heart.'"

"Stop." Lucy squeezed her eyes shut.

"That sounds nice. She loves you."

"Not the same," Lucy challenged.

"'Each with my whole heart,'" Calaca countered.

Where was all the luscious green she'd been steeping in? Where was the swirl of love and possibility that Calaca's brew had stirred up in her? *Poof.* Gone. In its place were some hard truths from the horse's mouth. Sara being a horse this time, not a toucan.

"'Faith, you were my rock,'" Calaca read.

Lucy's heart dropped like a rock. She wanted to lie back down and pull the covers over her face.

"Should I stop?"

"Go ahead." Lucy would be brave. Get it over with.

"'Lucy, no matter how far you strayed, you were always in my heart.'"

Lucy's anger flared at the word "strayed," mostly to distract her from the tenderness of "always in my heart." She desperately wanted to be in her mother's heart, but was afraid of what might come next to undercut that.

"'And Lucy, my dear,'" Calaca read, "'I know that even if you couldn't say it, you loved me too.'"

Lucy pictured the soft down on her mother's face. The slope of her cheek like the curve of the world seen from space, back when Sara was Lucy's world. And much later, after mother and daughter were all too separate, how heartbreakingly fragile Sara had been, dying in the downstairs room.

"I did," Lucy said quietly. "I do."

"Of course you love her," Calaca said. "She's your mother."

Now the tears fell. They were different from the easy tears Lucy had shed earlier. These made her face ache.

Calaca got up out of the chair and perched on the bed again. "It's okay," she soothed. There's only a little bit left. Do you want me to read it?"

Lucy nodded.

"'You are such good girls,'" Calaca read. "'You are mine. I am yours.'"

Love for her mother flooded Lucy's heart with such force that it actually hurt. For a long time, she had protected herself from what she thought was her mother's lack of love for her. Feeling that love now was almost more painful than sticking to the story that it didn't exist.

For with that love came the full impact of what the loved person had done. Even if Sara had been trying to protect her from Gabriel, there was no excuse for keeping from Lucy that he was her father. Her mother had quite literally denied Lucy her birthright. She withheld crucial information about where Lucy came from, who she was, and who she might become. She'd even denied Lucy the choice of which country to do that becoming in.

Lucy had missed her chance to know her father. Whatever he had wanted—and he might have been as ambivalent about being part of her life as Sara was about letting him—Lucy should have been able to decide whether to seek him out. At some point, the child grows up, finds her voice, and gets to say what she wants, no matter how slim the chance of getting it.

"Are you okay?"

Lucy nodded.

"You need to sleep."

Lucy slid down in bed and pulled the sheet up to her chin. The wind was picking up again, whipping the trees around. Light and shadow splattered the white walls. Lucy thought Calaca was going to tuck her in, but instead she lay down next to her, putting her arms around her as well as she could with Lucy under the covers.

"Don't worry," she said. "Todo va a salir bien." *Everything is going to be all right.*

Despite her aching heart, Lucy felt a level of comfort and safety she hadn't experienced in years, if not decades. Quicker than she'd imagined possible, she slipped toward sleep. But just before her conscious mind blinked out, she realized there had been nothing in Sara's letter to suggest their mother wanted Faith to have the family house.

When she heard Lucy snoring, Calaca went to where Beto was recuperating. He was also in bed. And as she'd done for Lucy, Calaca read him a will of sorts: papers they'd found tucked into the waistband of his shorts when they'd pulled him out from under the villa.

"You get all of it," Calaca said, sliding to the edge of her chair. "That is, if this isn't one of Don Martin's tricks."

Beto couldn't believe that after all she knew about him, his mother still called the man by the honorific "Don." But then he couldn't believe a lot of things: that he'd managed to build the gate, hack the website, and stay alive. He felt good. Tired and banged up, but pretty damned good.

"Look for yourself," she said, thrusting the pages into his hands.

The papers said that Martin bequeathed the Rancho Dulce Vista to him, Beto.

To Beto, it didn't seem possible, or even desirable. Why would he want to stay in the place that had been his undoing? Of course, the same could be said for the town itself. Beto held the papers between thumb and forefinger, as if they'd been dipped in cat piss. "No," was all he could manage.

His mother took them from him and looked them over for herself. "It's a quit claim," she said after a while. "I think that means he can't take it back."

Beto shook his head.

"We'll get it checked out. But it looks real to me. Which means, I guess, that it was all worth it."

Beto snorted.

"I didn't mean it like that."

"Did you see my gate?"

"It's better than what you would have gotten, and still might get, from your father," Calaca said.

"My gate?"

"The Rancho."

"My gate is better than what I could have gotten from either of those *hijos de puta*." It was the second time in his life he'd felt it so strongly: Finalmente, soy yo. The verb in Chorotega: Cejo. *Finally, I am me*. This time it wasn't someone else who'd made him feel that way. It was Beto himself.

Calaca nodded, though Beto could see that his mother had no idea what he was talking about.

Someone was shaking her, gripping her shoulder. "I must insist." A male voice, accented English, formal. Lucy opened her eyes halfway to see a pair of battered black shoes. Shoe polish emphasized rather than hid the cracks in the leather, like heavy makeup on a wrinkled face. Blue-gray pants. White short-sleeved shirt.

It was José the policeman, AA member in good standing, officer of that slippery thing called the law, and Martin's henchman, if every single person in town was to be believed.

The woman from the lobby was back at her bedside. "She needs to rest."

"Where's Calaca?" Lucy asked.

"She went home to get clothes for Beto," the woman said. The sheet had fallen to the floor. Lucy wore a T-shirt and nothing else. "Let me at least put some pants on her."

"Quickly," José snapped.

"He says there's been a complaint," the woman said, helping Lucy into a pair of pants. To the policeman, she said, "Let me go with her."

"No."

The woman threaded a pair of flip-flops onto Lucy's feet. "I'll go to the American Embassy!"

"Do you know how far you are from your embassy? From your country?" His English was good when he needed it to be.

José the policeman walked Lucy out of Villa 3 like a nurse walking a patient down a hospital corridor. Up ahead, Beto blocked the path, bare feet planted in mud. He was shirtless, and a bruise like an undiscovered continent spread from his ribs down past the waistband of his low-slung shorts. His ear plugs were gone; his earlobes dangled. The golden nimbus emanating from his head told Lucy there was still some of Calaca's medicine in her system. Beto looked like some sort of martyred saint.

Staring José down, he let loose with a torrent of Spanish that Lucy didn't even try to follow. She looked into his handsome, complicated face and smiled, rather foolishly. My brother, she thought.

The policeman responded with a few carefully chosen words that seemed to hit Beto hard. But Beto rallied, and said, in English, "I'm coming with you."

José was surprised, and Beto noticed his surprise. "Your boss is gone," he said. "We ran him out of town."

In Lucy's altered state, she thought she could see power—undulating purple shot through with veins of gold—flowing out of José and into Beto. Not only that, but she felt all of Palmita tremble underfoot as old alliances and assumptions collapsed, and new ones sprang up. Where would she land in this seismic rearrangement?

Right then, she just wanted to be with her brother.

CHAPTER 24

> Say a species is pushed out of its habitat by heat, rising seas, deforestation, or dwindling breeding opportunities. When they get to the new place, are they an invasive species or are they refugees?
>
> — *Lucy's bug & bird notes*

"Can we switch?" Lucy asked.

She and Beto were shoulder to shoulder and thigh to thigh, squeezed into the only spot that wasn't heaped with everything from big jugs of cooking oil to boxes of imported whiskey. They were in the battered van with the Rancho insignia on its side, heading, it seemed, to the police station in Bocas. The unfamiliar road wound through trees and mud embankments.

"I get carsick," Lucy said. "And this side is where it hurts." She tilted her head toward where she was jammed up against a box.

Beto glanced down at his own beat-up chest.

"We're both pretty banged up," Lucy allowed. "And if you want the window, that's fine."

"'I get the window!'" Beto quoted. "Someone once told me that kids in the US always want the window seat on a car trip." That someone had been Martin. Against his will, Beto felt a pang of loss, knowing the man was gone for good. Martin had been good to him. Sort of. Long ago. Martin had loved him, at least a little. Hadn't he?

Maybe the real sorrow was that Beto had ever believed that.

"I don't mean that I get it automatically." Lucy sensed she was being tested. "I'm just asking for it." When he didn't reply, she mumbled, "I think your mom's brew is still in my system. In my stomach, at least."

Beto snorted. "Let me guess. Sleep tea? She can't stand when I do drugs, but she's the biggest pusher in town."

His voice had something in common with Calaca's: an underlying growl that would be at home in any jungle. She flashed on talking to him at the beach party, how they shared a similar rhythm and flow of conversation.

"Okay," Beto sighed. "We can switch. You do look a little green."

He made her do all the work. She got onto his lap, holding the roll bar. His bare chest was warm against her back. She thought of how he had come from Calaca's body, and of how well she'd known that body once upon a time.

"Scootch over!" she coached.

"What is *scootch* and how can I do it with you on top of me?" She heard the hint of a smile in his voice.

She eased off his lap and into the newly vacated spot by the window.

"¿Qué pasa?" José yelled from the driver's seat.

"Nada," Beto yelled back, then turned to Lucy, as much as their close quarters would allow. "Happy?"

She shoved at a latched window that opened only a few inches.

They rode in silence. The fresh air helped. Soon Lucy's nausea was gone.

"I liked your gate."

She felt him brace as if for a blow.

"I've never seen anything like it. It's like, you go through the gate, and you can finally see Palmita."

Beto cleared his throat but didn't speak. In her peripheral vision, she saw he was crying, not making any sound. She was surprised she had any tears left, but his crying made her cry too. They cried together but apart, facing front, making no noise and making no move to comfort each other. Being side by side was comfort enough.

They'd been driving for an hour when they turned off the main road. Beto raised an eyebrow and nodded. Lucy wasn't sure what that was supposed to mean.

They rendezvoused with a truck. Two young men in ragged pants and tank tops approached the van. Lucy grabbed Beto's arm as one of the men yanked open the side door. But the men weren't interested in them; they went for the cargo, unloading the van and carrying everything to the back of the truck.

José was having a smoke with the driver of the truck, a well-groomed, middle-aged man with a new-model cell phone tucked into his shirt pocket.

"I miss my family," Lucy said softly. "Back home," she clarified, not wanting him to think she was saying the two of them weren't family too. But suddenly she ached for her mother and nephew and, yes, even her sister. She thought of her mother's letter: *You are mine. I am yours.* Did all the hurt and doubt and love boil down to that?

"But you left them to come here."

A fly buzzed at the seam of the windshield. "I had to know about Gabriel, and look who I found."

"Who?"

"You."

His face lit up.

"But also, I think I'm here to avoid the real issue."

Beto tried to cross his legs but there wasn't room. "What is the real issue?"

It amazed Lucy how short the story was in its essence. She'd taken on a foreign quest to avoid a more domestic one, she explained. Her sister claimed the family house after their mother died. She should have stuck around to see what that was about. Whether it was true. Whether she wanted to fight it.

"But problems that involve passports and end-of-the-road beach towns are so much more romantic than ones set in your hometown," Lucy said.

"I wouldn't know."

"I know it sounds like I'm an entitled gringa—"

"And you're not?'

"Looking for a father I didn't know I had didn't feel so great, but maybe being able to come looking for him is, I don't know, entitled. But then I find out I'm too late, and the mess he made turns out to be even messier than the one back home. Now I have another dead parent, and a delinquent—"

She stopped herself. "And another fight over another will."

"Your mother gave everything to your sister? Sounds familiar."

"Yeah," Lucy allowed. "I get that. And now I'm not even sure that's what my mom wanted."

"I have an idea," Beto said. "I go to California and fight for your house, and you stay here and steal mine."

She felt pulled up short, like he'd jerked on her reins. But a smile started to creep up on her. Soon she was laughing out loud, and Beto was laughing too.

"Perfect," she said. "I finally learn how to stay put, and you—"

"I get the hell out."

"Get out." Officer José's tone was more weary than brusque. He was not by nature a bully, a diplomat, or a wheeler-dealer. The job forced him to be all three.

They'd arrived at the police station. Beto climbed out of the van, then helped Lucy down. She smiled her thanks.

"What the hell?" Rafa and Isa rushed down the station's cracked cement steps. Rafa didn't know where to look first: at the angry bruise covering half of Beto's torso, at Lucy's paler-than-usual face, or at the state of the Rancho's van, front end accordioned, one headlight dangling like an eye out of its socket.

"Why are you still here?" José had assumed Rafa and Isa would be long gone. He'd counted on it.

Isa raised her chin. "Your wife invited us for breakfast. Then she needed help with the heads."

In the back of Rafa's pickup were two of the town's giant carnival heads. Lucy knew from previous visits that at certain times of year, men donned the papier-mâché heads and reeled along the parade route. One was nothing but a stump: the headless priest of Cartago who'd lost his head to his brother's wife. Another was the mythic La Cegua, a woman transformed into a dead horse with putrid breath who punishes men for taking advantage of girls and women. Looking at the heads, Lucy wondered if she'd ever understand this country.

Inside the station, the smell of fried plantains and reheated gallo pinto lingered.

"You're free to go," José told Rafa.

"I'm free to stay," Rafa said. "And to know why Lucy and Beto are your prisoners."

"Beto is not a prisoner."

"But Lucy is? What is her crime?"

José told Rafa what he'd refused to tell Beto and Lucy. Pilar's parents had complained that Lucy was harassing their daughter.

"What?" Lucy was outraged.

"The parents also claim you told their daughter she should go to school far away, where you are a teacher."

"No," Lucy protested. "I mean—just no. And you know what? They're terrible parents. She'd be lucky to get out of this place."

Everyone looked at her, and she wished she could take back her words. She thought of the white woman at the Rancho, assuming Calaca was the help, and of how Beto had implied that she was an entitled gringa. No way did she want to be that, but here she was, reciting lines she didn't really believe. Pilar's parents weren't her version of great, but the kids here seemed happier all around than the kids back home.

"That's not for you to say." If the admonishment had come from the policeman, it would be one thing. But it came from Rafa.

"There's another problem." José's self-importance added a few inches to his height. "She does not have a passport."

Lucy rallied. "I have a passport!" This was a problem she could solve. "It's at Hilda's."

José looked at Rafa. "No doubt she knows that Hilda's office is, well, not what it once was."

"No," Lucy said softly, slumping into a plastic chair.

As if pulling words from the bottom of a well, Lucy explained what had happened the night before. The town meeting. Hilda and Lucy holing up in the hotel office, an angry mob outside. Lucy escaping and riding to the Rancho.

Isa chimed in, describing how they didn't find Martin but they did find Beto. "He was tied up." She smiled at Beto, who had grown in her esteem by having stood up to Martin.

"I was supposed to find help," Lucy said. "I fell off a horse." She shuddered, remembering the impact. "Calaca went to Hilda's this morning, I think."

Lucy watched from her chair as Rafa, Beto, and Isa conferred in heated whispers in one corner. Then suddenly Isa and Beto were out the door, without a glance in Lucy's direction. Lucy was hurt as well as confused. Hadn't she and Beto just made some progress in figuring out how to be siblings?

Rafa stayed. He convinced José not to put Lucy in a cell. He said he would help her understand the seriousness of the situation.

Lucy looked at them both dully. Her own contusions had started to pulse. Her head too. "I understand the charges," she said. "I understand they're a bunch of Third-World crap."

Oh, God. Not again. Would she forever be her own worst enemy?

* * *

Isa drove her father's pickup, the giant heads rolling around in the back. A three-way fork in the road was coming up fast. Going right would take them to the doctor her father said Beto needed. Straight would take them to Palmita, where they could check on Calaca and Hilda. Left was the way Martin had no doubt gone, heading for the border.

At the crossroads, Isa started to drift left, looking at Beto. They hadn't talked about going after Martin, but somehow they each knew what the other was thinking. He nodded.

"Fuck Palmita," Isa said, taking the turn fast. "Let the old people sort out their shit." She was mad at her father for staying with Lucy. What had the gringa ever done for him?

"Damn right!"

They felt a joyride giddiness, roaring away from the town that hemmed them in.

For a while they were quiet, taking it all in—the rain-wet trees and fields, the skinny golden cows, the lonely clusters of bedraggled houses, and the occasional grandiose gate to some hotel or rich person's spread. The tires hissed on the wet pavement.

"This road has come a long way in the last few years," Beto mused. "Meanwhile, I haven't gone anywhere."

"We're going somewhere now." Isa pounded the steering wheel. "Maybe we'll never go back!"

"What's funny is that finally, I might have a reason to stay." He told her about Martin handing over the Rancho Vista Dulce.

"No fucking way!"

Beto shrugged.

"Think of everything you could do with that place," Isa said. "It could be a hangout for locals, with free drinks.

"Maybe I'll sell it," Beto said. "But then some other *hijo de puta* would probably buy it. People with money think they can own everybody." He gazed out the window. "What I really want is to have a place where people who know the old ways can come. There must be people left who know the right ceremonies, the lost language. They could teach us how it used to be.

How it could be again."

"You could teach art," she said, "and I'll teach—soccer! Calaca can teach cooking. For things like math and reading, well, Pilar wants to be a teacher. We just have to wait until she's old enough. Each subject would be taught in a different villa. During recess we'll swim in the pool. It could be the best. School. Ever."

"What about taking off and never coming back?" Beto swiped at the condensation on the windshield. The defroster only worked on the driver's side.

"Or, like you said, sell it. Then travel. Stay in really expensive hotels until the money runs out."

"You're so practical. Maybe you should be the Rancho's manager."

Isa laughed. She'd like to see Deysi's face if she became the boss.

Thinking of Deysi, Isa remembered telling her friend about the Rancho job interview. How she'd taken off her clothes for Martin's photos, thinking that keeping her underwear on was some sort of triumph. She gripped the steering wheel until her brown knuckles were white. "I hate that fucking place."

Isa closed her eyes, and the car starting drifting into the opposite lane.

"Isa!"

Her eyes flew open. She pulled over onto the dirt shoulder and turned off the car. Sighing, she rested her forehead on the steering wheel.

Beto put his hand on her shoulder. "It's ok," he said. "I hate that place, too. Or I hate the man who made it. But think about it. The place could be good for us. For Palmita."

Isa raised her head. "We're never going to find Martin, are we?"

"Maybe we have better things to do."

Isa turned the car around, and they headed home.

DAY EIGHT

SATURDAY, AGAIN

CHAPTER 25

> When we inherit genes from our parents, that's vertical gene transfer. When we get genes from other species, it's called horizontal. Almost ten percent of the human genome has come at us sideways, mostly through microbes. We inherit who we are and how we operate not just from our parents, but from the whole living world.
>
> — *Lucy's bug & bird notes*

If you ever find yourself under arrest, Faith once told Lucy, stay calm. Be respectful, but don't give up your power. Her big, bad little sister with a badge. She liked to give Faith grief about being sheriff, but Lucy was proud of her. Had she ever told her that?

"I would like to see the complaint against me." Lucy kept her voice low and pleasant, hoping to sweep them past her *Third-World crap* comment.

"See it?" José frowned.

"There must be a written document."

"What we would like you to see," the policeman said, "is that we will protect our children from outsiders with all the tools at our disposal. Outsiders like Don Martin. Outsiders like yourself."

Lucy's face flamed at being lumped in with Martin.

"You said you would make her understand," José said to Rafa.

"I understand," Lucy said, desperation creeping into her voice. "But what you need to understand is that I need to catch a plane. Also—" Her hand went to her side. "I'm injured. I may need medical attention."

When no one said anything, she added, "Do I need to pay a—fee?"

José shook his head in disgust.

"Please leave us alone for a few minutes," Rafa said to him.

"You can't just keep me here. You can't throw me in jail for nothing."

On his way out of the room, José turned to Lucy. The fury looked out of place in his bland face. "You know, of course, that your country has the highest rate of incarceration in the world?" He turned to Rafa. "Five minutes." José left the room.

"How do you reorient someone's worldview in five minutes?" Rafa muttered.

Lucy's heart sank at his judgment of her. "I don't know what I'm supposed to do. Should I demand to call the embassy?"

"Maybe it's time to stop demanding."

Lucy nodded, waiting for more. "But shouldn't I stand up for myself? For my rights?"

"You North Americans."

What had happened to them being fellow Americans meeting on the bridge between continents?

"You gringos are big on rights. Maybe you need to think about your responsibilities."

What came to her at that moment was the conversation they'd had a few days earlier, riding in Rafa's truck. She'd said something about Beto probably not being related to her. Rafa had snapped back with a reversal that hadn't quite sunk in at the time: that if she and Beto weren't related, it would be Lucy who wasn't related to Beto. She saw it now: Beto at the center, Lucy an outlier. He was the one with his feet in the soil and sand of Palmita; she was a ragged kite so far up that she was almost out of sight.

"There's claiming the land," Rafa went on. "Then there's the land claiming you."

"Umm," Lucy murmured.

Rafa's sigh made Lucy feel that once again she didn't get it. "Maybe you have a legal right to the land," he conceded. "But you act like you deserve it. Like you earned it."

She took a step toward Rafa, but he moved back to maintain the distance between them. "Maybe I did earn it. By not having a father."

"Maybe Beto earned it by having that same father."

Lucy thought about that.

"You're lucky," Rafa went on. "I feel bad saying that. Gabriel was a friend. But look what kind of father he was to Beto. What kind of man he was to Calaca."

"Did he—did he hurt them?"

"Not physically. But he cut them loose. So loose that they rattled around inside of themselves. Then Beto drifted up the hill. Gabriel could have stopped that."

"Calaca could have too."

Rafa nodded. "Maybe we all could have."

"I kind of like Beto now."

Rafa laughed, leaning toward Lucy just a fraction of an inch.

His tiny movement gave her a disproportionately large jolt of joy. Maybe he recognized her weaknesses, the gaps in her understanding of the world, but still hadn't given up on her. Was there anything more romantic than someone seeing how unlovable you are, but loving you—or at least liking you—just the same?

"I mean, I think we could be friends." Lucy was ostensibly talking about her brother, but the way she looked at Rafa told a different story.

When José came back into the room, the air had changed. When Rafa asked if he would release Lucy to him in exchange for her passport, José readily agreed.

"But my passport is at Hilda's. You said the office was—"

"Everything's fine at Hilda's," José said.

So the story about Hilda's office being "not what it once was" was pure invention.

"We'll deliver her passport," Rafa said. "Be assured that she takes the complaint against her very seriously."

Lucy's eyes opened extra-wide, but she managed to keep her mouth shut.

Rafa called them a taxi—a local who ferried other locals around for a fraction of what taxis charged tourists. On the drive back to Palmita, Rafa pointed out a flock of scarlet macaws as they rose from their burrows in a cliff. In the air they were beyond stunning, kin to dinosaurs, rainbows wheeling into the unknowable future.

Back in Palmita, Calaca was figuring it all out. If they somehow reclaimed the island as a cemetery, it'd be harder for Lucy, or anyone else, to make a legal claim on it. The dead had rights, sometimes more than the living. And all the energy she'd spent imagining her son's funeral? She would transfer it to putting Gabriel to rest, which was better than the man deserved. What he deserved was what he'd wanted when he swam out: to be drifting, forever, with no place to call home.

When the taxi dropped Lucy at the restaurant, Calaca was planning the funeral with three other local women. They sat around a table, nursing bottles of Fanta and Sprite, legs spread comfortably, wide feet slipping out of shoes. They'd pulled their chairs into the shadiest corner.

Calaca chin-pointed to a chair. The other women watched, stone-faced, as Lucy took a seat, then continued as if she wasn't there.

"No coffin," Calaca allowed.

Rafa had told Lucy that Calaca was hell-bent on having a funeral for Gabriel, and wanted Lucy to be a part of it. Lucy wasn't sure of her role here, but she was cautiously optimistic that the town no longer wanted to string her up.

"We can still have a procession," said a woman in a T-shirt with a sequined teddy bear on it. "There's no law against it."

"No civil law," pointed out a woman dressed like a modern nun: a sober skirt and blouse and low, lumpy shoes. "As a suicide—"

"We don't know that for sure," Calaca jumped in, though she herself had implied just that when she told them the story of Gabriel's last swim.

"The priest won't be able to make it on such short notice," said the fourth woman, "so we don't need to worry about it one way or the other."

If the town had had a city council, these women would be it.

"What about the idea of making this about more than Don Gabriel?" The teddy bear woman took a long pull off of her Fanta.

Lucy had been keeping quiet out of respect, and taking the temperature of the room. She was surprised when one of the women asked her what she thought.

"About what?" Lucy said gracelessly, then, "Thank you for including me in the discussion. How would the funeral be about more than Don Gabriel?"

"Your father."

Lucy's chin trembled in confusion and gratitude, that these women were acknowledging her connection to Gabriel, and, by extension, to the town. Calaca must have worked some magic on that account.

"My father," Lucy agreed, looking at Calaca.

"Lucy doesn't know the history of the island," Calaca explained.

"I know a little. Calaca, remember how we used to go out there? When we were girls?"

Calaca's face flushed brick red.

"You were friends," teased teddy bear woman. "That's—"

"Nice." The woman smirked, leaning forward so her face was no longer in shadow.

Color drained from Lucy's face. The woman was Pilar's mother. The woman who'd complained about her to the police.

Lucy stood up. "I need to go."

"Sit down," Calaca said. "No one here means you any harm."

"No harm? You know as well as I do why the police came for me."

"It was," Pilar's mother said, "a kind of, well, joke."

Lucy looked at Calaca, who shrugged.

"A joke." Lucy was incredulous.

"Maybe not at first," Pilar's mother allowed. "But then Calaca told me you meant well, but you were jealous of women with children." She looked Lucy in the eye. "Because you can't have any of your own, poor thing."

If children were bestowed on the worthy, Pilar's mom would be forever unencumbered. But then Pilar wouldn't exist, and Lucy loved Pilar, not like a mother but like a cousin or teacher, some bond not as fraught as parenthood, because it was true: Lucy wasn't mother material.

The women around the table probably thought it was because her body wouldn't allow it. But she'd been pregnant, and had been told she'd have no problem repeating the trick when the time was right. The time was never right. She could make excuses about not having the right job, partner, or bank balance, or of wanting to keep her independence. But the real, awake-at-three-in-the-morning reason was that she had a big hole inside her very being, and was afraid of passing it on.

Sara had never said much about her own mother, except that she came and went and then left for good when Sara was ten. "I took care of myself," Sara had boasted. "Just like you girls do."

A friend in college had once told Lucy that if your own mother didn't have a mother, she wouldn't know how to be one. The trauma of being left, even if she didn't recognize it as trauma, could be passed on to her kids. Those kids would feel orphaned in ways all their own, then pass that on to their own kids.

Lucy had told that college friend that orphaned insects made terrible parents too. For instance, earwig young could survive on their own if necessary. But female earwigs raised without mothers were shit mothers themselves. They forgot to feed their offspring and didn't protect them from predators.

"Well," her friend had said, "if imagining yourself as a neglected earwig makes your own neglect more bearable, more power to you."

"Who said anything about neglect?" Lucy had shot back. It had taken her years to understand that the word was all too apt.

Oddly, Faith had been clearer about Sara's shortcomings than Lucy. Not long after Sara's diagnosis, Faith had mused, "Funny to be caring for a mom who wasn't much on that account herself."

Sitting in an open-air restaurant in Palmita, the enchanted place Sara had given her girls and then taken away, two realizations collided in Lucy. One, Faith was somehow more of an adult than Lucy was, with a less charged relationship with their mother, maybe because Faith herself was a mother. And two, Lucy should have tried harder to help when Sara was dying. If not for Sara's sake, then for Faith's. And maybe for her own sake, too: to see her relationship with her mother through to the bitter and tender end.

"Yes." Lucy nodded at Pilar's mother. "Sometimes I'm sad I don't have children." She was surprised she could say it so simply, that she could take in the pain and still stay whole. She knew she'd made the right call, but there was no way around it: It was a loss.

The women—even Pilar's mother—melted. Tears sprang to their eyes. As a group, they herded her into a chair and gathered around, one hand smoothing her hair, another dabbing a napkin under her eyes though it wasn't Lucy who was crying. Soft, solid bodies braced her from all sides.

Had Lucy ever had so much flesh pressed up against her at one time? It was as if they were making her the baby, the baby she would never have. Lucy thought of how bird parents could be mated pairs, single moms or dads, even a group of unrelated individuals. There were so many ways to parent or to let yourself be a child, many of which had nothing to do with blood relation.

Sandwiched between the women, Lucy heard the clip-clopping of a horse. She could see just a sliver of the man on a gray mare as he approached and dismounted.

"Tell the gringa she can take Chan-Chan for a ride," he called cheerfully. "I don't want my horse to be the only one in town she hasn't fallen off of."

CHAPTER 26

> If plants and fungi can separately tolerate temperatures of up to 100 degrees, when the fungus grows inside the plant, together they can withstand temperatures of up to 160 degrees. Joining forces means we can better bear the extremes of the world.
>
> —*Lucy's bug & bird notes*

AFTER HILDA LET LUCY use her landline to postpone her flight home, the two women spent half the night talking. Lucy begged forgiveness for not bringing help, and Hilda admitted to not having a fresh and open heart where Lucy was concerned. Lucy pretended to scratch her foot to hide her smile.

Things had turned out fine, Hilda assured her. When there were just a few people left outside, she'd invited them in, breaking out her prized bottle of aquavit. They'd all been so chummy toward the end that they now had several ideas for going into business together, like growing organic microgreens to sell to hotel kitchens in Bocas, decorating lampshades with seeds and shells, or having marimba workshops for local kids and maybe even tourists.

"But I was so worried about Beto," Hilda said. She told Lucy how at first, people wanted to tear down Beto's gate, but that Don Diego had somehow convinced them it was the first step to reclaiming their town; Don Diego's cemetery gate would follow. They took the photos off the gate, and picked out anything that looked like a bone. Don Diego had to muster all of his eloquence to convince them that weaving bones into the gate—alongside flotsam and jetsam and glittery trash—hadn't been a sacrilege, but a tribute.

"I heard it myself, but I couldn't tell you what he said. Only that the old man was persuasive. You know, he used to be quite the charmer."

The conversation sailed along until Hilda asked Lucy how her heart was doing.

My heart? It was empty, and full to bursting. Limping along, and about to gallop out of her chest like a spooked horse.

"Fine," Lucy said.

In the morning, the women dragged plastic chairs out into the yard, drinking their coffee in the shade of a pochote tree, its spiny trunk doing nothing to deter the iguanas that lived in its branches. The women watched as one jewel-colored adolescent scrambled down headfirst and scuttled away.

It was then that Lucy told Hilda she was going to donate the land bordering the national park, so Hilda wouldn't have to worry about who might end up owning it.

Hilda was speechless. After a while, she said, "For such a big decision, you need to be grounded." She offered Lucy a private yoga session.

"I said I'd help with the funeral."

"Me too," Hilda said. "But they don't need us there so early."

"I don't have the right clothes."

"You can borrow mine."

Lucy was out of excuses. She gave the yoga session her best, though she hadn't known there was a wrong way to stand, sit, and breathe.

"Make the poses yummy," Hilda demanded.

Nothing felt yummy until the end, when Hilda let her lie down and relax.

"Spread yourself out," Hilda purred. "Let gravity have its way with you."

It was a beautiful morning. Birds sang as if they'd just figured out how.

"This is called corpse pose."

Lucy laughed. "How appropriate."

"No talking," Hilda said, but then curiosity got the better of her. "What do you know now?"

Lucy sat up. "You mean about Gabriel? I know he's dead. If I can believe Don Diego, he drowned. Beyond that, I don't know much. What do *you* know?"

Hilda rocked a little, arms encircling bent knees. "I used to think he and I were friends. Maybe more. He was big on a deliberate death. An earned death, as he used to say. Like how you earn corpse pose at the end of a hard yoga session. Then he wouldn't even say hello on the road. I think his world got smaller and smaller. Maybe he wanted to swim out to a bigger world."

Lucy thought about Gabriel, and about her mother, her ashes in the river. One parent in the river, the other in the sea. A sister up north and a brother down south. Where did that leave her?

Later, at Calaca's restaurant, Beto told Lucy he had something to show her on the island. They needed to go now, before the funeral started. He spoke and moved with a new authority, his eyes no longer going crabwise when you looked at him.

The rocky spine of the path to the island was still wet and slippery, but the sun was quickly drying it, the dark wet stone turning lighter before their eyes. Once on the island, they passed between two newly poured concrete pillars, rebar sticking up like rusty tentacles.

"For the new archway," Beto explained. "It won't be ready for today. Grandpa is taking his time. He won't know what to do with himself once he finally gets it built."

They went past men picking up trash and raking dirt. A lot of rubble had been cleared, but there were still broken headstones, pieces of crosses with seashells pressed into the cement, and dusty plastic flowers strewn about, as if by the wind. Someone in a straw hat waved them over.

"Big enough?" the man asked Beto, indicating a hole.

"Maybe a little bigger," Beto said.

"Boss man," Lucy teased.

Moving on, they ducked under an overgrown bush to enter a clearing the size of a large room. The view from here was out to sea.

"This is where the foreigners were buried," Beto said. He told her about Europeans and North Americans who'd come years ago, dying far from home. Most were men, and solitary. One guy loved his dirt bike so much, he had them press the tire tread into cement on his grave. Another had been a pilot; he had a real propeller as a marker. An Italian artist had a big fist made of marble, something he'd sculpted in art school and had shipped over. Back before they moved all the graves, people would come out to the island to party with the dead, snorting drugs off the marble fist.

"Foreigners are segregated in life and segregated in death."

Lucy sighed. "I know you think I don't belong here."

"It's funny. Foreigners want to be buried with a view of the sea. Locals want to look back at the mainland."

"Have you heard of the Golden Gate Bridge? In San Francisco? It's known for people jumping off it. Most of them, they jump looking back at the city. Not out to sea."

"Interesting."

"I think I have to go back there at some point, figure things out." She sighed. "It's like I have to decide which way to jump."

They looked at each other, and for a moment, everything else fell away: parents, countries, money, land. All that remained were the two of them, who would have to figure out what being related meant to them. Was it something inherent, something they'd choose, or both?

Faith was another puzzle. Could she and Lucy ever fit back together, like when they'd spooned on the couch as girls? Not likely. They'd both grown prickly, for good reason. Their bond might never be as strong as it once was. But Lucy knew now she had to at least try.

Beto led her around the perimeter. At one point, they stepped across a narrow inlet. He reached for her hand. She gripped his, hopping across. They came to a spot where a plot the size of a single bed was slightly raised.

"Well?" he said.

She looked at him blankly.

"You wanted to pay your respects."

Something rippled up her spine. Suddenly she felt her father there, at her feet. Planted. Grounded. Grounding her, Lucy, to this place.

"I knew it," she whispered, as if she might wake their dead father. "I knew he wouldn't leave me."

Beto snorted. "That's not how it was."

Beto finally told Lucy the story she'd been longing to hear.

"There was something wrong with Gabriel. I mean, apart from him being a lifelong bastard who wouldn't look at me because he thought *I* was the bastard. By the way, you know you're a bastard too, right?"

Lucy pawed the loose ground near the grave with a sandaled foot. She opened her mouth, then closed it without speaking.

"The doctors in the capital couldn't figure it out. I know because he talked about it all day at the bar. When people asked him what exactly was wrong, he roared at them. I mean, he *roared* like a howler monkey. Something in him was scrambled. I have to admit I didn't mind that he was suffering.

"He couldn't swallow, and his skin hurt. Months of bitching about that. But he had a solution. A burial at sea, as he called it. He wanted to swim out like a pirate, which makes no sense but that's what he said. Then he switched to sailors, how they were sewn into sailcloth shrouds and tossed to the sharks. That's how the Count of Monte Cristo escaped, wrapped in a shroud, weighted down, and hurled off a cliff. But the Count cut himself out of the shroud and kicked for the surface.

"I know," he responded to Lucy's quizzical expression. "Who cares about the Count of Monte-fucking-Cristo? But it gets worse. I don't know how many times he told us about Sir Francis Drake and his lead coffin, dropped off the coast of Panama. Or how Neil Armstrong, the first man on the moon, was buried at sea, the Earth's version of outer space."

Beto nodded to himself. "That, I liked. The first man on the moon wants to end his days not in space, but under the sea.

"Gabriel said he'd never liked the idea of being planted in the ground," Beto continued. There was nowhere to go after that. In the water, he said, the body was still alive, if only by virtue of its drifting.

"'By virtue of its drifting.' That's really how he talked. In English. What a show-off. I mean, my English got almost as good as his, but I wouldn't say something like that. Anyway, people let him rant. They never thought he'd actually do anything." Beto looked out past the graves to the sun's hard gleam on the water. He seemed to be gathering strength for the next part of the story. When he spoke again, his voice was small, and Lucy had to come closer to hear.

"He botched it. Lives here for decades and never gets a handle on the tides. The sea, it spits him back out."

Lucy thought of her own recent swim. Luckily, the sea had spit her out while she was still alive. It was as if the ocean had delivered her back to herself. Her father wanted the sea to be his final home. She wanted her bout with the sea to be the start of something entirely new.

"The first thing I think when I see him, before I know who it is? This is *my* beach. I figure some tourist got drunk, took off all of his clothes because, you know, he's sure this is his own private Eden where there's no shame, right? And falls dead asleep. I've been known to do the same. But I was up that morning. Hadn't been to sleep, in fact."

His look was a challenge, as if Lucy as the older sibling—almost as old as his mom, Lucy realized—might chastise him for staying up all night. She shrugged. She wasn't going to be the designated adult. She had enough of that as a teacher.

"Getting close, I see the man's eyes are open, and cloudy. He's curled up in a pile of driftwood and seaweed. Flies landing on his face."

Lucy shuddered at that detail.

"And then I see it's my *pendejo* of a father. Our *pendejo* of a father. I look at him a long time. He shows about as much recognition of me dead as when he was alive. You know, my mother never made any demands. Said if Gabriel wanted us, he knew where to find us. I had to be angry for the both of us.

"I remembered something else he'd talked about at the bar," Beto said, "about the dignity of a deliberate death, like his hero, Edward Abbey. Not much dignity in washing up naked as a skinned deer."

"Damn," Lucy said quietly.

"I met a man up at the Rancho," Beto continued in Spanish, as if all that English had worn him out. "This was long before Gabriel's last swim. The man told me, there's a tipping point, where son waxes and father wanes. He said I'd let my father define me and what we were to each other, which was nothing. He said I needed to rethink my position. I didn't know what he meant at the time, but when I saw Gabriel on the beach, I had to wonder: Am I, the unclaimed son, responsible for claiming the dead father who washes in with the tide?"

Much to her surprise, Lucy understood every word. She wondered if she was starting to regain the fluency she'd had as a kid visiting Palmita. Back then, Spanish had flowed like water for her.

"I called Rafa," Beto continued, still speaking Spanish. "He's my friend, even though he was also Gabriel's friend, which I could never figure, except maybe that they both loved birds. I told Rafa my idea, and he didn't laugh. He said a surfboard was a good way to get the body to the island. He said he'd bring the shovel."

Lucy's brain was on fire with this new story. She had lots of questions, but right now she couldn't get the image out of her head of their father dead on the beach.

"I'll be angry with you," she said, thinking of how Calaca had abandoned him on that front. "I mean, I'll be mad *alongside* you—not that I'll be angry with you."

He laughed. He told her how he'd tried to keep the secret of Gabriel buried on the island, but couldn't for long. "Of course, Rafa would have taken it to his grave. He's a rock. I'm not. I told my mother."

Lucy thought of her mother's last letter. Faith was her rock. Lucy wasn't. She envied how Beto was so matter-of-fact about what he was and wasn't.

Beto said that Calaca and Don Diego told him to decide whether to leave Gabriel's body where it was or to dig it up and put it in a box, rebury it with the entire town there. It was a new feeling, having his family trust him with such a big decision. He wondered if the new authority had to do with standing up to Martin and surviving it. He liked to think it also with his new way of carrying himself—no cringing, no apologies—but also knew the word had gotten out about how the Rancho might now be his. Soon, he might be the big man on the hill, dispenser of jobs and favors.

"I said we should leave Gabriel where he was," he concluded.

"I get it," Lucy said in English.

"Do you?" He switched to English too. "I told them he was gone, and we should let him stay gone. No digging the bastard up again."

With Lucy's mother, there'd been no burial, but she'd been digging Sara up at every turn, seeing her in the bushes, on porch railings, walking on water. She'd been regaling the poor dead woman with questions, none of which would ever be answered. Except maybe, *Did you love me?* Though Lucy still felt raw and done wrong, she knew in her heart now that yes, her mother had loved her. And she had loved her mother. With the simple love of a child, then with the complicated love of an adult child. But complicated love is still love, and love doesn't end just because someone is gone.

The last time she'd seen her mother, Lucy had brought Sara's favorite cinnamon raisin bread. Sara wasn't eating much at that point, but she wanted the bread, toasted and slathered with butter. Lucy could still smell the spicy sweetness and see the look of simple satisfaction on her mother's face. "That's so good," were her last words to Lucy.

Beto was looking at her expectantly. She pulled herself back to the moment.

"So Gabriel came back," Lucy said. "Like he still had business on land. Like maybe you needed to see him to do what that man up at the Rancho said: rethink your position."

Beto shrugged. But a tiny crack had opened in the story. He wouldn't mind thinking of it like Lucy did. To revise the story of his father. To rewrite history so he felt the possibility of connection. Maybe he could even claim the man's love now, without the obstacle of the man not wanting him to.

"And I came back," Lucy said.

He nodded, unsure where she was going with this.

"But I don't want to take anything that, by rights, belongs to someone else. I want you and Calaca to have most of—to have all of what Gabriel left. Because it was yours, or your family's, to begin with. Right?"

Beto kicked at the clods at the edge of the grave. It galled him that she got to play God. "We don't need your charity. In fact, I now own more land than Gabriel ever managed to pull out from under us."

He told Lucy about Martin willing him the Rancho.

"But that's not yours," Lucy protested. "I mean, even if it is now, wouldn't you also want what used to be your family's?"

"So you'd just go back home, like none of this ever happened?" The idea was a relief to Beto, but it also felt like abandonment. Had she come, assessed them, and found them so lacking that she was willing to give up what she'd inherited?

"I'd like to have a place here," Lucy said. She thought back on what Rafa had said at the police station. You can claim the land, or let the land claim you. Maybe the same was true of family, too. It was about being less grabby and more receptive. "But only if you and your mother want me to."

A part of him was suspicious. Did she actually mean what she said? And if she did, then he, and his mother, held her future—at least, her future in Palmita—in their hands.

"I don't know anything anymore," Lucy said, apropos of nothing. She watched a buzzard take off from the top of a palm tree, black against the blue of the sky. "I do know I'm glad he's not completely gone. Even if he was—"

"A steaming pile of monkey shit," Beto finished for her. They laughed, bonding over what a non-father their shared father had been.

CHAPTER 27

> Social species—bees, ants, humans—have their ways of dealing with the dead. Undertaker bees, about one percent of the hive, drag away the dead. Ants do the same, but they're so strong, they lift the bodies overhead. Hauled by bees, hoisted by ants, or carried out to the island: Bodies need a place to go. And we social species need a place to put them.
>
> —*Lucy's bug & bird notes*

CALACA PREPARED MORE FOOD than the town could consume in a week. Others brought their signature tamales, cabbage slaw, or a bottle of guaro. Besides sharing mountains of food and drink, the function of the gathering at Calaca's place seemed to be to give people a chance to talk about the funerals they'd attended and to recount harrowing stories of body transport.

One woman told of a friend who'd died on the Caribbean coast and was trucked back to the west coast. "But they didn't tie him down very well, and on every curve, he slams against one side of the truck and then the other. They didn't have the money for embalming, so they had to drive as fast as they could, get him in the ground before—"

"Stop!" said a man holding a plate piled high with chicken, pork, rice, and tamales. "You're ruining my appetite." But his fork never paused in its repeated journey from plate to mouth.

"He was worse for wear," the woman continued, "but when he got here, they put him in the coffin another friend made. You could see his face through the little window. His face looked okay, thank God."

"My aunt didn't have a window, and we missed her during the funeral," said a woman in a dark dress with discreet sparkles.

"They put him in clothes he never would have worn when he was alive," the first woman said, as if that were a bigger outrage than the man's death. She gestured with her empty beer bottle.

"Can I get you another?" Lucy coaxed the empty out of the woman's hand. Calaca had loaned Lucy one of her dresses, which Calaca herself never wore because it was stiff and hot. A thin stream of sweat trickled down Lucy's spine. She stood so the front of the too-big dress touched her in as few places as possible. She'd gotten dispensation to wear her own sandals, so at least her feet were comfortable.

The place was packed, but Rafa and Isabel hadn't yet arrived. Peering into the kitchen, Lucy asked Calaca if they were expected. Lucy plucked at the front of her dress, trying to let a breeze in. If and when Rafa came, she was going to be a sweaty mess.

"I burned the beans," Calaca lamented, stirring at the top of a big pot but not going deeper, fearing she'd dredge up the char. "I got distracted with the bones."

She had bathed a great many bones—the ones pulled from Beto's gate, and the others he'd still had in burlap sacks—in water perfumed with herbs and flowers. A few other women helped, rebuffing Lucy's offer of assistance. Lucy didn't know why this rather grisly chore had to be taken on right then, with so much cooking and party prep to be done, but she'd stopped asking for explanations. Calaca was too busy and stressed to answer her questions.

Lucy was glad to have a function: Make sure everyone has a full plate of food and a fresh drink. The few times people expressed their condolences, Lucy offered them more food or another bottle of beer. She appreciated having Gabriel acknowledged as her father, and it was right to mourn the man, but she didn't know how, especially not in public with people she barely knew. She also wondered if condolences extended to her somehow took away from what Beto—who'd stayed on the island—had been through.

"Sorry about the beans," Lucy said. "Can I help with anything else?"

"Rafa was supposed to make his *pinto*. It's the Nicaraguan *pinto* but still, it'll make up for this mess."

"So they're coming."

"Of course they're coming." Calaca slammed down the pot lid. "Everyone's coming."

Everyone, indeed. Even a couple of the guests from the Rancho were there. As provisional owner, Beto had brought back the staff, at least for this round of guests. Turned out he had access to the Rancho's payroll account.

Over near the pinball machine were the women who'd helped Lucy after she'd fallen off the horse, and baseball cap man, who'd dragged Beto from under the villa. They held plates heaped with food and looked delighted to be part of the scene, even if it was a funeral.

Rafa arrived, holding a big pot. Lucy went to him, reaching for it. Rafa held it to the side. "It's hot," he warned. "I'll take it in."

But he didn't move, and neither did Lucy. They looked at each other, foolish grin meeting foolish grin.

Calaca appeared, taking the pot from Rafa. A dish towel tucked into her waist sailed out to the side as she spun away.

Rafa was dressed as if for church, though he hadn't been in years. His hair gleamed wet against his skull, pulled back in an elastic band. He looked older somehow, and not quite as handsome as before.

That didn't put a dent in Lucy's attraction. It was a buzzing ache and a new taste in her mouth, as if he were already part of her. Despite or maybe because of that, she had nothing at all that she wanted to say. She tried and failed to curb the goofy look on her face.

When Beto arrived, it was time to take this show on the road. The tide was right, the island ready. Women gathered up flowers; men grabbed bottles. A fair number, both men and women, cradled clean canvas bags against their chests, the remains of loved ones who'd been dug up long ago. Calaca and Beto had cleaned and bagged the bones, hoping people wouldn't think too hard about how bags this size couldn't possibly hold a full skeleton, however broken down. The bags were meant as a gesture, a symbol, and people seemed to understand that.

Don Diego led the procession while Calaca brought up the rear, shooing stragglers as if they were chickens. Clouds massed to the west, but so far, the rain had held off.

On the way to the cemetery island, Calaca walked beside Lucy, talking a mile a minute. Her face betrayed impatience, as if getting Lucy up to speed was just one more thing on her very long to-do list. For her part, Lucy was thrilled that she understood every word of Calaca's Spanish.

The graves on the island had been dug up, Calaca said, because nobody fought hard enough to keep them undisturbed. Now the bodies were coming home. The old cemetery, an island except when it wasn't, was the perfect place to keep old friends and family who were no longer with us, except when they were.

Beto and Calaca had timed it flawlessly. The land bridge was several feet across now, the rock nearly dry. In single file, the procession made its way to the island. Sun sparkled on the water, and a breeze dried the sweat collecting in the smalls of people's backs.

The island looked better than it had in years, the trash cleared, Don Diego's unfinished arch festooned with gladioli spikes of blood red, vivid fuchsia, and a soft, buttery yellow.

Lucy trailed after Calaca, humid in her borrowed dress. Calaca herself wore a flowered cotton skirt and a sleeveless top, though her face was clothed in thick makeup, some of which had caked and cracked. When they paused while waiting for those in front of them to negotiate a narrow section, Lucy told Calaca to stand still so she could blend and blot some of the makeup with her spit-moistened finger.

"Does it look okay?" Calaca wanted to know.

"It's perfect."

It was a multi-part funeral and it took a long time.

The crowd gathered at the first grave, where Beto talked about

Chorotega ghosts, friendly ghosts, people who loved their dead so much they dug them up again after flesh and sinew were gone, rearranged what was left of them, bones woven into a thorny circle around the skull.

People looked at Beto with distrust. Calaca spoke next, acting as translator for her son's ideas. She toned down the Chorotega stuff and emphasized that their loved ones were coming home after a long exile. She didn't remind people that her father, Don Diego, had been the agent of that exile, or that her son had desecrated the remains. No doubt everyone knew, but their own guilt—they hadn't taken very good care of their people, either—kept them from casting blame, at least in public.

Calaca had presented people with washed, assembled, and bagged ancestors, to prevent them from looking too closely and seeing that maybe some other family's remains were jumbled in with theirs. Beto and Calaca had agreed it was important to mix up the bones a little, to make sure Palmita would hold together as a town and not just a random collection of individuals and insular families.

Each bundle had to have its due, had to be lamented, praised, apologized to. Those bundles that had no one left to mourn them took even longer, as people covered the bones' orphanhood with tendril-draped verbiage and theatrical tears.

Palm blades rustled. People waved off buzzards and kicked at crabs. Side conversations broke out on the way to the next grave. Couples sniped at each other. People were sluggish with all the food and drink they'd imbibed at the reception. But the island was getting back its freight of bodies, and it was appropriate that the living should be weighed down as well.

Gabriel's grave was the last. The sun went behind a cloud and the wind picked up. Waves broke on the dragon's teeth of rock that kept the island from being engulfed. Lucy's gaze skimmed over the water to what looked like a cruise ship, far out to sea. She felt no desire to escape. She was where she was supposed to be.

Finally, they squeezed into the area, enclosed by bushes and cacti, where Gabriel was buried. A cross had been erected, with a fist-sized glass decoration at the intersection of the two planks. It was gemlike, and caught the light. Coming closer, Lucy saw what it was: the lavender cut-glass doorknob she'd brought from home. Beto had somehow gotten his hands on it and—as artists did—made it his own. But what did a doorknob on a funeral cross mean? Lucy would ask him later. No doubt he'd have a lot to say.

Someone told a story about the time Gabriel poured sand in the gas tank of Martin's earth mover when it strayed over his property line. Lucy thought, I will know him mostly through other people's memories. Before the thought ebbed into sadness, the rain hit. A true tropical downpour, a weighted curtain dropping.

People huddled under scrawny trees, hoping it would let up.

It didn't. The wind sent waves sloshing across the land bridge. The window of opportunity to get back to the mainland was closing earlier than expected. People looked at each other, wondering how rude it would be to leave a funeral early.

Calaca released them. "We have put our loved ones to rest," she thundered over the sound of the rain. "They are happier now, and Palmita will be too."

"¡Viva Palmita!" People shouted. *Long live Palmita.*

Within minutes, almost everyone was heading back to the mainland.

Those who stayed—Don Diego, Beto, Calaca, Lucy, Rafa, and Isa—gave up on trying to stay dry. They let the rain have its way with them. It darkened the raised grave, more so than the surrounding soil, as if the weather were emphasizing the very plot they had gathered around.

Lucy welcomed the cool rain. She held her head high, letting the water hit her squarely and stream down her back and her face.

They stood around Gabriel's grave, each with their own thoughts blossoming in the privacy of their own noisy shroud of rain. Calaca remembered the man who had seduced her, or had she seduced him?

Beto didn't think much; he was exhausted after building a philosophical frame around the day's events that was then largely ignored. Rafa thought of the morning they buried Gabriel, of how hard the ground had been. Isa wondered what Beto was going to do with the Rancho, and if he liked her idea of making it a school.

Lucy marveled that she'd come all this way to find Gabriel but had also found Beto and, in a way, Sara, who she sensed in birds and kinkajous and behind every oversized leaf. There were still so many questions about what Sara had or had not done.

One Sara had lied to Lucy about her father and had possibly told Faith she could have the family house. But there were other Saras, too, like the one who'd yanked her girls out of their grade-school world and let them run wild in this one. What would any of the Saras make of this day, this place, these people surrounding the grave of a man who'd planted life in her? What would Faith say? Would she pretend to not be interested?

When the rain stopped, the sun made the new graves steam.

"Fantasmas," Isa said, widening her eyes in mock fear. *Ghosts*.

"They can't cross over to the mainland," Don Diego assured her. He was restless, going from one person to the next, touching elbows, looking into faces, looking for friends long since gone.

Lucy wondered if people were shaped by land as much as by blood or experience, and if some places had more power than others to make and remake us. Here, the sea whispered or shouted, according to your willingness to listen. Some heard the hot breath of boredom, some a warning to *Get out while you can*. Others detected a promise: *You could be happy here*.

Lucy wasn't sure what she heard in the slap of water against rock. She did know that the weight of the air, the quality of light, and the architecture of how water met land spoke to some deep part of her. Deeper than the redwood forests of Northern California? She wasn't sure yet.

How many landscapes can we hold in our heart at any given time?

The six laggards stayed on the island for a while longer, talking about Gabriel, tearing up, reverting to quiet. Each felt done at a different moment, and somehow it was okay to wander away. Beto walked the perimeter of the island, tamping down the earth here and there and wondering if they could find some of the old grave markers and bring them out here. Don Diego had a moment of confusion, and Calaca led him to a shady spot where he could regroup. Isa went after Beto.

They knew they were staying far beyond the time that the land bridge would be crossable. In fact, at this point it was safer to swim back, not risking the waves that might make them slip on the rock. When Calaca told her father the plan, she expected him to balk, but it was as if he'd been waiting for just such an invitation. He took off his shoes and lined them up neatly under a bush. Fully dressed, he launched into a perfect dive. Calaca blundered after him, in case he needed her. But his strokes were slow and sure, and he didn't look back.

Isa and Beto were talking on the far side of the island.

Rafa and Lucy wandered to a spot facing not the shore or the sea, but an outcropping down the coast. "This is a good place to go in," Rafa said. "No hidden rocks."

Lucy turned so he could unzip her. The air on her skin felt wonderful as she stood in her underwear and bra. She folded Calaca's dress carefully and placed it on a rock protected by exposed tree roots. She would come back for it.

He was taking off his shirt when Lucy made a sound for him to look. She chin-pointed at a roseate spoonbill taking off with a leisurely flap of its huge pale wings. Somehow, she'd absorbed, or remembered, that pointing with a finger was considered rude here.

Rafa smiled that now it was she pointing out birds to him, and in the manner of a local, though the gesture was usually reserved for human beings.

Lucy wanted to go to him but instead she launched her body into the water and started to swim.

Enjoy more about
You Could Be Happy Here: A Novel
Meet the Author
Check out author appearances
Explore special features

ABOUT THE AUTHOR

Erin Van Rheenen writes fiction and nonfiction that explores family dynamics, cultural difference, and the power of place. Her work has been anthologized and published in *Bellevue Literary Review, Atlas Obscura, BBC Travel, Fiction, The Sun,* and *Best Women's Travel Writing*. After earning a BA from UC Santa Cruz and a master's from City University of New York, she left the US to see the world. She ended up in Costa Rica, where she lived for several years, soaking up the green and researching her relocation guide, *Living Abroad in Costa Rica*, and her children's book, *The Manatee's Big Day*. For ten years she was Senior Writer at The Exploratorium, a science museum. Erin now lives in San Francisco.

ACKNOWLEDGMENTS

When you publish a novel you've been working on for almost two decades, there are a lot of people to thank. If I mentioned everyone by name, this section might rival the length of the book. It would include not only those who helped bring this particular story into the world, but also all of the teachers, students, and random strangers who have surprised me with their wisdom, encouragement, and inspiration. And it would have to feature the whole of the natural world, from trees to birds to rivers, for grounding and guiding me as I learn what it means to be a writer: someone who finds meaning in describing the world, as it is and as it could be.

I owe a huge debt of gratitude to the many writers' groups I've been a part of, especially the Las Vegas Show-Don't-Tell Girls—Ellen Neuborne, Debbie Daughetee, and Pat Murphy—who got me thinking outside of the genre box and who read countless drafts of this novel.

Thanks to Sibylline Press, and especially to my sister Sibyls—a wonderfully talented group that I am honored to join. Thanks to Julia Park Tracey for the title, Alicia Feltman for the cover, and Vicki DeArmon and Suzy Vitello for keeping everything on track. I'm grateful to the Pirate's Alley Faulkner Society, who awarded me their novel-in-progress prize the year that Oscar Hijuelos judged the contest. That prize gave my confidence a real boost! I've also been generously supported by retreats and conferences such as Hippocamp, Community of Writers, and the wonderful Cottages at Hedgebrook.

Most of all, I feel a bone-deep gratitude for my friends and family, who generously offered places to write, material support, and belief in my abilities even when I myself was in doubt. A big shout-out to Gianna DeCarl and Adam Cavan, Gwyneth Horder-Payton, Gabrielle Glancy, Laura Jacoby, Kathy (my mother), and my brothers, Brian and Derek. Most of all, I thank my spectacularly supportive and just-plain-fun husband, David Webster Smith, to whom this book is dedicated.

STUDY GUIDE QUESTIONS

1. What is the significance of the title? Would you have given the book a different title?

2. Were there any plot twists that surprised you? Did they affect your understanding of the characters?

3. Which scene resonated the most for you on a personal level?

4. Think about the characters: who do you love/hate/find boring? Why? Who would you cast in the movie version of this novel?

5. How do the characters change in the course of the story?

6. Does Lucy belong in Palmita? Why or why not?

7. How did the setting (time and place) influence the story?

8. What is the significance of the bug (and bird) notes at the beginning of each chapter? How do they relate to the rest of the book? Why does Lucy begin with bug notes and gradually come to write about birds, too?

9. Some say there are really only two storylines: "An individual ventures out into the world" and "A stranger comes to town." Which does You Could Be Happy Here most closely resemble?

10. Were you satisfied with the ending? Did it feel conclusive or open-ended?

Sibylline Press is proud to publish the brilliant work of women authors over 50. We are a woman-owned publishing company and, like our authors, represent women of a certain age.

ALSO AVAILABLE FROM
Sibylline Press

Other People's Kids: A Novel
By Kim Culbertson
FICTION
392 pages, Trade Paper, $22
ISBN: 9781960573438
Also available as an ebook AND AUDIOBOOK

After a violent incident at her prestigious Bay Area school, English teacher Chelsea Garden returns to her rural hometown seeking refuge and a fresh start. There, she reconnects with a burned-out principal and an old flame, both working at the local high school. *Other People's Kids* follows three educators at different stages of their careers as they navigate second chances, personal crossroads, and the risks of starting over.

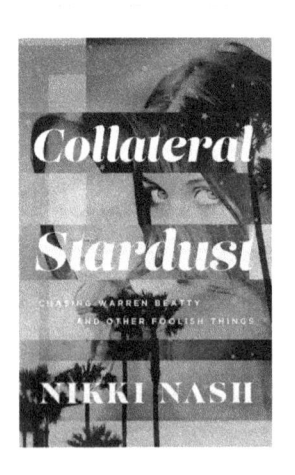

Collateral Stardust: Chasing Warren Beatty and Other Foolish Things
By Nikki Nash
MEMOIR
280 pages, Trade Paper, $19
ISBN: 9781960573421
Also available as an ebook AND AUDIOBOOK

Raised in a chaotic, bohemian Hollywood household, teenage Nikki Nash becomes fixated on a bold mission: meet and win over Warren Beatty. With determination and a detailed plan, at eighteen, working in a restaurant near the Beverly Wilshire, her long-shot dream collides with reality. While Warren remains ever present in her life, this is really the story of one woman navigating Hollywood as a producer, comedian, and actor in the eccentric fringes of L.A., brushing up against fame, danger, and dysfunction.

Seeds of the Pomegranate: A Novel
By Suzanne Samuels

HISTORICAL FICTION
416 pages, Trade Paper, $22
ISBN: 9781960573445
Also available as an ebook and audiobook

After illness derails her dreams of becoming a painter in Sicily, Mimi Inglese immigrates to New York, only to be dragged into her father's criminal underworld. When he's imprisoned, she turns to counterfeiting to survive, using her artistic gift to forge a path through Gangland chaos. As violence closes in, Mimi must risk everything to escape a life built on desperation and reclaim the future she once imagined.

The House of Cavanaugh: A Novel
By Polly Dugan

FICTION
248 pages, Trade Paper, $18
ISBN: 9781960573469
Also available as an ebook and audiobook

In 1964, Joan Cavanaugh has a secret affair that leads to the birth of a daughter whose true paternity she takes to the grave. Fifty years later, a Thanksgiving reunion unearths the buried truth, shaking the foundations of two tightly connected families. *The House of Cavanaugh* is a gripping story of hidden pasts, unraveling loyalties, and what it really means to be family.

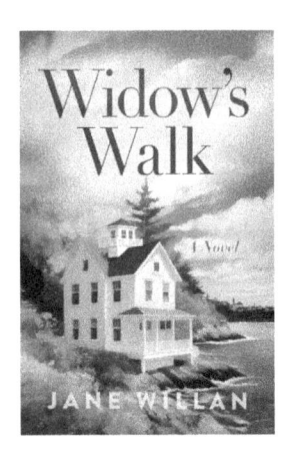

Widow's Walk: A Novel

By Jane Willan

FICTION
336 pages, Trade Paper, $20
ISBN: 9781960573452
Also available as an ebook and audiobook

When new Reverend Miranda McCurdy brings progressive change to a tradition-bound coastal church in Maine, her efforts spark fierce resistance—especially after she challenges the town's beloved Thanksgiving pageant. As the congregation splinters and a woman seeking sanctuary raises the stakes, Miranda must choose between fleeing back to her old life or staying to fight for the community she's slowly come to love. A stray dog and a mysterious stranger may tip the scales in this story of conviction, belonging, and second chances.

Reviving Artemis: The Making of a Huntress

By Deborah Lee Luskin

MEMOIR
280 pages, Trade Paper, $19
ISBN: 9781960573759
Also available as an ebook and audiobook

At sixty, longtime writer, gardener, and teacher Luskin feels a wild new calling: to leave the safety of her garden and learn to hunt deer. *Reviving Artemis* follows her late-in-life transformation as she confronts fear, embraces the forest, and reclaims a primal connection to nature. Blending humor, vulnerability, and myth, it's the story of a woman choosing to age on her own fierce terms.

For more books from **Sibylline Press**, please visit our website at **sibyllinepress.com**

www.ingramcontent.com/pod-product-compliance
Lightning Source LLC
LaVergne TN
LVHW050722140825
818505LV00022B/108